P9-CKL-157

JAN 0 8 2023

NO LONGER PROPERTY OF
SEATTLE PUBLIC LIBRARY

THE LONG WAY OUT

THE LONG WAY OUT

Michael Wiley

**SEVERN
HOUSE**

First world edition published in Great Britain and the USA in 2023
by Severn House, an imprint of Canongate Books Ltd,
14 High Street, Edinburgh EH1 1TE.

Trade paperback edition first published in Great Britain and the USA in 2023
by Severn House, an imprint of Canongate Books Ltd.

severnhouse.com

Copyright © Michael Wiley 2023

All rights reserved including the right of
reproduction in whole or in part in any form.
The right of Michael Wiley to be identified
as the author of this work has been asserted
in accordance with the Copyright,
Designs & Patents Act 1988.

British Library Cataloguing-in-Publication Data
A CIP catalogue record for this title is available from the British Library.

ISBN-13: 978-1-4483-0984-9 (cased)
ISBN-13: 978-1-4483-1012-8 (trade paper)
ISBN-13: 978-1-4483-0985-6 (e-book)

This is a work of fiction. Names, characters, places and incidents
are either the product of the author's imagination or are used fictitiously.
Except where actual historical events and characters are being described
for the storyline of this novel, all situations in this publication are
fictitious and any resemblance to actual persons, living or dead,
business establishments, events or locales is purely coincidental.

All Severn House titles are printed on acid-free paper.

Typeset by Palimpsest Book Production Ltd.,
Falkirk, Stirlingshire, Scotland.
Printed and bound in Great Britain by
TJ Books, Padstow, Cornwall.

In memory of Philip Spitzer, among the great ones.

Acknowledgments

Thank you to Kye Gibbs for expertise on chicken farming and to Stefanny Carranza for help with Mexican Spanish slang and idioms. Soledad Castillo's *Guardian* article, 'At 14, I walked through the desert to reach the US. My story didn't end there', was especially important to me as I wrote about the Soto family's immigration experience.

The talk, laughter, and friendship of Reed Farrel Coleman, Matt Goldman, Charles Salzburg, and Tom Straw have blown away the gloom of the plague years. Julia, Isaac, Maya, and Elias – 1 would travel with you anywhere. Thank you for being mine and letting me be yours.

Greatest thanks to Lukas Ortiz – and to Joanne Grant and all the amazing people at Severn House Publishers.

ONE

Two hours before dawn, the Cardinal Motel seemed to exhale. The huffing, the fake ecstasy, and the wall-pounding laughter quieted. Skinny-armed men slunk from the rooms, along the sidewalks, and into the dark. Girls, clutching fistfuls of twenties, climbed into the passenger seats of idling cars. A boy stopped howling in the room on the end. The last of the nighttime semis passed on Philips Highway. A hundred yards beyond the highway, a freight train stood silent on the tracks, where it would remain until the railroad bridge over the St Johns River came down after a barge went through.

If I stepped from my room, I would smell the rich vegetable rot of the lowland trees and river mud.

I sat on my bed and opened the vinyl case Music Time threw in for free when I bought a French horn. I touched the bell, the slides, the valves, the levers, the leadpipe.

No fake ecstasy.

I brought the mouthpiece to my lips.

What did freedom sound like two hours before dawn?

I made a sound – a note, not much of one.

I made another.

When I was a kid, my sixth-grade music teacher Mrs Wendorff taught our class 'Across the Stars' from *Star Wars* and gave me a solo in the spring concert.

Later, during the summer after I finished high school, Detective Bill Higby taught me other songs, chiming to metal bars and doors. I yelled against that music, but it played and played for eight years – three on death row, five in Supermax – until Judge Peterson said, *Get out of jail free*, and everyone else said, *How could we have let this happen?*

An eight-year-long jingle grows from an earworm into a dragon – and shrivels back into a soul-eating parasite. Tell the Raiford guards you need to go to the medical center for *that*, and they'll clank their batons along the steel bars like a xylophone, singing, *This will be the day that you . . .*

Behind those bars, I dreamed of the French horn day and night – promised myself *if I ever got free* . . . Other prisoners sang *their* songs. We sang in the prison yard, sang in the cells. You'd have thought you walked into choir practice.

Sitting on my bed in the Cardinal Motel, I tried to recall 'Across the Stars' one false note at a time. I touched the horn, and I made sounds – something like the notes I'd known from before Higby – but other notes clanged over them, dropping steel pipes on concrete.

The difference between harmony and cacophony . . . Mrs Wendorff told the class.

My friend Stuart at Raiford said the CIA crushed captives with sound torture in Iraq. He said, before that, the ATF and FBI played Nancy Sinatra's 'These Boots Are Made for Walking' mixed with rabbits getting slaughtered to shake David Koresh and the Branch Davidians at Waco. Stuart said, *Keep it together, Franky. Think good thoughts. Whistle a happy tune.*

I whistled 'Across the Stars' until the guards brushed their batons across the bars.

Now, two hours before dawn, sitting on my bed in the dark, I blew the horn across the galaxy, closer and closer to the hot center where gravity crushes like a fist on Q-Wing, where men wait the last days before the Death House and the prison tailor comes, humming that incessant music, to measure them for execution suits. Stuart said, *I don't sugarcoat it, Franky. You know I'm a straight shooter*, with that big, gentle laugh, *which is what got me in this predicament to begin with*. He fooled the tailor and the executioner at last, dying of three-hundred-pound diabetes before they could find a vein.

In my room at the Cardinal Motel, I played across the sky from Polaris to Sirius, Antares to the Pleiades, though sixteen inches of plaster ceiling, beams, and rooftop gravel separated me from the stars. The shapes of constellations made no sense. The universe never ticked like a clock. If you hold a star map up close to the face of a star, it'll burn. A well-ordered universe is a lie we tell to make ourselves feel good. The sooner we all agree on that, the better. Then we can get on with it.

I got through four measures, more or less recognizable, when Jimmy and Susan pounded on the wall next door. 'Four thirty in the morning! Don't you know it's against the law to kill a cat?'

I yelled back, 'Kind of ironic after you bang your bed all night. Who do you think you are with that moaning and groaning? Beyoncé? What office are you running for? Hypocrite in Chief?'

I hadn't slept for three days and nights, and the Raiford music was winning in my head. Crushing me.

Jimmy and Susan must've sensed the danger because Jimmy – who usually liked a fight – yelled, 'Nothing I hate more than a bully, man.' Five minutes later, Mr Hopper, who owned the Cardinal, knocked at the door.

'What are you doing, Franky?' he said. 'You know we can't have this.' He wore a black bathrobe, his chest hair – as gray and curly as the hair on his head – poking from the top. A cool November breeze blew into the room.

'I'll be quiet.'

'You will if you want to keep living here.'

'You'd kick me out for a little music after Jimmy and Susan shake the roof twenty hours a day?'

'Number one, what you were doing wasn't music. Number two, you're going to throw Jimmy and Susan under a bus?' Hopper was a born-again, who'd bought the motel on Philips Highway so he could rent rooms to people like me who no one else wanted, not even our families, on the principle that Jesus and Mary were undesirables and drifters too.

'Play that thing somewhere else,' he said. 'I'm trying to run a place.'

'Fine.'

He stared at my face. 'You look lousy.'

'I'm OK.'

He gazed past me into the room. 'You sure?'

'Yeah – I'm going to shower and go to work.'

'The cats?'

'Until something better comes along.'

'I don't like them. Not even in a circus.'

'Right.'

He nodded at the horn. 'You sure you're done with that?'

'Yeah, I'm sure.'

He scratched his chin. 'I like having you here, but maybe you're outgrowing this, you think?'

Everyone had been trying to pry me out of the Cardinal lately.

When Cynthia spent the night with me, she would lie awake, listening to the noise from the other rooms. 'This is a shithole, Franky. A very loud shithole,' she would say. 'Don't you think it's time to move?'

The truth was, after my time at Raiford, I liked it – the sound of wild living. The Cardinal Motel kept me on an honest edge.

'I'm good here,' I told Hopper.

'No,' he said, 'you don't look so good.'

TWO

N ine years earlier, Detective Higby testified, *so help him God*, that I killed Duane and Steven Bronson, ages fifteen and thirteen, on a rotten rainy night – me barely more than a kid myself. The judge and jury liked his lies. The blood of two young boys made them hungry for a reckoning, and one bowl of sugar tasted as good as another, even if it sickened them later.

The day after sentencing, as a van drove me to Raiford, I put my nose to the window and watched the highway-side woods like a kid on a school bus. The guard said, 'Take it all in now, son. Those are the last trees you'll see in this lifetime.' We passed an encampment where Mexican and Haitian migrants slept after grinding their knuckles in overheated farm fields. The guard said, 'There'll come a day when you envy them shit weasels. That day'll come real soon.'

Later, when Judge Peterson called the conviction a miscarriage and told my lawyers from the Justice Now Initiative that the State of Florida owed them a debt of gratitude for their persistence in righting a wrong, I wanted to go out in the woods and run and run until I lost myself in the green freedom. But the guard got the second point right – before then, I would've traded my cell for heatstroke and a plate of beans.

When I first came out, Dr Patel, my reintegration counselor, said, 'Give it time.'

I said, 'They took eight years of my life. I've got no time.'

'Nice and easy – that's the way.'

'You're asking too much,' I said.

'The odds are against you, Franky. You can't run away from your past, and you can't run toward the future. You need to deal with the present with your feet planted squarely on the ground.'

'You're wrong,' I said. 'I can run and run. When I was a kid, before they crammed me in prison, I ran the trails through the forest behind my house. Anything going on at home or school? It disappeared.'

'But you're no longer a kid, are you?'

I said, 'Once, when I was thirteen, I ran around a bend in a trail and came face to face with a wild hog and her piglet. Up until then, I never saw anything so ugly and scary. The mama hog's nostrils widened, and her eyes were like black holes. She didn't look angry. She looked curious. She seemed to be wondering how I could be so stupid as to stand there with my feet square on the ground.'

Dr Patel gave me a tight-lipped smile. 'You aren't unintelligent, Franky.'

'Funny thing is, my dad taught me that if I ever came on a hog that way, I should stand tall and calm and face it down like you say, and then I should back away nice and easy.'

'Did it work?'

'I don't know. I turned and ran. I went back down the path – then left it and pushed through the palmettos and staggerbush. Even after the mama hog cut from the chase, I ran.'

Dr Patel set his notebook on a side table. 'I guess it turned out for you that time.'

'I got lucky.'

He considered me. 'You like animals?'

'Not wild hogs.'

'How did you feel afterward – after you escaped?'

I had run, the fat leaves slapping my legs, my chest, my face, the ground soft under me, the mama hog at my heels, its fur as brown as mud and rough as thistle. I'd run, as if in a dream, chased by a fear that could tear me apart with its tusks and teeth. At some point, after the hog quit and trotted back to her piglet, I broke through the scrub into a clearing, and I seemed to pass from one dream into another. In the clearing, surrounded by miles of forest, the ruins of a wall rose toward the sunlight. It was made of oyster-shell tabby and seemed ancient. A glassless window – as high on the wall as a second story – looked into the woods, and the sunlight angled through the gap, tricking on dust and pollen. I stopped, gasping for air – if the hog had still hunted me, it would've ripped me apart – and for a moment, I thought I saw heaven.

I told Dr Patel, 'I felt fine. Relieved.'

'Naturally.' He picked up his notebook and wrote in it. 'I can make a call. I think you would benefit from an activity that fills your need for a certain intensity but also refocuses your energies from your own pain on to alleviating the sufferings of others. I think this might be therapeutic for you, yes?'

'A job?' The work I'd done with the Justice Now Initiative when I first came out from prison blew up when I went after Higby instead of doing what they assigned me to do. I exposed the detective for what he was. Later, I found the man who murdered the Bronson boys.

'You need one, yes?'

'What's the pay?' I said.

'Are you in a position to haggle?'

'Being at a disadvantage hasn't stopped me before.'

He set up an interview at Safe Haven, south of the city, in wetlands where a plantation once farmed slash pines for the pulp mills. Safe Haven rescued big cats from private owners and roadside zoos. They'd pulled an albino leopard from a cage behind a Jiffy Lube where one of the technicians had kept him since winning him in a bet. Judy Pollard ran the refuge, funded by her family, who owned the land.

Safe Haven locked a chain across the end of a gravel road. In heavy rains, the road flooded, stranding Judy, her wife Diane, and their eighteen-year-old assistant, Zemira. They neutered the male cats. When an animal died, they buried it in an acre-wide cemetery planted with wild flowers. They banned visits from the public.

The eighteen-year-old, skinny in overalls, let me in through the gate. She eyed me like I was more dangerous than lions or leopards. I drove a half mile to a wooden house where the three women lived surrounded by a compound of cages, enclosures, and work sheds. They'd landscaped the area with angel's trumpet and African tulip trees, elephant ear plants, palms, and, between the leopard and tiger enclosures, a bamboo grove. Orchids hung from hooks on the sides of the work sheds. A space to the side and behind the wooden house looked like a little junkyard with trucks on blocks, others parked side by side, and, tucked under an aluminum carport, a rusty GMC Sierra Grande pickup that seemed most of the way to being an antique.

Judy and I sat down at a picnic table in front of the house. She said, 'I hate people,' as if that was her first interview question.

'Looks like this is the right kind of place for you,' I said.

'I run Safe Haven because I'm done hurting,' she said. 'And I'm tired of watching people harm others. What do you think of that?'

'Anyone who says she's done hurting must be hurting badly,' I said. 'Anyone who stops caring about others must be hurting even worse. You can't turn that off.'

'I can try.' She pulled a pack of Marlboros from her vest and lit one. 'You're talking from experience?'

'Is that what Doctor Patel told you?'

'He may have hinted.'

'If you don't mind my asking, how do you know him?'

'He comes out once a month,' she said. 'My brother insists on it if I want my family to give me money for this place.'

'What do you think of your brother doing that?'

'To hold on to Safe Haven, I would deal with the devil.'

'I'd like a job if you can use me,' I said.

She gave me the keys to a Ford F-150 they used to pick up chicken and goat carcasses. 'The cats wake up hungry, and that means you work early. Can you handle that?'

An hour before dawn on the morning when Jimmy and I shouted at each other through the motel wall, I stood in the shower humming 'Across the Stars,' the mental clank of metal sinking in the drain.

Then I drove the Ford out on Philips Highway.

A mile north, the brilliant orange and white lights of Sahara Sandwiches shined from the roadside. I swung in close to the front door. Except for a hooker who sometimes stood inside the front window with a shoulder-high walking stick, I seemed to be the only one who ever came in an hour before sunrise. I ordered a fried egg sandwich from the bald counterman and said, 'You ever think of playing music? Warm up the place?'

He looked as if I'd suggested putting a plate of sample turds on the counter. He went to the grill.

When he handed me my sandwich, wrapped in waxed paper, he said, 'I like it quiet.'

Thirty minutes later, I pulled from a narrow highway into the drive at Chartein Poultry Farm, which supplied about half of the meat for the Safe Haven cats. A singlewide trailer stood by the entrance, across from a large sign with the farm name and a painting of a white hen pecking corn from the ground and a black hen craning its red-combed head back, its yellow beak open so wide it seemed it could pluck clouds from the sky. The hens looked real enough to be photographs, but the clouds and sky were too brilliant, overexposed with whites and silvers, as if brightened by a double sun.

The lights were on in the kitchen of the singlewide. The farm manager, a wiry fifty-year-old named Everett Peters, lived in the trailer with an old German shepherd he treated better than his workers. Normally at this hour, the six chicken houses at the end of the drive were dark, the only sound from them the thick, low whine of industrial fans mounted in the back. This morning, two pickup trucks and a car stood in front of Chicken House Three. The exterior lights on the building and the ones to either side of it – typically used only when a coyote or fox had been burrowing under the flooring – shined over a dozen men and women.

When I climbed from the Ford by the singlewide, Peters came out with a mug of coffee, followed by the old dog. He squinted up the drive at the chicken houses, then came down his wooden steps.

'Ninety birds for you in the cold shed,' he said.

If a chicken died, the processing plant refused it. The farm buried it in a compost pit or gave it to Safe Haven.

A car door slammed by the chicken houses. 'What's up?' I asked.

Peters frowned. 'One of the Mexicans ran off and got lost.'

'Who?'

'The girl.'

'Antonia?' Fourteen years old, Antonia would watch me as I loaded carcasses on to the truck bed. She would ask questions or tell me about herself. She had come from Jalisco with her mom to be with her dad when he found year-round work at the farm. She had a loud, startling laugh. Her dad sometimes called her a simpleton

– an *imbécil* – because she talked to men like me too quickly. But she'd always seemed clever to me.

'That's the one,' Peters said.

'She ran away?' Twice in the past month, she'd wanted to hitch a ride with me back to the city instead of going to school. I'd turned her down and told her that kids who skipped school found sorrow nine times out of ten.

'What did they find the tenth time?' she'd asked.

'Aren't you afraid?' I'd said.

She would rather die than be afraid, she'd told me, and I got the sense that her life had already given her plenty to be scared of if she'd given in to it. Anyway, she said, the kids at school were dumb, and so were the teachers.

Peters said, 'She went out last night and didn't come home. Her family's been making a racket since two in the morning.'

By the time we finished loading the birds into the back, the morning sun hung low in the sky, and most of the people by the chicken houses had driven or walked away.

Antonia's mom and dad stood by a remaining truck, along with a thick-shouldered Haitian I recognized as one of the dad's friends and a short, gray-haired man named Harry, who was Mrs Chartein's brother. I'd met Antonia's dad, Martin Soto, once or twice. I knew her mom was named Alejandra only because Antonia had told me.

But when I climbed from the Ford, Alejandra rushed to me and took one of my hands in hers. She had Antonia's wide face and large eyes. 'Franky?' she said.

'Sure.'

'You are *asesino*, yes? You kill?'

'No,' I pulled away.

'You were in jail? The boys?'

'I didn't do it.' I'd never told Antonia about my past, but any school kid with five minutes on the internet could find out about the conviction. Or maybe everyone at Chartein Farm knew.

'You find the man who kill the boys? That is you?'

'I helped.'

She smiled. '*You* will find Antonia.'

Not a chance. Last time I tried to help strangers, stopping when Duane and Steven Bronson broke down while joyriding in their mom's car, eight years of my life fell into a hole and kept falling. Before my life went to hell, my dad used to say, *Never answer the phone if you don't know who's calling. Don't answer the door if you don't know who's knocking.* I'd told him that was a rotten way to think, not to mention impractical, but since then I'd come around.

'What happened?' I asked Antonia's mom.

Half in English, half in Spanish, she made me understand that Antonia had gone dancing at Bar Deportivo with her cousin Clara. Alejandra and her husband had prohibited her from going, but after dinner Antonia walked out to the highway, where Clara – who was twenty-four and reckless – picked her up. There was a boy Antonia wanted to see. He was supposed to be at the bar after he got off work at a restaurant, but the manager kept him late. At midnight, when Clara looked for Antonia, she was gone.

'You checked with the boyfriend?'

'*Por supuesto.* Of course.'

Antonia had told me about him too – a nineteen-year-old named Carlos, who'd also come up from Jalisco. He served burritos and pitchers of margaritas seven nights a week at El Jimador, three miles to the south of me on Philips. 'You're a kid,' I'd said. 'The guy is five years older?'

She'd laughed. 'He's very immature.'

I asked her mom, 'Does she have a phone?'

'No – Martin, *mi esposo* – my husband – he has the phone. It is too much. *Es muy caro*, do you understand?'

'Too expensive, yes.'

'You will look for her?' she said.

Don't answer the door. 'There's nothing I can do.'

She seemed confused, angry. 'Why do you stop the truck if you will not help? Why do you get out?'

'I like Antonia.'

'You *like* her?'

'I'm sure she's fine.'

'No,' she said, 'no, she is not fine. They know who she is. The children at school.'

'I don't understand.'

'They call her the names. They threaten her.'

'With what?'

Her mother leaned toward me. 'She come home with a paper.

They say what they will do to her. They draw pictures. But what can we do? We cannot complain. We cannot tell the police. We stay quiet. Now she is gone.'

As she talked, a Jeep drove toward us on a dirt road from the brick house at the far end of the property, where Douglas and Bella Chartein lived. During one of my early-morning pickups, Mr Chartein had told me he grew up on this land when it was little more than trees and scrub. Before marrying, he built the first of his chicken houses. Over the following decades, he put up six long aluminum sheds and became one of the biggest poultry producers in North Florida. He and his wife, who grew up a half mile away, started out in the singlewide trailer where their manager now lived. As the business grew, they built their brick house and, behind it, three cottages, along with housing for their workers. Two of the cottages were empty. They let Harry live in the other in exchange for handling the farm-to-plant logistics, a part-time job he combined with a house-painting business he ran from a van. Harry dressed like the other workers, but Mrs Chartein wore dresses and creased linen pants, Mr Chartein khakis and loafers.

The Jeep stopped by the men, and Mr Chartein climbed out and clasped the hand of Antonia's dad, pulling him near to speak into his ear. Mrs Chartein got out and went to Antonia's mom. She drew her into a hug and said everything would be all right – children did this kind of thing.

I climbed back into the truck and started the engine.

Don't answer the phone. Don't open the door. Nice and easy. That was the way.

THREE

That night, I told Cynthia about Antonia. We sat on my bed at the Cardinal, eating China Joy takeout. When Cynthia was unsure of something, she had a habit of raising her left eyebrow, which she'd pierced with three rings. She wore a gray button-down shirt with a cotton tag that said *Bourne-Goff Storage* in block letters and, on the other side, *Cynthia*.

She ate a piece of orange beef from a cardboard container and said, 'You owe her nothing.' She raised the eyebrow.

'What can I do?' I said.

'Nothing. Unless you ask around, like at the bar.'

'Why would I? No one would talk to me at a place like that.'

'Maybe not.'

'She's with the boyfriend,' I said. 'She snuck out to see him, right?'

'Makes sense.' The eyebrow.

We dropped it. When we finished eating, Cynthia gave me her Coke cup and took off her jeans. The skin on her legs was mottled red and gray – scarred from a house fire when she was eight years old. I touched an ice cube to each of her thighs the way she liked. I drew the ice from her left knee to the leg band on her underwear and back to her knee. Then I drew it up and down her right leg. When the ice melted, I used another cube.

The first time she'd had me do this, a month after we got together, she'd put ice in her mouth and kissed me with her cold lips. She'd tried to explain the heat she felt inside, as if her skin was infected, feverish, a fire burning in the muscle. She'd kissed me again – touching her cold tongue to mine – and said, 'Some nights, I dream of ice. The whole world. The sky. The land. I'm lost in it. I can't see my feet.'

'Sounds like a nightmare.'

'I'm obliterated. I don't mind. I'm alone.' Then she'd put the ice from her mouth into my hand and said, 'Touch me.'

Her doctors had a word for what made her hurt. Hypermetabolism. Cynthia said they could screw themselves with their medical studies and prescription pads. All she wanted was ice.

She dried her legs on my bedsheet, and we dumped the takeout boxes in the bathroom garbage can. Then she linked her phone to the TV. After I got out of prison, we'd met at the Regency Cineplex, where she sold popcorn and Junior Mints. Later, she quit the job for the one at the storage facility, and we spent most evenings streaming movies in my room or, if her parents were out, at her house.

The previous night, we'd watched the 1940s black-and-white *Wolf Man* with Claude Rains and Bela Lugosi, and now she loaded the remake with Anthony Hopkins. We sat against the headboard, nestled close, the lights off except for the bright TV. When Jimmy and Susan started fighting next door, and one of them slammed against the wall, Cynthia moved closer, and I held her and she held me. We seemed to be nowhere and everywhere, in a space away from all our troubles. The world could do its worst, because we were gone. For an hour and a half, I didn't care that a third of my life had been sucked into a darkness so black I still doubted my eyesight. I didn't care that when Cynthia's dreams of ice ended, fire would chew at the edges of her sleep, swallowing the carpet and curtains, turning the bedsheets into a grill. I didn't care that a fourteen-year-old laughing girl went dancing – looking for love – and disappeared.

When Anthony Hopkins battered his wolf-man son with a silver-tipped cane, Cynthia reached for my belt and undid my pants. Anthony Hopkins turned into a wolf man too, and he and his son fought, tearing fur and flesh from each other's body, and she slipped off her underwear and unbuttoned her work shirt. The son threw the father into a fireplace, incinerating him, and she climbed on top of me, her lips and tongue hot. The world could burn. It could freeze from pole to pole. I didn't care. Not tonight. Not now.

FOUR

The next morning, Judy waved me over as I drove past her house at Safe Haven. She asked what I'd brought.

Under a tarp in the back, I had the offal from a dozen Jenquist Meat Company lambs and a whole goat from Ron Heckscher Organics.

'Take it back to Zemira – she's with the lynxes. Did you see what happened with that girl from Chartein Farm?' Judy wore heavy cotton pants, a sweatshirt, work boots, a sunhat over her graying hair.

'Sure, she ran away.'

She looked at me sideways. 'You don't watch the news?'

'Depends on the night.'

'Yesterday afternoon, a couple of motorboaters found her in Clapboard Creek, out by the Intracoastal.'

I felt a punch in the gut. 'Antonia Soto?'

'That's the one. You know her?'

'Yeah . . . yeah, I met her a couple times. You sure it was her?'

She looked at her watch. It was almost eight o'clock. 'When you and Zemira finish with the cats, come over. We'll see what the news says at noon. Get going now.'

But I pulled out my phone and looked up Antonia's name. Two of the local TV stations had online stories repeating what Judy had told me.

Judy said, 'The cats are hungry, and I'm not paying you to make them wait.'

I opened a third story, from the *Times-Union* newspaper. It said what the TV stations said. I looked at Judy. 'She was a kid.'

'Sad,' Judy said.

I went to find Zemira, who was shoveling out the lynx enclosure. She wore oversized mud boots around the bottoms of her overalls. She usually talked to me only to tell me something I was doing wrong. We would work silently side by side through the mornings. When we were done, she would go back to the house or walk into the woods.

This morning, when she climbed into the passenger seat, I drove to the refrigerator shed. She pulled the goat from the truck. She went to the shed for an axe, severed the head from the body, and cut off the legs. With each blow, I thought of Antonia and heard her startling laugh.

When Zemira tossed the legs into a wheelbarrow, I said, 'You hear about the girl?'

She carried the axe to the hose, washed it, and returned it to the shed.

We went to the tigers. As the cats watched from behind gates, we set a pile of meat on three concrete pavers. Zemira released the latches, and the animals rushed in.

Next, we fed the lions, setting food on a wooden platform and watching them gnaw and crush the bones.

Zemira fed the albino leopard scraps from the end of a wooden pole. He backed away as if she was about to shock him with an electric prod, crept near, dragging his belly close to the ground, and snatched the meat. He retreated to the back of the enclosure to eat before returning for more.

As we went to a plywood and steel-mesh building Judy had converted into a jaguar house, Zemira said, 'I saw.'

'Huh?'

'The girl. Antonia Soto.' Her voice was flat. 'I hate it.'

'Yeah, me too.'

'Right.' She sounded like she doubted me.

I felt her suspicion in my gut. 'I didn't touch the Bronson brothers.'

'That's not what people say.' She pushed the bloody wheelbarrow back to the hose station.

Through the rest of the morning, we hammered nails, dug post-holes, and poured concrete for an enclosure that would house a tiger Judy had agreed to take from Zooland Park, forty miles north of Baton Rouge.

At a quarter to twelve, I put down my tools and knocked on Judy's door. Diane – a narrow-faced woman with short black hair – let me in, and we went to the living room. Judy sat on a paisley couch with the TV on. Diane settled in next to her, pulled a can of Sprite from a box on a coffee table, and tossed it to me. 'We don't do a lot of company,' she said.

Action News at Noon led with Antonia's death. A bearded, sad-eyed anchor said the body of an undocumented Mexican child was discovered late the previous afternoon. The police were investigating her death as a homicide. He showed a map of the creeks and rivers at the northeast corner of the city, including a boat launch where I'd sometimes fished for flounder before I went to prison. To one side of the ramp, a winding waterway, too narrow and obscure to have a name, reached through marshes into a low forest. To the other side, Horseshoe Creek flowed into Clapboard Creek, which tentacled through more marshes and fed into the St Johns River, which emptied into the Atlantic Ocean. The anchor pointed to a backwater bend in Clapboard Creek where a young couple, out on their motorboat, found Antonia.

The station cut to a reporter in a blue dress for an exclusive interview with the couple, Rick and Kenyon Munro. Kenyon, small and nervous-eyed, and Rick, in a black ball cap and a black T-shirt, stood by a jon boat on an apartment complex parking lot. The husband said they'd gone boating with their black lab, letting themselves get lost as they sometimes did when they had an afternoon off.

The dog had nosed the air and whined.

'Then I smelled it,' the wife said.

'We both did,' the man said. 'Something terrible.'

'You don't mistake that smell,' she said.

'I thought it might be a dead deer,' he said. 'They stink like that. I pulled up my shirt so I could breathe.' To show the reporter, he pulled the collar of his black T-shirt over his nose.

'I wanted to turn around,' the wife said.

'There was nowhere to go,' her husband said. 'Quicker to round another bend – we'd be out of it in a minute.'

'The dog went wild,' she said.

'Yeah, I saw something in the water,' he said. 'It looked like a tree trunk. I thought it might be a dead dolphin.'

'Which was ridiculous,' she said.

'It was the girl,' he said. 'She had on a yellow dress.'

When the camera cut back to the anchor, Judy said, 'Shame,' and Diane took her hand.

I could hardly breathe, hardly move.

The anchor said *Action News* had reached out to Lieutenant Detective Deborah Holt, who was leading the investigation, but the detective hadn't returned calls.

'Hell,' I said. Deborah Holt was Bill Higby's partner in the homicide unit. When I came out from Raiford, she'd tried to help him lock me back up before changing her mind about me.

I left the living room, went out of the house. Breathless, sweating, I stopped at the pickup truck and leaned against the hood. I sucked air deep into my lungs.

Zemira, who was pushing her wheelbarrow toward the work shed, stopped and watched. She wiped sweat from her forehead with the back of her hand and said, 'What?'

If I opened my mouth, I might scream. I got in the truck and started the engine.

'Hey,' Zemira said, 'we have a fence to finish.'

I hit the gas and barreled out over the rutted drive.

* * *

A half hour later, I pulled into the Cardinal Motel parking lot and slid into the spot outside my door. Susan was coming out of her room in jean shorts, a Jack Daniels T-shirt, and white platform sandals. She gazed at me through the windshield, shook her head, and walked toward the vending machines outside Hopper's office.

I went in and locked my door. I set the window AC low and turned the fan high. My heart was racing. I stripped off my shirt and pants, ran in place, fast, for five minutes, then did a hundred jumping lunges. I ran another five minutes and did more lunges. When my legs ached, I lay on the carpet and did a hundred pushups, a hundred and fifty sit-ups, and more pushups. I kept at it for an hour until my muscles burned and my skin was slick with sweat. Then I showered, shedding a film of salt and dirt, as if the jets from the showerhead could penetrate to my nerves and course through my blood, cleaning me of all I remembered, all I knew.

I dried and, though I'd promised Dr Patel at my last reintegration appointment I would find healthier ways to fight bad thoughts, climbed into bed. I pulled the pillow over my face and held it so I couldn't breathe. When I ripped it away and gasped, I forgot myself for a few seconds, forgot Antonia Soto and the Bronson brothers, forgot Bill Higby insisting, insisting, *insisting* until his words, his goddamned certainty, got inside my head and I believed them for long enough to repeat them, long enough to put me in a cage for eight years. Now, another child was dead. The world seemed full of dead children, a parade in time and space, the little feet marching.

In my few seconds of relief, I turned from the parade. I receded from the world. My ears rang and my body buzzed as I gasped and gasped.

Then I held the pillow over my face and did it again.

Dr Patel called it autoerotic asphyxiation, but he was wrong. When I held the pillow over my face, I approached death – I held it in my body for long enough that I wasn't afraid of it. When I breathed again, for a few seconds, the living world didn't terrify me either.

At four in the afternoon, Cynthia called.

I told her I'd left Safe Haven early and needed a night on my own.

'What's wrong?' she said.

I said Antonia was dead. I said Deborah Holt was leading the investigation. I said, 'It's all too close.'

'Where are you now?' Cynthia said.

'I just finished working out.'

'That's not what I asked.'

'I'm in bed.'

'*Franky?*'

'I'm fine.'

Forty-five minutes later, she knocked on the door.

I opened. 'I don't need you to save me.'

'We need each other.' She pushed past, into the room.

'*Out,*' I said.

She went to the bed and pulled off the sheets, throwing them on the carpet.

'Goddammit.'

She stopped. 'You look bad,' she said. 'And you smell like shit.'

'I showered.'

'Shower again.'

'Get out.'

'Don't be a baby.' She went to the AC and turned down the fan. Then she unbuttoned her Bourne-Goff Storage shirt and took off her bra. She undid her pants and slid them off.

'What are you doing?' I said.

'You aren't the only one who's messed up.' She went into the bathroom and turned on the shower.

I dialed the AC fan back to high and put the sheets on the bed. I lay down and waited.

A half hour later, I was still waiting.

I went into the bathroom and opened the shower door. 'What are you doing?'

Her wet hair hung down her neck. Her scarred legs glistened red. 'What do you *think* I'm doing?'

I gazed at her. 'I hate myself,' I said.

'Don't,' she said.

I stepped into the shower. Another slick of sweat sloughed from me. We stood together. As she watched, I soaped myself. She turned the water hot and hotter, until it stung my skin.

I asked, 'Does it hurt your legs?'

'Yes,' she said.

'Why do you do this?'

'I don't have a choice.'

When we got out, we lay on my bed together. In the cold wind from the air conditioner, she said, 'Tell me.'

I told her how Judy Pollard hit me with Antonia's death as I arrived at Safe Haven, how we watched the interview on the noon news. I tried to explain my panic when I heard Deborah Holt was in charge. The rest of it, I said, I couldn't explain.

'Turn over,' she said.

I did, and she held me from behind, and though I wanted to kick free and run and run, I let her hold me.

'You need to do something,' she said.

'Like what?'

'You can't let it go. It won't let you.'

'I'm too late,' I said.

'When you got out of prison, you refused to let Higby beat you down. You showed him. You showed everyone. You made things right.'

'Things are never right.'

'Right enough. Do what you would've done if you'd tried to find Antonia when you thought she'd run away.'

'Why?'

'Because what else are you going to do?'

Sweat broke from my skin. 'No.'

'You can't hide.'

'Watch me.'

We were lying there still, naked in the cold room, when my phone rang – then rang again, and again.

'Answer it?' Cynthia said.

'No.'

She reached to the bedside table, swiped the phone, and handed it to me.

Dr Patel was on the other end. 'You can't just walk out on a job in the middle of a day,' he said.

I closed my eyes, opened them. 'Everyone's telling me what I can't do.'

He said, 'Judy took you on as a favor to me.'

'Like another beat-up animal? Feed me raw meat and hope for the best?'

'You aren't at fault, but men like you don't get a lot of chances.'

'Why don't I? I'm free, right? The judge exonerated me. Why shouldn't I get chances?'

'You know it doesn't work that way, Franky.'

'Exactly.'

'You can only control what *you* do and what *you* think about yourself.'

I laughed at him. 'You think I can control that?'

'We can give you the tools. That's what we're working on.'

I breathed hard. 'Tell Judy I'm sorry for leaving.'

'No, Franky – you tell her. Take responsibility for your actions.'

FIVE

When I pulled the Ford into the Chartein Farm drive in the morning, the kitchen light in the manager's singlewide was off. I stopped and let the engine idle. After a few minutes, I touched the horn.

The kitchen light went on, and Everett Peters stumbled out the door. His old German shepherd came out behind him, stiff-hipped.

'Running late this morning,' he said as he got in on the passenger side. 'Cops tied us up all day yesterday. Let's go to the cold shed.'

'The woman detective here?' I asked.

'Holt? Sure. Talked to everyone but the chickens. Jesus Christ, you'd've thought the president got assassinated.'

'What did she say?'

'She didn't. But a deputy told me Antonia got shot in the back of the head.'

'What else?'

He glanced at me in the dark cab. 'Do blood and guts turn you on? I've heard about you.'

My belly tightened. 'I feel for her, that's all. Her and her family.'

'Well, *she* doesn't feel anything anymore. The deputy said something chewed on her out there. In the water less than twenty-four hours, but the fish must like Mexican.'

I hit the brakes hard, and he slammed into the dashboard. 'You think this is funny?'

He glared and drew a sharp breath. 'You want my chickens, *never* do that again.' He leaned back in his seat. 'Jesus – are you crazy, boy?'

I drove to the shed, and he unlocked the door. 'Load them yourself,' he said, and walked back toward his trailer.

By the time I'd put the dead birds into the truck bed and tied the tarp over them, the sun was coming up. The big bay door on Chicken House One was open, the lights bright inside. Mr Chartein stood in front of Chicken House Three alongside Antonia's parents and a heavyset Black man with braided cornrows.

Then a van, with a broadcasting mast and a *First Coast News* logo, came up the drive, followed by a little white Miata. Mr Chartein waved them over, and two women climbed from the van with a camera set-up. One had the group move to the side of the chicken house. The other positioned a camera tripod. A small man with gelled hair got out of the Miata.

I went over to watch.

The small man glanced at me as if he recognized me, then fixed his face with a gentle smile and went to Antonia's mom and dad. He shook hands with the Black man, who introduced himself as Demetrius Jones and said he was an immigration advocate.

The interview of the Sotos lasted less than two minutes. As the advocate stood off camera, the reporter asked Antonia's mom what happened on the evening her daughter disappeared.

Wide-eyed, clutching her husband's arm, she said Antonia went out with friends – her cousin and others – and didn't come home. 'She go to dance.' She seemed about to smile, but her mouth fell, as if she struggled with the memory of her daughter dancing. 'She is a child. Why?'

The reporter expressed sympathy and asked if she had any words for the person who'd killed her daughter.

She looked confused. 'No – no. ¿*Por qué?*' She let go of her husband and leaned toward the camera. 'What good?' It was an angry demand. The blow of Antonia's death had shattered her inside, but it was clear that she'd been struck before and learned to absorb terrible pain.

'Mr Soto?' The reporter held the microphone to Antonia's dad.

Antonia's dad put his hand on it as though it could keep him from falling. 'If I find the man who did this, I will kill him.'

Demetrius Jones stepped in. 'You'll cut that part,' he told the reporter.

The small man asked Antonia's dad, 'Do you want to try again?'

He did. Once more, he clasped the microphone. 'Who did I hurt? Who did Antonia hurt?' His anger, so powerful a moment before, seemed gone. His eyes were wet. 'Why? We only wanted to live. We wanted to work and eat – and live. Was that too much?'

'Thank you, Mr Soto.' The reporter looked at the camera and said, '*Why?* That's the question the distraught parents of Antonia Soto are asking law enforcement this morning. From the northwest side, this is Chris Arnaud.' The camera cut, and the reporter turned back to Antonia's dad. 'Wow – that was great.'

Martin Soto looked like he wanted to take him by the throat.

Demetrius Jones put a hand on the grieving man's shoulder.

Walking back to the Miata, the reporter paused and pointed at me – hesitating as if he could almost recall my name – then climbed in and started the engine.

As the camera operators packed their equipment into the van, another car came up the drive. I knew the car from before – a black Mercury Grand Marquis – and I rushed back toward the pickup.

But Antonia's mom saw me. 'Franky.'

I kept going.

'Franky?'

I stopped and she came to me.

'You do not need to run away,' she said. '*No te culpo.* They do this – not you.'

I looked at her, this broken but powerful woman. 'When you asked me to look for her, you said she brought a piece of paper home – with threats and pictures. What were the threats? What were the pictures?'

'They are terrible pictures. I will not . . .' She seemed to pull herself together. 'They say they hurt Antonia. Do you understand? They tell her what they do to her.'

'Who are *they*? Kids from school?'

'*Tal vez.* I don't know. They are sick.'

The Grand Marquis stopped beside the news van. Detective Holt got out of the driver's side – a solid, olive-skinned woman with black hair in a ponytail. She looked around as if she'd landed on a strange planet and needed to assess the dangers. When she saw me, she cocked her head, perplexed.

I looked back to Antonia's mom. 'I'm sorry to ask this, but did they say they would shoot her? Did they say they would put her in the water?'

She shook her head. 'It does not matter now.'

'Do you still have the note?'

'I give it to the police.'

I nodded at Holt. 'That one?'

'Yes. Yesterday.'

'All right,' I said. 'I'll see what I can find out.'

Her eyes showed her pain. 'Why? What difference now?'

'I'll go to the bar.'

'It is too late.'

'I also need to talk to her cousin. Can you tell me how to find her?'

'Clara? She tell you nothing.'

Then Bill Higby climbed from the passenger side of the Grand Marquis.

I made myself breathe. 'Please,' I said to Antonia's mom. 'The cousin.'

The woman sighed. 'She live in the blue house that way.' She pointed down the narrow highway. I had passed a robin-egg-blue house, two miles to the south, on my runs between Safe Haven and the chicken farm.

Higby glanced around. He was a big man with thinning hair. When he'd first arrested me long ago, he'd carried most of his weight in his chest and shoulders. During my time at Raiford, it had settled into his belly.

Spotting me, he looked as perplexed as Holt. Then he charged toward me.

'What the hell are you doing here?' He stepped between Antonia's mom and me.

I hated everything about him. 'Look in my truck. Climb under the tarp if you want some company.'

'I asked what you're doing here?' He touched his hip, where he sometimes carried a service pistol, though his belt was bare now.

'I'm picking up chickens. It's my job.'

'Since when?'

'Did you come here to talk to me?'

Antonia's mom asked him, 'Do you know something about Antonia?'

He glanced at her, unsettled. 'No . . . no.' He softened. 'I'm sorry . . . we have more questions.'

'Be careful what you tell him,' I told her.

He glared. 'Get going.'

I said, 'Don't trust this man.'

He turned on me again. 'You can leave now or ride out of here in the back of our car.'

'For what?' I walked away.

As I climbed into my truck, Higby was asking about Antonia's boyfriend, Carlos Medina. Was her mom sure he'd told her he was working late at El Jimador when Antonia disappeared from Bar Deportivo?

I drove to Safe Haven.

I set chicken on the concrete pavers for the tigers and lions. Zemira fed the albino leopard with her wooden pole. We finished sinking posts for the new Zooland tiger enclosure and put up the fencing.

When I apologized to Judy for leaving the previous day, she said, 'The animals need to eat. They need a place to live. Without us – without the work we do – they die. I won't allow that.'

'I left for one afternoon,' I said.

'Are you going to argue with me? We're talking about responsibility.'

'Yeah,' I said. 'I know.'

SIX

The dance floor at Bar Deportivo was empty except for a couple doing the salsa to Oscar D'León's 'Llorarás.' A red-filtered spotlight shined on them from a rig of strobes. Three bartenders, dressed in ruffled shirts, stood at a long bar. A bank of large-screen TVs silently streamed a soccer game, a telenovela, and an animated show with a blue bear and a beady-eyed man in a black top hat.

I went to the bar. 'A Tecate, please.'

None of the bartenders moved. They watched the dancing couple, stone-faced.

'*Por favor.*'

The bartender on the end yawned, went to the taps, drew a beer. I gave him a ten. 'Antonia Soto,' I said.

He leaned against the bar. 'You don't belong here. Guys like you, we get them all the time. You want to get laid by a hot Latina, am I right? Maybe you dig the music?'

'Did you see Antonia?' I asked. 'Before she disappeared?'

He glanced at the other bartenders. They stayed put. 'Drink your beer and leave.'

'I'm a friend of the family.'

He almost smiled. '*You* are?'

'Alejandra and Martin Soto. Out at Chartcin Farm.'

'I don't know about that.'

'And Antonia's cousin, Clara.'

He lowered his eyelids. 'You know Clara?'

'Antonia's mom told me about her. She said the two of them came here together.'

He glanced at the other bartenders again. 'Maybe you can find Clara in there.' He gestured at a door to a side room.

'You saw nothing?'

'*Nada.* It gets rowdy here after ten. Drinking, dancing, maybe some kissing in the corners. I watch the beer and the cash register. Then I close my eyes.' He nodded at the door to the side room. 'I wouldn't stay too long. When it gets rowdy, someone might kick your ass.'

I carried my drink to the other room.

Six men and four women played pool on red felt tables. The men were thick-legged and wore faded jeans and untucked T-shirts, as if they'd worked long days and – except for a squirt of cologne and a change into cowboy boots – couldn't be expected to make an effort for a night out. The women wore tight dresses and red lipstick, their hair hanging loose past their shoulders – all but one, who'd cut hers short, bleaching it dirty blond. That one wore big hoop earrings and a black leather choker studded with a piece of amethyst.

When she leaned over her table to shoot, the others watched.

One of the other women, who played with a burly man at the last table, looked like she could be Antonia's cousin. I crossed the room and stood by an old *Cinco de Mayo* poster, waiting for a chance.

Then the blond woman sank a bank shot, and another woman laughed and said, '*Clara*,' so the first syllable rhymed with *star*.

Clara was playing against a large man in his forties, his jeans tight against big legs, a leather cowboy hat on his head.

When I said, 'Excuse me,' he sucked in a slow breath as if I'd made a mistake.

'Are you Antonia Soto's cousin?' I asked her.

She nodded. 'Who are you?'

'My name's Franky Dast. I knew Antonia at the farm. I do pickups there.'

She eyed me dubiously. 'OK.'

'Can we talk?'

She handed her pool stick to the man in the cowboy hat and walked into the main room.

We sat at a table by the bank of TVs, and she asked, 'What do you want?'

'I told your aunt I would see if I could find out what happened to Antonia.'

'Why would she want *you* to do that?'

'A year ago, I got out of prison for something I didn't do. Then I found the guy who did it. I was in the news for a while. She must've found out.'

She tapped a fingernail on the table. 'What did they arrest you for?'

'They said I killed two boys.'

'Big time. So you came here looking for me?'

'I came because this is where Antonia disappeared. I didn't expect to see you.'

She leaned across the table. She had the same wide eyes as Antonia, so dark the pupil blended with the iris.

I said, 'Someone was threatening her – with a note and drawings. Maybe kids from school.'

'No way. I saw the note. Fourteen-year-old kids don't know that stuff. They don't think that way. A man wrote it. A real *hijo de puta*.'

'What did it say?'

She shook her head. 'Antonia was grown-up for a fourteen-year-old. Coming across the border, she saw a lot of things – a lot that a kid should never know about . . . what happened to my Aunt Alejandra, her mom. But this note? It terrified her.'

'What did it say?'

'It called her an animal. It said they would slaughter her like a pig. She would be sacrificed – tied down and gagged, so when she squealed like a pig, no one would hear. You know, in Spanish the word *sacrificar* also means *butcher*. There was a drawing of it in case she couldn't imagine it.'

'Did it say she would be shot?'

'No – nothing that simple.'

'Anything about the creek where the boaters found her?'

'No. It was just crazy stuff. Sick. Someone wanted to scare her.'

'She had no idea who wrote it?'

'Oh, she had an idea.'

'Huh?'

'But she wouldn't tell me. She knew that if she did, I would go after him. Whoever wrote it wanted to scare her.'

'She was too scared to tell you who wrote it but not too scared to show it to you?'

'When you're fourteen years old and undocumented, everything in the world should scare you. But if you let your fear become bigger than you – if you're paralyzed by it – you might as well lie down. So you make choices. What to tell. What to keep to yourself. You live on top of your fear, not under it. Sometimes you laugh at it.'

'I loved her laugh,' I said.

'Yeah,' she said. 'Me too.'

I looked at her. Antonia's mom thought she was reckless, but she seemed thoughtful. 'Do you mind if I ask what you do?'

'You mean when I'm not hustling suckers on the pool table?' She smiled. 'I'm a teacher. Callahan Middle School – seventh-grade math.'

I must have given her a funny look.

'Not only white boys go to college.'

'I didn't.'

'Well, I did. I grew up here. When I was a kid, I went to the same school where I teach. My dad came twelve years before his brother – Antonia's dad. My family has the same stories, the same experiences. But I got lucky – I was born here.'

Her eyes made me think she'd faced down some fears too. I said, 'Could her boyfriend have done this? Carlos?'

She allowed a sad smile. 'The boy she *wanted* to be her boyfriend. Carlos is gentle. Not so smart, but very kind.'

'There was nothing between them?'

'A fourteen-year-old's hopes and dreams.'

'How about Everett Peters – the Chartein Farm manager? He seems like a racist and a prick.'

'If every racist prick killed us, there would be no Mexicans in this country.' She stood up. 'Do you know how many undocumented kids die or disappear every year? Do you know how little time and money the police spend trying to figure out what happened?'

I must have given her another look.

'You seem like a bright guy. Look it up. That's probably why my aunt asked you for help. She knows what she'll get from the authorities. Antonia was a pretty girl. She'll be in the headlines for a few days, but then watch what happens.' She walked back to the room with the pool tables.

I finished my beer and went to the bar again.

The bartender came over. '*¿Muy bien?*'

'Yeah, thanks. Do you keep security video of the parking lot?'

His friendliness evaporated. 'What do you think, *compadre*? If our customers drive down the street with a broken taillight, the cops put them in jail. If they stay home, ICE kicks down their doors. Should we put cameras outside so maybe the cops and ICE can have easier jobs?'

'Sorry.'

'Don't be sorry. Just go.'

A half hour later, I lay on my bed and called Cynthia.

She was at home with her parents after a day at Bourne-Goff Storage. I told her about running into Holt and Higby, about apologizing to Judy Pollard, and about talking with Clara Soto and the bartender.

'How are you feeling?' she asked.

'Pretty good.'

'Yeah?'

'Yeah,' I said. 'Now tell me something boring and normal.'

'A creepy guy came in today and asked me out to dinner.'

'I meant something nice.' Cynthia worked alone at a reception desk between the two halves of the business – one side with self-storage units for individual renters, and one side with warehouse space, cold storage, and blast freezers. She answered the phone, rented lockers, and cut locks for clients who lost their keys. Once or twice a week, a customer would ask her out. He would usually be sweaty from lugging an old easy chair or his grown children's bikes.

'Expensive blue suit,' she said. 'Good shoes. Gray hair – very distinguished. I told him he was too old for me. He said I hurt his feelings, and anyway he had a BMW and a couple of other fancy cars that he drove like a kid. He said he would treat me better than a boy with a smelly truck.'

I felt a sting. 'He meant me?'

'I don't think he was being specific. The funny thing is, he didn't have a storage unit – at least I didn't recognize him. I think he came in just to flirt with me.'

'Tell me something nicer and more boring.'

'My dad's freaking out again. I don't know how much more of him I can take.'

Years ago, he'd dropped a cigarette when he fell asleep, starting the fire that burned her legs. Since then, he'd swung between guilt and anger, as if his pain from having hurt her became too much for him, and then he would lash out against her as the source of his shame.

I said, 'You can come here.'

'If I spend more time with you than I already do, he'll kick me out.'

'That would solve the problem.'

'It would make it worse. He told me twice tonight that he would never hurt me. I didn't know what to say. I feel like I owe him something.'

'I know.'

When we hung up, I stared at the blank screen on my phone. The motel was quiet – no banging on the walls, no hollering from outside. I could imagine I lived far away. Then a siren whined in the distance. Far away had its tragedies too.

At eleven o'clock, I turned on *First Coast News* to watch the reporter interview Antonia's parents. The program led with a press conference at the Sheriff's Office. The sheriff stood at a wooden podium and said the police were searching for a person of interest. He said Carlos Medina had been Antonia's nineteen-year-old boyfriend and should be considered dangerous. The news showed a still image of a long-faced man with golden-brown skin, thick eyebrows, and a big-toothed smile – then a picture of Carlos and Antonia together, his arms wrapped around her from behind.

'Well, shit,' I said. So much for what Antonia's cousin knew about them.

The news anchor recapped the story of the killing and then cut to a city council member named Randall Lehmann, who also had something to say about it.

About sixty-five years old, he was new on the council, winning a special election to replace a member who'd had a heart attack. He had promised to protect what he called the cultural integrity of the city. So far, that meant opposing plans for a homeless shelter in his district and supporting not only keeping statues of heroes from the old South but putting up new ones.

On TV, he wore a white Oxford shirt, with the sleeves pushed to his elbows, and a neatly knotted yellow tie. He said, 'As sad as the death of this young woman is, it should surprise no one. When you live outside the law, you assume risks. We're sympathetic people, but we shouldn't waste our sympathy. Let's think about *innocent* victims.' Then he called for Immigration and Customs Enforcement, with the assistance of the Sheriff's Office, to conduct a countywide sweep of factories and farms.

'Asshole,' I said, and turned off the TV.

The day had been too much.

I got down on the carpet and did pushups, stopping at thirty. I lay on my belly, then got up and opened my French horn case.

I tried a couple of notes.

I ran through a scale.

I played the opening of 'Across the Stars' – and stopped. Hopper had no sense of humor. I put on a coat and carried the horn out to my truck.

I drove over the St Johns River, went north, crossed the Trout River, and cut east toward the ocean. A half hour after locking my door, I went through a lowland cedar forest and rolled to a stop by the boat launch into Horseshoe Creek. Ten years earlier, I would come at midnight and, standing on the shore beside the ramp, cast a hook baited with shrimp and reel in fish after fish. But two days ago, a nervous-eyed woman, her husband, and their dog had boarded a jon boat, drifted into Clapboard Creek, and smelled a terrible stink.

I got out with the horn. The night was cool and clear and quiet. A three-quarters moon hung over the marsh. The black ghost of a night bird cut across the sky. I went down to the boat ramp. The water was still, the pavement damp where an ebbing tide had slicked it. Beside the ramp, up in a sandy area, someone had planted a white wooden cross and laid two bouquets of flowers by it.

I held my horn to my lips. I tried to play 'Llorarás' from Bar Deportivo. I tried 'Across the Stars.' The music sounded nothing like it should except as I bent the noise in my imagination. Next to the ramp, on a strip of sand and broken shells, tiny fiddler crabs skittered in the moonlight, ducking into holes, the males battling for territory with their big claws.

I said, 'I don't care.'

I tried the horn again. More noise.

I shouted, 'I don't care.'

I blew the horn with all my might.

SEVEN

The next morning, I woke up twenty minutes late. Jenquist Meat would turn me away once their day shift started, and I knew better than to go to Safe Haven with an empty truck. As I pulled on my pants, someone knocked on the door.

I froze.

Don't answer if you don't know who . . .

At five in the morning, don't answer at all unless someone yells murder.

I pulled back the window shade.

Demetrius Jones, the immigration advocate, stood outside my door. He wore a black windbreaker and carried a briefcase.

He saw me at the window.

'Franky Dast?'

I opened the door. 'I don't have time.'

'Right. Alejandra Soto said you work early. I hoped I'd catch you.'

I let him in and put on my shirt. 'What do you need?'

He gave me a business card. He was a lawyer specializing in immigration appeals with an organization called Vanguard Reform. 'We're working with Antonia's parents,' he said. 'I understand you also offered to help.'

'No – Alejandra asked when Antonia first went missing. I turned her down . . . until it was too late.'

'If it's too late, why did you agree to help now?' Each braid of his cornrowed hair ended with a single black bead.

'Why do you care?' I put on my boots.

'Vanguard is committing to the Sotos. We need to know who we have on our team. I looked you up yesterday evening, and, to tell the truth, you sort of scare the hell out of me. Having you on our side might be as bad as buying the Sotos tickets for the border.'

I went to the door. 'I've got to go.'

He walked with me out to the truck.

'The thing is, Alejandra Soto wants you involved,' he said. 'I don't know why. But as a matter of respect, we try to follow family wishes.'

I climbed in and started the engine.

'We can't pay you,' he said. 'Even if we had the funds, you have no credentials for the work she wants you to do.'

'I agreed to help for free.'

'I understand that,' he said. 'But her employers would like to give you something – I guess we could call it an honorarium. Nothing official.'

'The Charteins want to give me money?'

'I tried to persuade them out of it. If they want to help the bigger cause, they could donate to Legal Aid or the Immigrant Coalition – or us. But they aren't interested in the bigger cause. They want to help the Sotos.'

'Generous.'

'They seem like good people,' he said. 'They take folks in. They keep the Sotos and other undocumented families even though that could put them at risk. They pay OK, and their housing is better than it might be.'

'How much do they want to give me?'

He pulled a check from his briefcase. It was for three hundred dollars.

He smiled. 'It's the thought that counts, right?'

'I don't want it.'

'Well, that's foolish. No strings attached. They gave it to show they support the Sotos. If you don't like it, you can give it back yourself. Just don't do anything that makes the situation worse than it is already.'

'Why are you taking the Sotos on as a cause?'

'They're visible right now, and they have an important story,' he said. 'People will fight over them. They need supporters.'

'I saw that city councilman on the news last night.'

'Randall Lehmann? He's a son of a bitch.'

'Does anyone listen to him?'

'A couple of ICE agents went to Chartein Farm three hours after the police left yesterday. Lehmann tipped them. The bastards thought yesterday would be a good time to check up on a mom and dad who'd just learned their daughter was murdered. You know, get 'em while they're hot. They don't care about Antonia. She's one less Mexican to bus back across the border. The only way you matter in this country is if you're sweet and white.'

'I don't feel so sweet either,' I said.

'You're a special category – white ex-cons. You're what happens when the sugar goes bad.'

'Cute. Do the cops really think Antonia's boyfriend did it?'

'Carlos Medina?' he said. 'That would be convenient, wouldn't it? Mexican-on-Mexican crime. Immigrant-on-immigrant.'

'Then he didn't do it?'

'Hell, no. But let's say for a moment he did. How does a guy who's scraping by on tips from his restaurant job find a boat to dump her body in a backwater creek – and why does he bother? Carlos is easy pickings, that's all. Throw him in jail, kick Antonia's mom and dad out of the country, and the police can be done with it.'

'Yeah, I know something about being an easy target.'

'That's what I saw online.'

'The detective who went after me is the partner of the lead detective on Antonia's murder.'

'Yeah, I saw that too. Bill Higby.'

'He likes low-hanging fruit. Can't resist it. Deborah Holt is better. She might be tempted, but she'll think twice.'

Twenty minutes later, I drove up to a bay door at Jenquist Meat. As I climbed out, their morning work whistle blew, as it had blown every morning since the packing house opened a hundred years earlier. The Jenquists had owned the plant since the beginning, and the fourth-generation owner had gone to high school with Judy Pollard. His name was Ollie, and she called him one of the good ones, a group that seemed to include only a handful of people in the city. His day-shift supervisor had warned me twice to show up before the whistle or not at all. But inside, a logistics clerk led me to a pallet of assorted pork and lamb scraps and called over a hard-hatted woman to forklift it into the back of the pickup.

Another twenty minutes later, when I pulled into Safe Haven, Judy, her wife, and Zemira remained in the house. I drove to the refrigerator shed and carted the meat inside.

When Zemira came out, she was uncharacteristically cheerful.

'What happened?' I asked.

'We're getting two tigers instead of one from Zooland Park.'

'Hooray?'

She gazed at me as if trying to get inside my thinking. 'This is good news, Franky.'

'Zooland just happened to find another tiger?'

'They were hoping to hold on to their last one. But the Department of Agriculture threatened to take away their license unless they closed the tiger exhibit completely. We'll give them a good home.'

'A cage is a cage.'

Her smile fell. 'Do you think so? The cats we take have been crammed into tiny pens and concrete pits. Abused.'

'So we put them in bigger pens, talk to them nicely, and change their water twice a day.'

'What should we do? Free them? Ship them to a jungle and release them? They would starve unless they got lucky and other animals killed them first. There's no such thing as getting out of a cage for them, but there are better cages and worse.'

She'd never said so much to me at one time. 'I like you better when you're quiet.'

She shook her head. 'I know you've had it hard, but that's no excuse for being a jerk.'

'I don't like cages.'

'Yeah? Well, welcome to the world.'

That evening, I met Cynthia for dinner at El Jimador.

The wall inside the front door displayed hundreds of snapshots of customers eating chimichangas and giant burritos, drinking margaritas out of oversized glasses. Some customers wore a sequined El Jimador sombrero while downing shots of tequila. Carlos Medina – tall, thin, his big-toothed smile stretching across his long face – appeared in many of the photos, gripping the tequila bottle, laughing wide-mouthed.

The hostess took us to a table across from the kitchen, and I glanced around the room. 'Where's Carlos?'

She handed us menus and walked away.

Cynthia said, 'You're fooling no one.'

When a busboy poured our water, I asked, 'Is Carlos here tonight?'

'*No sé.*' He left to get our chips and salsa.

'Tell Carlos to stop by if he's here,' I said, when he returned.

He disappeared back into the kitchen.

Cynthia said, 'Why are you doing this? You know he won't be here.'

'Something I learned in prison. If you ask a question often enough, you'll make someone mad or find someone to talk to you. Usually both.'

After a while, a short woman in a blouse embroidered with flowers came to take our order.

'Tacos al pastor,' Cynthia said.

'Enchiladas Suizas,' I said. 'Carlos around?'

'Not tonight,' she said, and darted into the kitchen.

A few minutes later, a heavy man with a wide black leather belt, the top buttons on his shirt open, came to the table. 'What?'

'Are you the manager?'

'One of the co-owners. Why are you asking about Carlos?'

'Nine years ago, a cop arrested me for a crime I didn't commit. I spent eight years in prison before anyone realized I was telling the truth. Some people still suspect I did it.'

'So what?' He carried his belly as if it was muscle. There were men at Raiford like that, some of the deadliest.

'So, did Carlos Medina kill Antonia Soto?'

'Why do you care?'

'Antonia Soto's mom asked me to help.'

He looked as if he'd spent a lifetime of tolerating hustlers and fools and he'd run out of patience. 'No, she didn't.'

'You ever meet Antonia?' I said.

'Maybe I did.'

'Lived out at Chartein Farm with her mom and dad. Dad's name is Martin. Mom's name is Alejandra.'

He still looked suspicious.

'Cousin's name is Clara,' I said. 'She's a school teacher.'

He let out a breath, then pulled an empty chair from the next table and sat down. 'What they say about Carlos – it is not true.'

'What do they say?' I said.

He considered me. 'The police are looking for him,' he said.

'He told them he was here on the night Antonia disappeared. But was he?'

The man looked impatient again.

I asked, 'Then how do you know?'

'I hired him when he first came,' he said. 'He's a good person. He's funny, you know – wants to have a good time. It's always a party. Everyone likes Carlos. Everyone.'

'Where is he?'

He shook his head.

'Wherever it is, if he didn't kill Antonia, he needs to stay there,' I said. 'If the cops stop saying he's a person of interest but they still want to talk to him, he should keep hiding unless they've arrested someone else.'

'You don't think he knows this? When you're in this country like Carlos and the Sotos, you always look for a hole to hide in if the authorities come.'

'Good,' I said. 'Do you have a pen?'

He gave me one, and I wrote my phone number on a paper

napkin. 'Get this to him. I can't do much, but maybe I can put him in touch with someone who can.'

He stood up. 'Why do you care about Carlos?'

'I'm just trying to make sense of things.'

He looked doubtful. 'Do you think you're a hero? Are you going to ride in on your horse and save him?'

'Not me.'

'Because we don't need horses in here. They break the tables and make a mess.'

EIGHT

E arly the next morning, I turned into Chartein Farm and drove past the chicken houses to the cold shed. Next to the shed, by a tool and equipment building, Everett Peters and Mrs Chartein's brother Harry had Harry's house-painting van up on blocks. On the side, the business name, *Reclamation Painting*, stretched over the image of a brush dripping blue paint. The hood was open, the engine running. Peters was lying on a creeper dolly. When I got out, he slid under the van.

'Good morning,' I said.

Harry smiled a hello. He was pale and slack-muscled, and he held his eyes in a cheerful squint as if he'd looked too long at the sun. With his sunburned cheeks, he reminded me of a cherub.

I called under the van. 'Any chickens for me?'

Peters was silent.

Harry grinned as if the manager was pulling a joke.

'I'll tell Judy you had nothing,' I said.

A set of keys flew from under the van and landed by my feet. 'Bring 'em back when you're done,' Peters said.

Harry followed me to the cold shed.

We carried plastic bins of chicken to the pickup, dumped them on to the truck bed, and tied the tarp. When we finished, we sprayed down the bins at the hose station. I asked, 'How well did Peters know Antonia?'

'Him? Can't say. But she grew up here. Got in everybody's

business – played at our feet until she was old enough and then worked alongside us. Sure, he knew her. We all did. But I can't say how well. Why?'

'Seems he has something against Mexicans.'

He laughed. 'Nah, more like he's got something against the world. Try to get that man to smile. But he's all right. He does his job.'

We walked back to the tool and equipment building. Peters remained under the van. I tossed the keys on the dirt by the dolly. 'Thanks.'

I knew better than to suspect a person without good reason. I'd spent eight years in prison because of that kind of suspicion.

But as I drove out past the chicken houses, I checked my rearview mirror. The tool and equipment building blocked Harry's van.

I cut toward Peters's trailer and parked at the side.

I sat in the cab thinking about what it meant to be a good man and what it meant to be a hypocrite. But I felt like I was where I needed to be, doing what I needed to do. I got out of the truck.

If Peters's door had been locked, I would have turned away.

The door was unlocked.

The main room smelled like oil and sawdust. A green leatherette sofa stood against one wall. In front of it, on a gray area rug, there was a glass-topped coffee table. Standing against the opposite wall, a kitchen table was bare except for a clay salt-and-pepper set molded in the shape of Dalmatian puppies. A painting of Peters's German shepherd, with the same precise lines and the same overexposed, too-bright background as on the Chartein Farm sign out at the highway, hung from the wall. The dog that had followed Peters down the front steps was stiff and old, but here its muscles were taut, its eyes black, almond-shaped. The fine-lined fur on its back bristled. Its mouth bared long teeth and, lurking inside, a black tongue, as if the painter saw in the tired animal a wolf-like violence. In the kitchen, which opened to the living room, a coffee cup and a single plate were perched in a drying rack by the sink.

A narrow hallway led past a closed bathroom door on one side, a washing machine and dryer on the other. I opened the bathroom door.

The German shepherd sprang out, knocking me into the washing machine. I yelled and fell. It leaped at me, its old eyes clear and vicious.

I yelled again – and the dog stopped. It tipped its head curiously.

I stood, slowly.

I inched away, back toward the main room.

It followed calmly.

I stopped at the door to the front porch.

It stared – curious.

I went to the refrigerator and found a pack of hotdogs. I pulled one out and tossed it. The dog snapped it out of the air.

I went back to the narrow hallway and past the bathroom, the German shepherd trailing me.

The bedroom had space for a queen-sized bed, but Peters's mattress was barely wider than a cot. Along with a night table, there were two lamps and a dresser. Peters lived simply – hardly seemed to live at all. I opened the dresser drawers. The top three held folded shirts and pants, neat stacks of underwear, balled socks. The bottom drawer had the kinds of things he might want if the power went out or he took a day off – a flashlight, an extension cord, a roll of duct tape, a two-pack of candles, an old pair of binoculars, a rusty Zippo lighter, a sheathed fishing knife, a roll of string, a wind-up alarm clock. Scattered on top, as if thrown into the drawer in anger or panic, were about a dozen photographs of a blond-haired girl, maybe three years old. She posed in a tiny bikini at a beach. She stood naked in a bathtub smiling at the camera. She danced in a pink leotard. She lay nude, asleep, on a mattress.

I made a sound. I didn't know what the sound meant. But it hurt like a broken bone, a torn muscle.

Then a voice spoke from the hall. 'You robbing me, boy?'

Peters stood there. His hands and face were filthy from Harry's van. He held a hammer.

'A little girl?' I said. I wanted to crush him to the floor.

He came at me, but instead of hitting me, he kicked the drawer closed, cracking the base molding. He gripped the tool. 'Get out.'

I backed into the hallway.

'Stay away from this farm.' His voice was flat. He followed me into the main room.

I reached for the door. The German shepherd stood between us, and for the first time it barked.

Then I was outside, and then I was in the pickup. I crammed the key in the ignition, and, seconds later, I was barreling south on the highway from Chartein Farm, my hands shaking on the steering wheel.

A mile down, I pulled to the side and got out, stumbled toward the line of cedars beside the road, and vomited.

When I was a kid, my teachers told my dad I was smarter than I acted. I had the *raw goods*, they said. The *nuts and bolts*. But I lacked *application*. Now I figured I was the stupidest man on the planet.

I breathed hard, sucking in the sharp smell of cedar.

What had I seen?

What did it mean?

I knew Everett Peters was a bitter man. He lived a tightfisted existence in a trailer scrubbed clean of the dirt and blood of the poultry farm. In that tiny space, he seemed to squeeze himself smaller – one coffee cup, one plate, everything stacked and orderly, all but the jumble in the bottom dresser drawer. The girl in the photos – who was she to him? Naked, dressed like a dancing doll, costumed, posing . . . for him?

But except for the pictures, his life looked like a more extreme version of my own. As far as I could see, though, no one had forced it on him. He seemed mean-minded enough to want that life. To choose it.

I went back to the truck and leaned against the hood.

I pulled out my phone and dialed the Sheriff's Office.

When a receptionist forwarded me, Holt answered her phone by spitting back my name as if it tasted rotten in her mouth. 'Franky Dast – to what do I owe the pleasure?'

I said, 'Why do you think Carlos Medina killed Antonia Soto?'

We'd been through enough together after I got out of prison that she must have thought I deserved more than a hang-up. 'Why do you think that's what I think?'

'You need to look at Everett Peters. The manager at Chartein Farm.'

'What are you talking about?'

'He has pictures of a girl. He's a sleazebag. Talk to him before you nail Carlos Medina.'

'You make no sense,' she said.

'I went into Peters's trailer. I searched it.'

She became quiet. 'Did he invite you in? Did he *let* you search it?' When I said nothing, she went on. 'Whatever you think you know, you don't.'

'Talk to him.'

'Thanks for calling, Franky.'

'Don't put me off,' I said.

'I'm not. But I'm busy.' She was kinder than most cops. 'You understand that, right?'

'I hope you're smarter than Bill Higby.'

'You just insulted both me *and* my partner. I don't appreciate that.' She hung up.

I drove to Safe Haven and unloaded the chickens into the refrigerator shed. Then, as I pushed a wheelbarrow past Judy's house toward the lion enclosure, Diane came out to the porch. She said good morning and asked, 'You all right? You're sweating a storm.'

I forced a smile. 'When do the cats come from Zooland?'

'Beginning of next week. Monday or Tuesday, depending on how they handle the move.'

'Zemira around?'

'She went to the city. You're on your own this morning.' She gave me a funny look. 'You get along OK with her?'

'We get along fine.'

She looked out across the open area between the house and the cat enclosures. 'Judy took her in the same way she took in all these injured animals. You too. Zemira has sharp claws, no question about it.'

'I suppose we all do if life makes us bare them.'

She cocked her head. 'Do you care for her?'

'I'm sorry?'

'Do you like her?'

'Not particularly.'

She nodded. 'Some people are more difficult to like than others.'

All day, I expected Judy to get a call from Chartein Farm and then to fire me.

At lunch, I Googled *Everett Peters*. Then I added the word *arrest*.

Everett Peters – forty-three years old, Caucasian, brown hair, blue eyes, five eleven, a hundred and sixty-five pounds – had three arrests, the first of them seven years ago, the last, five. The charges included disorderly conduct, DUI, resisting an officer, and an assortment of drug possession violations. No luring girls into a car or exposing himself on a playground. No shooting someone in the head – no gun charges or assaults of any kind. Even the resisting-an-officer charge went down as *without violence*.

Why didn't he hit me with his hammer when he caught me rooting through his bedroom? He could've justified knocking out my teeth. If he shot Antonia, why was there no gun in the trailer, not even a rifle to put down raccoons and possums that raided the farm? Why didn't he report me and get me fired?

He could have broken me and no one would have blamed him.

When I drove out from Safe Haven that afternoon, I'd convinced myself twice that Peters had killed Antonia and twice that he hadn't. My belly twisted with shame and anxiety and fear and I didn't know what else.

I wanted to shower and lie on the floor, rocking and rocking. But Cynthia and I planned to go to the Cineplex.

I called her and said, 'Let's hang out in my room tonight instead, if that's all right.'

'Sure. Why?'

'No reason,' I said. 'Staying in sounds good, that's all.'

'Don't do that,' she said.

'Do what?'

'Lie.'

An hour later, we ate gyros from Sahara Sandwiches on my bed. I told her everything.

'Will you go back to the farm?' she asked.

'I have to.'

She touched my forehead, as if thinking how easily a hammer could crush it. 'He must've done it.'

'I don't know.'

'The pictures,' she said.

'They could've been anyone – a daughter, a niece.'

'Nude pictures? Bikini shots?'

'They weren't necessarily like that.'

'What were they like? You wouldn't just chuck pictures of your own kid in a drawer.' She picked up a tomato slice and ate it.

'I don't know.'

She gazed at me.

'What?' I said.

'You're the best person I know,' she said.

'What did I do?'

'You broke into his trailer. You crossed the line.'

'Most people would count that against me.'

'Not me. You took a risk.' She kissed me. Then she told me that the creep who'd come into Bourne-Goff Storage to flirt with her earlier in the week had returned. 'He said he could help me out.'

'What does that mean?' I balled the sandwich foil and tossed it toward the bathroom door.

'That's what I asked him. He said if I ever got in trouble, he had friends. Friends and power. I asked him if I looked like I was in trouble. He said I looked like *a lot* of trouble. Then he said everyone has a kink. He asked me what mine was. I told him if he didn't have a storage unit, he should leave.'

'Good.'

'So he said I should go out with him. I told him my boyfriend would be jealous. I was sitting at the front desk and I had my phone in my lap, ready to call nine-one-one. He went to the door and said I didn't know what I was missing. I said I could live with that. He said, "Don't be so sure of it." I asked if he was threatening me. He said any girl who goes out with an ex-con doesn't need to worry about a harmless old guy like him.'

A jab in my belly. 'He meant *me*?'

'He must have.'

'How would he know?'

'That's what creeps me out. It's like he's been looking into me.'

'Yeah.' I got up and put the ball of sandwich foil in the bathroom garbage can. 'There's a security camera, right?'

'Video. No sound. If he comes in again, I'll get him with my phone.'

When I first came out from Raiford, everyone seemed to know who I was, from the guy at the deli counter to people on buses. The news couldn't get enough of me. I was the man who had talked himself out of a double killing and was hunting for the real killer. Strangers watched me as if they suspected I might explode with anger. Although most backed away from me or changed seats, putting me at a safe distance, a few seemed attracted to the danger. Now and then at the Cardinal, Hopper would deliver a letter a woman had addressed to the front office inviting me to hook up or come over when her husband was out. Now and then in a restaurant or a bar, a man would stand chest to chest with me as if he wanted to butt heads. A year after my release, except for one woman who sent cards from Arkansas, I'd stopped getting the mail, and, even in a crowd, men had stopped hassling me. But I still felt eyes on me.

'Keep your finger on nine-one-one,' I said.

Then we stripped off our pants, and Cynthia linked her phone to the TV. '*Frankenstein* or *The Blob*?' she said.

We sat on the bedspread, waves of cool air breaking over us from the window AC.

Cheerful music by Burt Bacharach played from the TV speaker. Red circles expanded over a black screen, as if an animator dropped pebble after pebble into a puddle of blood. Opening credits appeared on the puddle. *Steven McQueen, Aneta Corsaut, Earl Rowe . . . Color by Deluxe*. Then throbbing bold black letters replaced the names. *The Blob*.

As the movie opened, Steve McQueen kissed Aneta Corsaut in an open convertible high on a hillside lovers' lane. He called her *Janie-girl*, and she insisted he call her *Jane*.

Cynthia ran her fingers up my leg and said, 'You can call me anything you want.'

An hour and twenty minutes later, as we lay under the sheet, Steve and Jane were trapped with a crowd of townspeople in a burning diner. The Blob oozed through cracks and crevices, coming to get them, thriving on the heat and smoke. Then Steve sprayed a fire extinguisher at the flames, and the Blob recoiled from the blast. At the end of the movie, a military airplane airdropped the Blob on to Arctic ice.

Cloud-like white letters appeared over the Arctic. *The End*. But just before the screen went black, the letters curled into a big white question mark.

NINE

On most fall weekends during deer hunting season, Judy sent a truck an hour north to Brunswick, where a wild game processor saved organ meat for her. She called the offal *home cooking* and would feed it to the big cats herself. But that Saturday, with the Zooland tigers arriving in two or three days, she sent me for wire mesh to roof in the enclosure. The manufacturer that made the thick-gauge stuff was on the city's northwest side, out near Chartein Farm. I was waiting in front at eight a.m., when they opened.

Driving back with rolls of mesh in the truck bed, I cut over to the narrow highway that passed the farm. Barely visible from the highway, the bay doors on Chicken Houses Four and Five were open.

Two miles down the highway, beyond an easy bend, I passed the blue house where Alejandra Soto said Clara lived. A brown two-door Ford Ranger pickup with a beige topper over the bed stood on the driveway behind a Taurus.

I drove another half mile, then made a U-turn. Back at the house, I pulled in behind the Ranger.

When I knocked, Clara answered.

She wore a terrycloth bathrobe, and her short hair looked mussed by sleep. She had on the same black leather choker, studded with amethyst, that she'd had on at Bar Deportivo. Her dark eyes looked vacant. She said, 'What?'

'When we talked the other night, I asked if Carlos Medina could have killed Antonia. You said he was her boyfriend only in her dreams.'

'That's not quite what I said, but what about it?'

'You lied. The news showed pictures of them together.'

'I *lied*?'

'Was it the truth?'

She screwed up her mouth. 'Just because a man puts his hands on a girl doesn't mean he wants to be with her.'

'Why did you tell me there was nothing between them?'

'No, why are *you* asking these questions? Why are you bugging me at . . . what time is it? Aren't you, like, the delivery boy? You pick up the chickens, right?'

'The Charteins gave me money to ask around.'

She seemed to consider me. 'The other night, you called the manager a racist prick. Does doing this make you feel good?'

'Huh?'

'Does it make you feel righteous?'

'It's something to do, that's all.'

'Because *I* don't think it's righteous. I think you're only a guy who tries to make himself feel better. You're wasting your time.' She closed the door.

I spoke through it. 'Whose truck is on your driveway?'

She opened again. 'What business is that of yours?'

'I thought it might be one of your suckers.'

She gave me a caustic smile. 'Yeah, maybe. Maybe the world's full of suckers.'

'I can't figure you out.'

'Don't try.' She shut the door again.

I went to my truck. What did I know?

I pulled out and drove back toward Chartein Farm. Then, just before the bend, I pulled another U-turn. I steered on to the shoulder, where I could see the front of the blue house.

If I'd shaken up Clara – if she had something to be shaken up about – I wouldn't need to wait long.

Three minutes later, her front door opened, and a tall, long-faced man came out. Carlos Medina.

I hit the gas, and, before he could get into the truck, I pulled in behind him on the driveway.

At the sight of my pickup, he ran back into the house.

Clara opened the door when I knocked. 'You little bastard.'

'Liar.'

I expected her to slam the door. Instead, she opened it. 'Come in.'

She'd painted the living room strawberry-red, as bright as the blue outside. The kitchen behind it was brilliant yellow, the hallway lime green. The living-room couch, two armchairs, and a wooden credenza were nothing fancy. A striped rug, as bright as a cheap serape, lay on the floor.

Carlos Medina sat on the couch, his elbows on his knees, his chin in his hands. He wore gray sweatpants and a matching gray sweatshirt.

I walked around the room, glanced into the kitchen, up the hall, out of the front window. 'You know the cops are looking for you.'

He glanced at Clara, then me. 'Yes, I know.'

'But you're hiding. Why?'

'I didn't kill Antonia. I would never hurt her.'

'Fine. You told her mom and dad you were working late on the night she went to meet you. But you weren't. Where were you?'

He glanced at Clara again. 'Here.'

I shook my head. 'Clara was with Antonia at Bar Deportivo. Why would you come here?'

'I was afraid.'

'Of what? A fourteen-year-old?'

He made a sound that could have become a groan.

Clara said, 'Antonia was pregnant.'

'Huh,' I said.

'She just found out.'

I pointed at Carlos. 'Yours?'

'Yes,' he said.

'She was a kid,' I said. 'You know what that makes you—'

'It looks bad,' he said.

'No, it *is* bad.'

'We loved each other,' he said.

'Fourteen-year-olds don't get to be in love. Not that way.'

'I'm sorry,' he said, miserably.

'Sorry won't do it.'

'I didn't kill her.'

I'd said words like his to Bill Higby as he'd grilled me about the Bronson brothers. *Admit it*, Higby had said. *Admit it or prove you didn't do it.* He'd come at me hour after hour, until the ideas of *did* and *didn't* twisted in my ears and my head like a sickness, and I could no longer tell the difference. I'd confessed to what I never could have done. I would've put a gun to my own head before I killed those boys, but there were my words on paper, my name signed under them, and, echoing from my ears to the jury's, there was my voice on the recording.

I said to Carlos, 'They're going to get you.'

Clara said, 'A couple of teenagers . . .'

'No,' I said, 'a nineteen-year-old man and a kid.'

Carlos said, 'It wasn't—'

'Yeah,' I said, 'it *was*.' I looked from him to Clara. 'How about the two of you? How long have you been together?'

Clara opened her eyes wide. 'Us? I let him sleep on the couch.'

'Liar.'

'He can't go back to his apartment,' she said. 'He can't go to work. Where else would you have him stay?'

I looked at him. He had the sad eyes a fourteen-year-old might fall in love with. 'Maybe it's time to run.'

'Clara knows a lawyer,' he said hopefully.

'Yeah?'

'I went to college with her,' Clara said.

'Good luck,' I said.

'I didn't do it,' he said again.

Clara asked me, 'What are *you* going to do?' Which I took to mean, would I tell the police where Carlos was?

I had no reason to believe anything she told me and no reason to trust him. She'd lied, and he'd gotten Antonia pregnant and gone into hiding. But people lie easily to protect someone they care about, and, whether or not Carlos killed Antonia, he had plenty of reason to be scared.

Clara said, 'You know what will happen if you turn him in.'

'Maybe,' I said.

'Give us some time,' she said.

I asked him, 'You think time will help?'

He blinked.

'Right.' I knew the look on his face – the look of a man who's screwed no matter what he does. I knew I must have looked like him as I'd tried to retract my confession about the Bronsons in the Sheriff's Office, and again as Bill Higby testified against me in court, and again and again during my first years in prison when I wrote letters explaining my innocence to anyone I thought might listen, laying out what happened on the night the boys died in detail that no one with open eyes could deny, though thousands of other prisoners protested their innocence every day to a thousand eyes, and who has time for all that?

I said, 'You know about a guy named Demetrius Jones?' I took his business card from my wallet and had Carlos and Clara put his number in their phone contacts. 'He's an immigration lawyer, helping Antonia's parents. You might want to call him. Maybe he can do more than talk a judge out of a speeding fine.' Then I had them give me their phone numbers. 'In case,' I said.

Carlos stared at me with something that looked like trust. 'Do you believe me?'

'I don't know what I believe,' I said.

That night, *First Coast News* ran an update on Antonia's killing. As Cynthia and I sat on my bed, a reporter said Antonia had no papers. He called Carlos an illegal. He showed a picture of her, at age nine or ten, riding a brown horse, her face caught in that startling laugh. He showed a picture of Carlos with a bottle of tequila in one hand and the sequined El Jimador sombrero in the other. The reporter called her a child and him a man. In a prerecorded video, Antonia's high school principal said how much her classmates and teachers were hurting.

I told Cynthia, 'The classmates bullied her. She thought the teachers were stupid. She played hooky whenever she could.'

'We called her our rough diamond,' the principal said. 'She was so bright. With the right breaks, she could have been brilliant.'

'Who knows,' I said.

A second reporter said the police were working on a tip that Antonia had been seen on the Bar Deportivo parking lot talking to a man in an SUV or pickup truck. Then he said counseling was available to Antonia's classmates. Her family would hold a private memorial service on Monday. 'In the meantime,' the reporter said, 'City Council member Randall Lehmann is proposing measures including fines on local businesses that employ undocumented workers, as well as restricted access to public education for their children – measures that he claims will reduce crime and keep the next tragedy from happening.'

The news cut to a clip of Lehmann. Again, he wore a white Oxford shirt, with the sleeves pushed to his elbows. He said, 'If we suspend business licenses and revoke liquor licenses—'

Cynthia jerked toward the TV. 'Son of a bitch – that's him.'

'Who?'

'The guy who's been hassling me at work.'

'Are you sure?'

She glared at me.

'If I go out for a taco,' Lehmann was saying, 'whose hands do I want preparing the ground beef? Do I want my tax dollars paying for after-school athletics for kids who've trained by running from border agents and swimming across—'

Cynthia yelled at him, 'Asshole.'

The reporter asked Lehmann, 'How do you answer someone like Martin Soto, the girl's father, who says all his family wanted was to work and eat – a simple life?'

'They always want more than they say.'

TEN

The next evening, when I steered into the parking lot at the Cardinal after work, Deborah Holt's black Grand Marquis was idling outside my door.

Every impulse told me to turn around and speed back on to the highway. But I parked next to her and got out. Her window rolled down.

'What?' I said.

'I was about to leave.' She looked me over. 'You've got good timing.'

'What do you want?'

She nodded at my door. 'Can we go in?'

'I see no reason to.'

'Then climb in.'

Nine years earlier, the Sheriff's Office had sent a car to pick me up when I called to say I saw something on the night the Bronson brothers died. I'd climbed in, ready to help. Then I'd spent eight years in prison.

I went to my door and unlocked it. Holt followed me inside.

She glanced around. 'You ever going to get out of this place?'

'What do you want?'

'I mean, it's been a year . . .'

'You're selling houses?'

She sighed. 'I went to Bar Deportivo. The bartenders say you came in, asking questions.'

'So?'

'So don't do that,' she said.

'What's this about Antonia talking to a man in an SUV or pickup outside the bar?'

'It's nothing. The witness wasn't sure it was her. And half the vehicles in this city are SUVs or pickups – in that parking lot, more like nine out of ten. Anyway, it's none of your business. I also heard you're pushing your luck at Chartein Farm.'

I tried to keep the fear from my voice. 'Everett Peters?'

'The manager? No – are you hassling him?'

'Have you seen his pictures of the girl?'

She sighed. 'What's going on in these pictures? Are they sexual?'

'The girl is posing,' I said. 'She's in a bathtub.'

'Most kids don't bathe?'

'They're worse than that.'

'How much worse?'

'I don't know,' I said.

'You push your luck,' she said.

'Look at the pictures.'

'I'll do what I can,' she said. 'You know I'm making an effort with you.'

'Who's complaining about me at Chartein Farm?'

'No more questions, Franky.' She smiled kindly. 'I'm just telling you to watch what you're doing.'

'I'm waiting for the *or else.*'

'No *or else.* A friendly warning. Antonia Soto died. Sticking your nose in the middle is a bad idea. This isn't playing around. I don't want you to get hurt.'

'You know how funny that is, don't you?'

'Yeah, I do – too little, too late. But I also know you can get hurt again. Guys like you who've already been hurt badly can become prone to it. Why would you want that?'

'Who says it's about what I want?'

'You need to stay out of the way. I'll investigate what happened, and I'll arrest the one who did it.'

'Carlos Medina?'

'He looks good for it.'

'Because Antonia was pregnant?'

The question stung her. 'How the hell do you know that?'

'The thing about you guys is just because you tied me up once and convinced a judge to put me behind bars, you think I'm stupid.'

'I asked you how you know.' She was angry. 'We haven't even told her parents. Only a few of us have seen the lab report.'

'Arrest him for sex with a minor,' I said, 'but don't accuse him of what you can't prove.'

She bit her lip. 'You could mess this up badly if you start spreading rumors. Carlos Medina could get—'

'He didn't do it.'

'Yeah? I'm pretty sure he did. Do you know about his background in Mexico – what he did before coming here?'

'No.'

'Good. Look, whatever you're getting out of this, find it somewhere else. You don't want people to think the wrong things about you. You know about arsonists who offer to help investigators work out who's been torching buildings.'

'You've got to be kidding.'

'I'm saying you should do your own thing and let us do ours.'

'Are you talking about Higby?' I was furious. 'Does he think I'm involved? Because that would be seriously fucked-up.'

'He thinks you're a nuisance. He doesn't understand your behavior, and, to tell the truth, I don't either. But I don't need to. All I'm saying is stay out of the way. Do whatever you were doing before. Live your life – your *own* life, no one else's.'

When she left, I locked the door. I stripped and ran in place – sprinted – until I was breathless and slick with sweat. I dropped to the floor and did a hundred pushups and a hundred sit-ups, then another hundred of each, and another hundred, and then my muscles were on fire and ached deep to the bone. I showered and, after toweling dry, lay on my bed naked.

I closed my eyes and thought about Holt's advice.

Live your life.

As if that made any sense. As if it was possible.

I thought about other advice I'd heard since getting out of prison.

Move on.

Make the most of your second chance.
Count your blessings.
The truth will set you free.
What doesn't kill you makes you stronger.
Time heals all.

A thousand other clichés – words on words on words, piling up and cascading down, a shuddering, shaking mountain of bullshit.

ELEVEN

The Sotos held the memorial for Antonia on a stretch of grass in the back acres of Chartein Farm, across from a row of little houses the Charteins rented to their workers. It was scheduled for a half hour after dawn, giving everyone time to complete early-morning chores, wash up, and change clothes. Except for the low whine of the great industrial fans in the chicken houses at the other end of the meadow, the farm was silent when the priest started to speak.

He greeted us with a sad smile, then rested his eyes on Antonia's parents and said, 'Señor Soto, Señora Soto, may the Father of mercies, the God of all consolation, be with you.'

The Mexican workers mumbled something in response.

The priest said, 'God, the almighty Father, raised Christ his Son from the dead. With confidence, we ask him to save all his people, living and dead.'

He stood behind a table where the Sotos had placed some of Antonia's belongings – a plastic model of a trotting horse, a pair of black shoes with low heels, a red sweater, a math book, a bracelet of green beads. On either side, there was a votive candle. Nested in the middle, there was a framed picture of the Virgin Mary.

The priest spoke for a while in Spanish. Mr and Mrs Chartein stood with Harry and Peters the manager, who hadn't bothered to change out of his jeans and boots. Demetrius Jones and a dark-haired woman who'd come with him listened from the side. Clara, in a blue dress, was alone. Deborah Holt, in a black pantsuit, and Bill

Higby, in the only tie other than Mr Chartein's, watched from behind the others. Two reporters with camera crews shot video. Demetrius Jones had convinced the Sotos that news coverage would pressure the police to solve their daughter's killing.

Martin and Alejandra Soto – his leather belt cinched around his belly, her hands clasped so tight her knuckles looked as if they would burst – stood in the middle of it all.

The priest said, 'God, our shelter and our strength, you listen in love to the cry of your people,' and a tear rolled down Alejandra's cheek.

Then, her mouth barely open, she started to wail. The sound rose inside her and spread over the farmyard, blanketing everything. No one touched or comforted her. Maybe the others respected her pain and knew there was nothing – nothing at all – they could do to lessen it. Maybe they were afraid if they touched her, she would shatter.

The priest said, 'Hear the prayers we offer for our departed daughter. Cleanse her of her sins and grant her the fullness of redemption.'

That was it.

He reached under the table for an old boom box, set it among Antonia's belongings, and hit the play button. A woman sang 'Dios Nunca Muere' from tinny speakers.

For a moment, no one moved. Then some of the farm workers wandered toward the Sotos' house, where a breakfast was set up in the kitchen. The priest left his spot behind the table and went to Antonia's parents. Although Judy expected me to bring a truckload of meat by nine, I stayed in the warmth and goodness of the mourners.

Then a heavy hand gripped my shoulder from behind.

Higby.

'Franky Dast,' he said. 'In all the best places.'

'Higby,' I said. 'Shameless as ever.'

'Last time I saw you here, didn't I tell you I'd drag you to the station if you came back?'

'No, you said to get moving. But I have another truckload of chickens. You want to see?'

'I want to see you get in your truck and drive away.'

'Sorry,' I said. 'I'm a friend of the family.' I turned.

He grabbed me again.

I shook free. 'If you touch me, you'd better mean it. I have nothing to do with you. Do your job and leave me alone.' I walked away.

He called after me, 'I keep thinking you *are* my job. One of these days, you'll prove me right.'

I went back. 'You must think I humiliated you by showing everyone how you screwed up when you arrested me. But I didn't. You humiliated yourself. Maybe one day you'll see that and leave me alone.'

'Don't hold your breath,' he said. 'After dealing with degenerates like you for as long as I have, I know evil when I see it.'

'You've got serious problems,' I said.

'Just one,' he said. 'And I know his name.' He went back to Holt.

The boom box started into 'Un Día a la Vez.' Demetrius Jones came over. He gestured at Higby and said, 'That looked like fun.'

I said, 'That cocksucker locked me up for eight years.'

'He's the one?'

'He wants me for another eight, unless he can have me for life.'

'Some men can't let go.' Demetrius looked out at the others. 'I tried to convince the Sotos to hold this thing in a public place – on the steps of the Sheriff's Office maybe. They said they wanted to do it at home. They're fifteen hundred miles from where they were born. They don't own the land they work on or the house they live in. Half of America wants to get rid of them, and most of the rest of us wish we could ignore them. They're lonely for the family and friends they left behind. But here they are, and they aren't budging if they can help it. Can you believe that?'

'There's no explaining people.'

'It's gratitude,' he said. 'They think they owe the place something for giving them a life. Or maybe it's just stubbornness. I don't know, but I've got to admire it.'

'I need to get going, OK? I have a delivery.'

'Are you OK?'

I forced a smile. 'Couldn't be better.'

As I walked to the pickup, I passed Mrs Chartein's brother, who winked at me and then went back to talking to the dark-haired woman who'd come with the immigration lawyer.

'Hawks take the chickens during the daytime, owls at night,' he said. 'But possums, they're the real nuisance. They're like piranhas on legs.'

'Is that a fact?' she said.

He smiled. 'As God is my witness.'

Then a white Lexus came up the drive, passed my truck and the other cars, and drove across the grass toward the reporters, who were breaking down their equipment. Randall Lehmann got out, wearing his white Oxford with the sleeves rolled to the elbow.

The news crews recognized him. The camera operators slung cameras back on to their shoulders, and the reporters fumbled with microphones, holding them to Lehmann's face.

Mr Chartein left the mourners and went over. I followed him.

As if Lehmann knew he had limited time, he talked fast, running sentences into each other, giving the reporters no chance to respond. 'Where's Immigration Enforcement this morning?' he asked. 'Someone should investigate whether agricultural transportation lines are being used to smuggle methamphetamine, cocaine, and opioids. Americans need to wake up to this danger. It's already snuck in through our back doors, and it's lounging on our living-room sofas.'

Mr Chartein stepped in front of the cameras and asked Lehmann what he was doing on private property.

As Lehmann grinned and started to answer, I moved in and slugged him in the jaw.

He stumbled but stayed on his feet. His TV face dropped into anger, and I thought he would come after me.

But he recovered as fast as he broke. He looked at the cameras again and said, 'This is the kind of lawlessness we're up against. I'm here as an elected official, encouraging the enforcement of legal policies meant to protect the people of our community and our country. I'm exercising my first amendment rights, rights guaranteed to *legal* citizens of the United States. Then I'm physically attacked by' – he turned his eyes to me, and the cameras followed – 'a felon. Yes, I know you,' he said. 'A felon. Here at an event that – I would be willing to bet my city council seat – is attended by men and women who are in the country illegally.'

I lunged at him again, but hands grabbed me, hands I knew well.

Higby said, 'Uh-uh, enough of that,' and pulled me away.

Lehmann recognized a scene ender when he saw one. 'That's it,' he told the cameras, as if the reporters were asking for more.

Higby held me by the collar. 'Is this my lucky day?'

But Deborah Holt came over and drew him aside to talk.

When she got done with him, he went to Lehmann, who clapped him on the shoulder and shook hands with him.

Then Higby and Holt came back to me. Higby said, 'I guess it's *your* lucky day. Seeing that Mr Lehmann was trespassing and isn't interested in pressing charges against you, we're letting you go.'

'The key word being *go*,' Holt said.

Higby said, 'Sooner or later – I'm guessing sooner – you and I are going to spend some quality time together. On your way out, tell Mr Lehmann you're sorry.'

Holt frowned at me. 'Do it.'

I walked over to the man – not to apologize but to confront him about harassing Cynthia.

He also stepped toward me. There was a welt on his jaw where I'd hit him. 'Yeah, I know you,' he said again.

'I know you too.'

He leaned in. 'And I know how to get to you.'

'I don't think you want to do that.'

He touched his jaw. 'Because what? Will you hit me again? You know, next time I might hit back.'

I turned away. As I walked to my truck, Doris Day sang 'Que Sera Sera' from the boom box.

TWELVE

Zemira and I were sanding the raised wooden platform for the new tigers when Zooland called Judy. The transport trailer had broken an axle as it crossed the Pearl River from Bogalusa into Mississippi. The tigers would come midweek because of the repair delay.

After the memorial service and Lehmann, I had little patience for Judy's irritation. When she complained that the wood filler over one of the screws in the platform was loose – and exposed metal could cut the cats – the wail rising from Alejandra Soto's chest still filled my ears.

'Fix it,' Judy said, and Lehmann's threat – *I know how to get to you* – echoed in my head.

I went to the work shed and came back with more sandpaper instead of wood putty.

'What am I paying you for?' Judy said.

'I have a therapy appointment at noon,' I said, and walked back to the pickup. If she didn't have to answer to Dr Patel to keep family funds flowing into Safe Haven, she probably would have fired me.

'You look miserable,' Dr Patel said, when I sank on to the couch in his office. High in the Baptist Hospital Medical Services Building, he'd made a burrow of plush cushions, thick carpet, and soft lighting.

'Good thing I don't come to you for self-esteem,' I said.

'What's wrong?'

I told him.

He seemed less concerned about Higby's insinuations and Lehmann's threats – or even Antonia's death – than how I was handling them. 'Have you been getting off on asphyxiating yourself?'

'Thanks for putting it that way,' I said.

'You may think there's nothing sexual in it, but you're wrong. Eros and Thanatos – love and death – they're an odd couple, but they get along fine.'

'No, I haven't – though I'm still exercising in my room.'

'Does that make you feel better?'

'Sure. I work out so hard I feel nothing but muscle ache.'

'Comfortably numb?'

'My question is, why is Lehmann hassling Cynthia? It must have something to do with me.'

'Does everything have to do with you?' He left his notebook on his side table.

'This does, yeah. He slammed ex-cons when he talked to her at Bourne-Goff.'

'Are you the only ex-con?'

'Don't be stupid,' I said. 'He showed up at the memorial service when I was there.'

'He's making a name for himself as a bigot. He couldn't resist the memorial.'

'He said he knows me,' I said. 'He said he knows how to get to me. Why?'

'Did you ask him?'

'I punched him in the face.'

'Why?'

'I needed to do something,' I said.

'Do you think you need to fix the world? You might want to work on yourself first.'

When I left the appointment, I had three choices. I could go back to Safe Haven. I could lock the door in my room and turn the AC on high. Or I could deal with the questions needling me – what happened to Antonia, how to get Higby to take his hands off me, why Lehmann was bothering Cynthia and threatening me.

I Googled Rick and Kenyon Munro, the couple who found Antonia in Clapboard Creek.

They lived in a strip of townhouse apartments called Villages of Baymeadows, on the southside. I drove out of downtown and, fifteen minutes later, coasted along a winding asphalt road past a playground and a sandpit volleyball court. I pulled into a visitor spot across from a line of interconnected brown two-story units, each with a peaked brown-shingle roof. At the far end of the parking lot, a jon boat stood on a trailer, a little Evinrude outboard clamped to the transom. Longleaf pine trees towered over the lot. A layer of pine needles covered the ground.

The doorbell at the Munros' apartment buzzed softly, and a dog barked from a back room. When no one answered, I peered through the shade on a tall window beside the door.

Then a woman's voice spoke from inside. 'What?'

'Kenyon Munro?'

'Yes?'

I told her who I was and said I knew Antonia. 'Could I talk with you and Rick for a few minutes?'

'Rick's at work, and I'm about to leave.'

'I have a couple questions.'

'No, I'm sorry.' In the television interview I'd watched after she and her husband found Antonia's body, she'd looked nervous. She sounded nervous now.

I said, 'To tell the truth, I don't want to be here. But if I didn't come – if I didn't do this – I don't know what I would do. Probably break in pieces. This shook me up.'

She was silent on the other side of the door.

I said, 'There's a cop – really two cops, but mainly one – he doesn't want me here either. You've probably talked to him and his partner. Bill Higby and Deborah Holt. You've probably told them everything you know. But he's an asshole. She's OK.' I didn't know why I was telling her this. Maybe because I heard fear in her voice. Maybe because I needed a stranger to listen to me and let me know whether I was talking sense or cracking up.

Silence.

'Then, there's this guy – this man – he's harassing my girlfriend – and he was there again at Antonia's memorial this morning. Maybe he has nothing to do with—'

The door opened, and Kenyon Munro said, 'He's harassing your girlfriend? About Antonia?' She wore black pants and a white chef coat with a fish insignia where a pocket would go. She'd banded her dark hair in a ponytail.

'I don't think so—'

'Because an old guy's been bothering me at work.'

'What kind of old guy?'

'I mean, not *that* old. You know, gray hair.' Twice, at the end of an evening, he had waited for her in the parking lot, she said. Since then, the manager had walked her to her car, and the man hadn't returned.

'Is he stocky? Does he wear his sleeves rolled up?'

'I don't know.'

I pulled out my phone and found a picture of Lehmann. 'Him?'

She barely needed a glance. 'No.'

'You sure?' I found another picture.

She studied it. 'No, that's not him at all.'

'Huh. What did he say? He talked about Antonia?'

'Not exactly. Maybe he just saw me on TV after we found her, but he seemed to know about me and Rick. He said he's more fun than a grease monkey. Rick's a mechanic.'

Again, that sounded like Lehmann. 'What did you say?'

'I told him I had mace on my keychain. He said he knew what to do with a girl like me. But he backed off.'

'Then he came again?'

'The next night. Waiting for me by my car. He said I looked like trouble – and he was trouble too.'

Like Lehmann. 'He said nothing about Antonia?'

'I don't know . . . I ran back to the restaurant. It wasn't so much what he said. It was what he did.'

'Yeah?'

She shook her head. 'Rick and I promised Detective Holt we would keep the details about what we saw to ourselves.'

'So don't tell me what you saw. Tell me what this man did.'

She looked a little embarrassed. 'He stared at my forehead.'

'Your forehead?'

'That's not where guys usually stare – especially not weirdos looking for sex. But this guy stared so hard, it was like he wanted to burn a hole in me.'

'What's that got to do with Antonia?'

Her voice quavered. 'I told Detective Holt . . .'

'Anything you tell me I'll keep to myself.'

She closed her eyes and held them closed. She spoke quietly. 'We saw her in the creek – floating face down. I wanted Rick to turn the boat around. I've never wanted to get away from a place so bad.' She opened her eyes again. 'But Rick said we needed to see. In case we could do something. In case we could help. We keep a paddle in the boat. Rick poked her with it. It was terrible. Her body seemed to . . .' She stopped, as if fighting down nausea, or tears, or both. 'She rolled in the water and came face up.' She bit her bottom lip. 'Her eyes and mouth – something had been feeding on her in the creek. But her forehead . . .' She touched her own forehead where the man outside the restaurant had stared at her. 'It had a cut in it. A big pink X. The water had washed it clean, but you could tell someone did that to her. With a knife. Or a razor blade. Someone marked her.'

'Oh,' I said.

'You can't tell anyone. I promised Detective Holt.'

'Yeah,' I said. 'No one will know.'

She held her hand to her mouth. 'After Rick and I pulled the boat from the water and went home, I showered. But if I think about her, I can still smell her.'

That night, a video of me slugging Lehmann led the news. The camera had the councilman in a close-up. Then Mr Chartein came into the picture, demanding to know what Lehmann was doing on his land. Then a fist broke into the frame, followed by the rest of me. I had to give the camera operator credit – he held steady. A moment later, Higby was there too, pulling me off the councilman.

A minute after the segment ended, my phone rang.

It was Demetrius Jones. 'You don't get it, do you?' he said. 'You gave him exactly what he wanted. Worse than that, you took the story away from Antonia and her parents. Do you want to know who loves that you punched Lehmann? All the jerks who think like him. We track the discussion board of a group of local fuckups who call themselves the Valknut. The FBI has looked into them, and the ACLU keeps them on a list of hate groups, but everyone's pretty sure they just get their rocks off by dreaming about an all-white America. Not me – *I* think they're looking for something to get excited about, and then watch out. Guess what? Your punch lit up their board. You turned an already bad situation into a fight between two men who want to show each other they have the biggest dick. This is a distraction. *You're* a distraction. We can't afford distractions.'

Although I'd hit Lehmann mostly because he was hassling Cynthia, I said, 'He was slamming your cause – and your people. We couldn't let him get away with that.'

'No,' Demetrius said, 'he was crashing a memorial service and talking like an idiot. No one would listen to him – no one who mattered – until you stepped in. We're in the right. He's wrong. But you made it look like a debate.'

'How did you get my phone number?'

'You're easy to find.'

His words reminded me of Lehmann saying he knew how to get to me. I hung up.

THIRTEEN

How did Lehmann know where the memorial service would be held? The news had mentioned that there would be one but had given no details. It was private except for Holt, Higby, and the reporters the Sotos had invited with the understanding that they would stay at a respectful distance. Could one of the news stations have tipped off the councilman to create exciting TV? Could Higby have tipped him off because he shared Lehmann's thinking and he was that kind of person? He'd warmed to Lehmann fast after pulling me off him. Maybe they were already friends.

Although I usually made runs to Chartein Farm every couple of days, the memorial had kept the workers from preparing a full load, so I went back the next morning. When I tapped the horn outside Peters's trailer, he came to the porch, threw me the keys to the cold shed, and disappeared inside again without a word.

I loaded the truck as the sun came up over the chicken houses. When I finished and was washing my gloves under a spigot, Mr and Mrs Chartein's Jeep came down the dirt road from their house. Mrs Chartein got out in brown slacks, a green blouse, and a strand of pearls. I said good morning.

She eyed me curiously. 'Yesterday was quite something, wasn't it?'

'I'm sorry I hit Lehmann,' I said.

'No, no,' she said, 'Randy needs a poke in the chin now and then.'

'Have you met him before?'

She smiled. 'I grew up with him. When we were young, his family lived just down the road from here. We all went to school together until seventh grade, when he moved downtown. He was a jerk then too – but he was bullied. I think the bullying may explain a lot of his behavior.'

'Immigrants and murdered girls picked on him?'

'No, but everyone else did.'

'I shouldn't have hit him.'

'Why did you?'

I shrugged.

She said, 'When Judy Pollard told my husband you would be doing the pickups, we looked you up online. My husband remembered you from when the Bronson brothers died and again when you got out of prison. Honestly, I didn't. Judy thought we should know who she was sending here. Not that you'd done anything wrong. Just that your experiences must have had an effect on you. I admire the work Judy does with the lions and tigers,' she said. 'And with people.'

'But?' I said.

'A few days ago, Everett Peters talked to me. He said he caught you in his trailer. What were you doing there?'

Sweat broke on my back. 'Looking around.'

She raised her eyebrows. 'He said you took nothing.'

'That's true.'

'I encouraged him to give you another chance.' She seemed to search my eyes. 'He also has faced hard circumstances.'

I thought about the pictures of the girl in his dresser drawer. 'Prison?'

'There are different kinds of prisons,' she said. 'They don't all have locks and bars.'

'Should I tell Judy to send someone else to pick up the chickens?'

'Why would you do that? All I want is to know that you're OK – and that there won't be more issues.'

'I'll do my best,' I said.

'That's all I ask. I'm not a stickler for rules or good manners, but I do expect people to be kind. You think you can manage that?'

'I'll try.'

She smiled. 'Feel free to make an exception with Randy Lehmann. He deserves what's coming to him.'

'Well, I'll let someone else give it to him.'

'That might be smart.' She turned toward the Jeep.

'Thanks, Mrs Chartein.'

'It's good to have you here, Franky.'

My hands shook on the steering wheel as I drove out to the highway. I breathed deep, rushing oxygen into my lungs until I felt I could submerge and stay submerged. Then I yelled, 'Fuck, fuck, fuck.' I willed my hands to stop shaking.

They shook.

I'd survived my first months out of prison by refusing to let the shaking stop me. I'd charged into houses and businesses where I didn't belong. I'd risked my life because Higby had ripped away eight years of it, and what I had back didn't quite feel real. I'd burst through doors until I put my hands on the throat of the man who had killed the Bronson boys.

Then, for a short while, the shaking stopped.

I got back my life – at least part of it. I had Cynthia. The Cardinal Motel was a shithole, but I returned there day after day because I chose to. I turned off the lights when I was ready. I turned them back on when I wanted. I ate, I showered, I made my bed or left it unmade. I held the key to my room on my keychain.

Then I had something to lose again.

Now Mrs Chartein called me out with a smile. She shook me by being kind. Because, as far as I could tell, she was a thoroughly good person – an innocent who let me know, calmly, that my wild, flailing blows had grazed her.

'Fuck,' I yelled again, and stepped on the gas. I was sick of shaking, sick of locking myself in my room with my key – my *own* key. Had I been wrong to go into Peters's trailer? Maybe, but I'd gone in after he'd showed no sympathy for Antonia. I hadn't known yet that Carlos Medina got Antonia pregnant. Anyway, what I saw in Peters's bottom dresser drawer justified me.

What about Lehmann? Was I wrong to slug him? I needed more time to think that through.

Pine forest, interspersed with farmland, little houses, and trailers, lined the highway south of Chartein Farm. I rounded the bend before Clara's blue house – and hit the brakes.

Her car was gone, probably to Callahan Middle School. Carlos's truck was parked off to the side, toward the back of the house, where cops would miss it.

I pulled into the driveway and walked to the door.

If I knocked, I would spook Carlos again. If I went in without knocking, I would break my promise to Mrs Chartein fifteen minutes after I made it.

I walked along the front of the house and peered in through a window.

Carlos slept on the couch in the strawberry-red living room, one long leg draped over the back cushions. A yellow bedsheet covered the rest of him.

I tapped on the glass, and he jerked up and looked around. I tapped again. He eyed me, pulled the bedsheet around him, and came to the door.

He looked up and down the highway, then beckoned me in.

I said, 'I hear you had a problem in Mexico. You want to explain that?'

His eyelids hung heavy. He shook his head.

'You know how screwed you are, don't you?'

'I didn't kill Antonia.'

'You don't seem too broken up about it, though. You're sleeping in, living easy.'

'You're wrong.' He went back to the couch and sat. 'I can't sleep at night. In the morning, I might sleep for an hour.'

'What happened in Mexico?'

'Why?'

'The cops are hunting for you, and when they find you, they're going to use whatever it is against you.'

He glared. 'I cut a boy with a knife. In Jalisco.'

'Why would you do that?'

'He threatened my brother.'

'Why?'

'Does it matter?'

I thought about Lehmann implying that Antonia's death was somehow connected to trafficking. 'Drugs?'

'You *gringitos*, man. You think everything Mexican is about drugs. My brother and the other kid both liked this one girl.'

'So you cut him?'

'I could cut him or he would cut my brother. Then I ran. The kid also had a brother – and an uncle. The uncle was police. That's when I came here.'

'Did the kid die?'

'No, man, he got six stitches.'

'You had nothing to do with Antonia's death?'

'I swear it.'

I'd known killers at Raiford who swore they were across state lines, or eating dinner with their moms, or sound asleep in their beds when their victims died. *I'd* also sworn, so help me God, that I didn't kill the Bronson boys. 'I don't know if I believe you.'

'Believe what you want. I was here by myself when it happened.'

'Even if that's true, you're going to need a better story if the cops decide you're the one they want.'

'I know,' he said. 'I'm screwed.'

Even as he admitted what he'd done, his distress seemed out of character. He belonged in a party hat, pouring shots, grinning ear to ear. He might have stumbled – or rushed – into bad situations, but there was nothing mean about him. He was a friendly fuck-up.

I asked, 'Who got the girl – the kid or your brother?'

'It was a waste of time. She liked a boy in another barrio.'

FOURTEEN

A Dodge Ram turned on to the gravel road to Safe Haven, dragging a rusty trailer. Inside the trailer, there were two cages, each holding a tiger. Although most sanctuaries, zoos, and safari parks crate-trained tigers before transporting them, Zooland had just shot them full of carfentanyl to sedate them. With the delay for repairs, the tranquilizers had worn off east of Biloxi. Judy looked like she would kick the driver when he said he didn't know if Sorrel, the older of the cats, had survived the final three hundred miles.

The driver removed a padlock from the trailer, and, with Judy guiding, we took out the cages on a rental forklift.

Sorrel was breathing hard, but the other cat, Rocko, barely lifted his head as we moved his cage across the lot to his new enclosure. Both were skinny, their fur matted, filthy from lying in their own urine for the past three days.

'Jesus Christ, when did they last get water?' Judy said.

'I don't know,' the driver said.

She moved close. 'If I had my way, I'd lock you up and let the cats run free.'

He was twice her size and half her age, but he backed away. 'I'm just the driver.'

After he left with the trailer, we eased the tigers from the cages into dark sensory-deprivation crates with water but nothing else.

When Judy saw my expression, she said, 'Only for a day or two. For their own good.'

'Solitary messes you up,' I said, and walked away.

She called after me. 'We're saving their lives.'

Three hours earlier, when I was getting dressed, I had turned on the TV. The story about me punching Lehmann was already old news, though the councilman was back. In a segment on the downtown homeless encampment he'd been fighting, he demanded that the police clear what he called *human refuse*. Before I could change the channel, the anchor cut to a developing story in the Mandarin Reach subdivision.

The on-site reporter, a grim-faced Asian woman, stood outside a community clubhouse. Late last night, she said, a man walking his dog discovered a body. The details were few, but neighbors said the victim was Kumar Mehta, in town visiting his son's family. The reporter talked to one of the neighbors on camera – a pale woman, who wondered how this could happen with a security booth checking the identity of everyone who came through the gate.

That was that, I thought. Antonia had died almost a week earlier, and the news needed fresh blood. A dead man on a tidy street of a gated community seemed just right to take people's minds off a girl whose existence, when she was alive, disturbed a lot of them anyway.

When the anchor returned, he said further reports would follow at noon and five.

Throughout the rest of the morning, as Judy, Diane, and Zemira watched the new tigers, I shoveled straw and animal shit from the other enclosures. I soaped the exterior fencing, leaving the scent markings on the sleep platforms and the old tires that Judy used to stimulate the cats.

In the afternoon, Rocko seemed to weaken, and Judy called for a vet, who worried about kidney failure and said the next forty-eight hours would tell. When I drove from Safe Haven at five o'clock, the others had brought chairs from the house. They would spend the night monitoring the arrivals.

Cynthia was going out to dinner with her parents and then sleeping at home, so I stopped at Sahara Sandwiches and bought a gyro and fries from the bald counterman.

'Music,' I told him. 'You need to liven up this place.'

Back at the Cardinal, I did sit-ups and pushups, showered, and ate. At seven-thirty, I turned on *Family Feud*. As the theme-song trumpets and trombones played, I settled back on my bed.

Then someone knocked at the door.

I pulled back the shade. Deborah Holt stood outside, staring at the ground.

'What?' I said through the window.

'Can we talk?'

'About what?'

'If you let me in, I'll tell you.'

'You can't call?'

'Some conversations are better in person.'

'Are you going to arrest me?'

'Why would I do that?'

I let the shade fall, turned off the TV, and opened the door. 'Next time, call first.'

'You know it doesn't work that way unless I want it to.'

'I know I can kick you out and go back to watching TV.'

She shrugged that off. 'You watching the news?'

'Not since this morning.'

'There's another killing.'

'The one in Mandarin Reach?'

She looked me in the eyes. 'I need to find Carlos Medina. I *really* need to talk to him.'

'I remember how that goes. You talked me into eight years in prison.'

'*I* didn't. Do you know where he is?'

'Why would I?'

'You've been asking around about Antonia Soto,' she said. 'You aren't stupid. Higby thinks you're smart enough to get away with murder. I just think you're smarter than you look. And people talk to you, God knows why – maybe they think that as bad as they've had it, you've had it worse.'

I said, 'What does Carlos Medina have to do with the man at Mandarin Reach?'

She stared at me, silent. I reached for the TV remote.

'Two people have died,' she said. 'I can't talk about any connections.'

'Who's the man?'

She told me what the morning news had already announced, adding a couple of facts that would probably come out on the news at eleven. Kumar Mehta – seventy-one years old – was visiting his son's family from India. 'Most nights, he would walk in the neighborhood,' she said. 'Last night, when he walked, he didn't come back.'

'Shot, like Antonia?'

She hesitated. 'No.'

'Did he get threatening letters?'

She shook her head.

'Then what connects them? They both came from other countries. Other than that, there's nothing?'

Her expression was noncommittal.

A couple of the people I'd talked to had resented or feared Antonia and immigrants like her. Everett Peters and Randall Lehmann stood out. Had they – or anyone else – done or said something that connected Antonia to a seventy-one-year-old on an evening stroll? As Higby had showed me when he'd held me against a wall at the Sheriff's Office and said, *You did it – admit it, dammit*, logic meant little if the police thought they saw a pattern in the evidence.

I said, 'Did the dog walker find the man floating face down in a ditch?'

'In Mandarin Reach? He was lying on a freshly cut lawn.'

I considered what Kenyon Munro had told me about finding Antonia. 'Did he have any marks on him?'

Holt's face fell. 'What kind of marks?'

I'd promised to keep the secret to myself. But now two people had tumbled out of the world. 'A cut?' I touched my forehead.

Holt's eyes filled with fury. 'Where the hell did you hear that?'

'Holy shit,' I said. 'He was cut too?'

'Goddammit,' she said, 'you can't know about this. No one can. Do you understand that? It's the one fact we know but others don't. Did Rick or Kenyon Munro tell you?'

'No,' I said.

She looked confused. 'Higby?'

'Are you kidding?'

'Who?'

'As you said, people talk to me.'

'Goddammit,' she said again.

'I'll tell no one.'

She breathed in deep. 'Jesus Christ. If you so much as—'

'What will you do?'

She sighed and seemed to bite back her anger. 'I need to locate Carlos Medina. *Now.*'

'Why would he kill the man at Mandarin Reach?'

'That's what I need to talk to him about.'

'He makes no sense.'

'Before he came here, he cut up a kid in Mexico. He has a history with knives.'

'I know,' I said. 'He was protecting his brother.'

'You know that story too? You've been in touch with him?'

'I didn't say that.'

'Whether he did the killings or not, I need to talk to him. I need to find out.'

'Will you hold him against a wall until he says he did what you think he did?'

'That's not my way,' she said.

'Do you know who you need to talk to?' I said. 'Everett Peters.'

'Already done.'

'You saw the pictures?'

'We've seen what we need to see. Not everything is as bad as you think it is, Franky. Or maybe it's as bad but in a different way.'

'Who's the girl?'

'None of your damn business. Really, you need to learn when to back off.'

I stared at her. 'Talk to Randall Lehmann,' I said.

She blinked. 'As in City Councilmember Lehmann?'

'He's been hassling people connected to Antonia's killing.'

'You're unbelievable. The only hassling I've seen was you punching him in the jaw. Where is Carlos Medina?'

'I don't know,' I said.

'Where?'

I hadn't even made a promise to him, but I felt I was keeping my word to him – and to myself. 'I told you – I don't know.'

*   *   *

When Holt left, pulling her Grand Marquis on to Philips Highway, I dialed Clara. Her phone rang four times and bumped to voice-mail. I said, 'Call me right away.'

I watched my phone for five minutes, then tried her number again. 'The police were here asking about Carlos. I hope you were with him all last night. If not . . . I don't know . . . Call me.'

I waited another five minutes. Then I grabbed the keys to the pickup and went outside. The night was clear and cool, the moon hanging in the sky as I drove to Clara's house. If Carlos had killed Antonia and Kumar Mehta, as Holt seemed to think, he might have taken a weapon to Antonia's cousin too.

When I turned into the driveway at the blue house, Clara's Taurus was parked in front. My headlights shined on Carlos's old Ford Ranger in the back. I took the lug wrench from my jack kit and headed to the house.

I rang the buzzer and pounded on the front door.

It opened. Clara wore jeans and a red blouse. She held a glass of wine. '*What?*'

'Where's Carlos?'

She eyed the wrench. 'In the back. Showering. Why?'

'You don't answer your phone?'

'What's going on?' She gestured at the wrench. 'What are you doing with that?'

'Where was Carlos last night?'

'Here. Why?'

'Are you sure?'

'Yeah – pretty much so. What's happening?' She blocked the door.

I dropped the tool on the front step, checked up the highway and down. 'Let me in?'

We went inside and she locked the door. 'Tell me what's going on.'

'The cops want to talk to Carlos about a second killing.'

'*What?*'

'You were here with him last night?'

'I went out for dinner with a friend, but then yeah—'

'How long?'

'What?'

'How long were you out?'

'A couple of hours. Three at most . . .'

'Goddammit.' I went to the front door, grabbed the wrench, and came back in. I headed for the bathroom.

'What are you doing?' she said. 'Stop—'

When I shoved the bathroom door open, Carlos was standing in front of the mirror in his underwear, a towel draped over his shoulders. 'What—?'

I said, 'Where were you last night?'

'Close the door.'

'Not a chance.' I held the wrench to let him know I would use it.

Then Clara came into the hall. 'Put it down.' She pointed a silver pistol at me.

I lowered the tool, let it lie at my side. I asked Carlos, 'Where were you last night?'

Clara said, 'Don't tell him anything.' Then to me, 'You son of a bitch, you come into my house – you threaten Carlos . . . you—'

I said, 'Shut up.' I tried Carlos again. 'Where were you?'

'Here,' he said. 'I was here. I didn't go anywhere.' He pulled a yellow golf shirt from a hook beside the shower.

'Who do you know at Mandarin Reach?'

He looked perplexed. 'What is Mandarin Reach?'

'It's where a man named Kumar Mehta died last night. If you've ever met him – if you've even served him a burrito—'

He shook his head.

Then the door in the front room burst open. Six men, dressed in bulletproof vests and Sheriff's Department uniforms, surged in. They yelled that they were the police. They told us to get down on the floor. They told Clara to drop the pistol, me to drop the wrench, all of us to get the fuck down.

As we lay with our faces to the floor, our hands cuffed behind us, Holt stepped into the house. She regarded us like we were animals that had been dragging livestock into the woods.

I understood then what had happened. Holt had used the same dumb trick I'd used on Clara and Carlos the first time I'd come to the house. After visiting me at the Cardinal, she'd waited for me to react.

I'd led her to Carlos.

She had lied to me. I was as stupid as I looked.

FIFTEEN

I might be guilty of obstruction for blocking Holt's investigation. I might also be guilty of simple assault for threatening Carlos with the lug wrench. But the police had named Carlos only as a person of interest, and, without formal charges against him, obstruction looked like a stretch. Simple assault was a misdemeanor, and since I was trying to make Carlos tell me what the police were trying to figure out too, the logic of arresting me got slippery. After making me sit in the back of a patrol car for an hour and then grilling me for another hour about what I knew and when I knew it, Holt set me free.

'You're almost as bad as Higby,' I said, when she was done with me.

'Go home,' she said. 'Or at least go away.'

I got back to my room at one in the morning. Next door, Susan was yelling at Jimmy. Their TV was blasting *Antiques Roadshow*.

I lay on my bed in my clothes, the lamp on, the overhead light on – everything on, my head revving.

Jimmy shouted at Susan, 'You bitch – you goddamned whore of a bitch.'

A TV voice droned, 'This one is in a pure state of preservation – there's nothing on it that isn't original.'

Susan yelled at Jimmy, '*You're* the goddamned bitch.'

A piece of furniture smashed against our shared wall.

I yelled, 'Cut it out.'

What was I doing?

The TV voice droned. 'It has a patinated surface.'

Why was I wrapping myself in others' troubles? I already had enough to smother in.

Jimmy yelled, 'Bitch.'

I got up and pulled the French horn from the closet shelf. I held it to my lips, silent.

Something smashed against the wall.

I carried the horn outside to the parking lot.

At two a.m., I drove back to the Horseshoe Creek boat launch. I went down to the bottom of the ramp, gripping the horn. The tide was slack, the air as still as the water. I brought the mouthpiece to my lips but couldn't bring myself to make a sound.

I went back up across the lot, where my truck stood alone. Behind the launch area, a dark wetland forest reached miles inland. Park rangers had carved hiking trails through the trees. I chose a path and moved blindly on to it.

Twigs scraped my face, and fat leaves licked my neck. My shoes sank into the sandy soil. Glimmerings of moonlight fell through the branches. I stopped. When I was thirteen and the wild hog had charged at me, I'd run, bursting through scrub, and I'd come to the tabby ruins with the window that seemed to shine with heavenly light. But on this dark night, if I ran, I would trip and tumble into a deeper dark. I would impale myself on a chest-high branch. I would crash into the tusks and teeth I was fleeing.

I listened.

Somewhere, not far away, an animal moved through the undergrowth.

Remember, it's more afraid of you . . .

A lie.

But on this dark night, I wouldn't give in to the fear.

If you give an inch, they'll take a mile.

Who were *they*?

You have no one to blame but yourself.

A lie too.

What was I doing?

I was trying to be free.

Freedom's just a word.

I went a hundred yards into the woods. I listened for the rush and rustle of the nighttime. I gripped the French horn, a weapon as lethal as a lug wrench.

I stopped and brought the mouthpiece back to my lips.

I tried and tried to make a sound. When it came, it was nothing like music. I tried again. Again.

You bitch.

Again.

Who could blame me?

After some time, I fingered through the first measures of 'Across the Stars.'

What was I doing? Why was I doing it?

I lowered the horn and stood in the silence.

The first time I went to Clara's house, she'd accused me of self-righteousness. Carlos's boss at El Jimador had accused me of something like it – of wanting to ride in to save the vulnerable, wanting to be a hero, a bright savior. I'd told them they were wrong.

The truth was I *did* want to help Antonia's family and protect Carlos less for them than for me. Helping them might keep me from crashing head-on into walls, tearing myself apart. The Sotos – and maybe Carlos too – were stronger and readier to deal with the world than I was. If sticking myself into their lives was selfish, then I was selfish. I would cross lines without worrying who drew them. I would hurt myself to make myself feel better. Hypocrite that I was, I might also hurt others.

A couple of months before Antonia died, I had explained impulses like these to Dr Patel, and he'd said, 'Surgeons cut off legs to save people's lives. Oncologists shoot bodies full of radiation to take out cancers. We hurt each other and ourselves all the time to take away pain and suffering. What else is sacrifice?'

I'd said, 'Nice try.'

But Clara had also talked about sacrifice. The Spanish word *sacrificar* meant *butcher*, she'd said.

If that was what Dr Patel meant by the word – something we do to ourselves and others with bone saws and cleavers – then maybe he had a point.

SIXTEEN

That Saturday, I woke before dawn. When Cynthia sat up in bed an hour after the sun rose, she watched me finish a set of jumping lunges. As I lay on the carpet, sweating, she said, 'Ever hear about the guy who pounded his head against concrete? It didn't move the wall and didn't help his headache.'

I said nothing.

'You need to breathe,' she said.

'I'm working on it,' I said.

We showered, then walked along Philips Highway to Sahara Sandwiches. The hooker who sometimes hung out on one of the stools in the front window was sitting on the sidewalk, leaning against a shady wall. Her wooden walking stick lay on the pavement beside her. The top of it was carved into the crude shape of a bear head.

She grinned up at me with big yellow teeth and said, 'Hey, baby.'

I opened the door, but Cynthia stopped. 'Hey.'

The hooker seemed to get a kick out of that. 'What's your name, honey?'

'Cynthia.'

The hooker grinned. 'You got a cigarette, Cynthia?'

'I don't smoke – I don't like fire.'

'Bring me a coffee?'

'I'll do that,' Cynthia said. 'You want something to eat?'

'No, honey. I live on cigs and caffeine.'

We went in, ordered egg sandwiches and hash browns, and a cup of coffee that Cynthia took outside.

She came back in and sat on the stool next to mine. 'Others have problems too,' she said.

While the eggs were cooking, the counterman reached into a stainless steel cabinet, brought out a laptop, and set it by the cash register. He fooled with it, and Dizzy Gillespie's 'And Then She Stopped' played from the built-in speaker. He glanced at me for a reaction, then turned to the griddle. 'You only see what you think you'll see,' he said.

As we ate, Cynthia said, 'I can't take much more of it.'

She meant her dad. Two nights earlier, when I'd been accidentally giving Carlos Medina up to the police, her dad had chewed her out about her job at Bourne-Goff Storage and about me. He'd made her sit at the kitchen table and told her he expected more from her – and for her. She asked, what if she already had what she wanted? He said she was young and had no idea what she wanted. She told him to fuck himself. He slapped her. She didn't flinch. Hadn't he already hurt her enough? He told her to get out of his house.

She stared at her hash browns as if she'd lost her appetite. 'I don't know what to do.'

Others' problems. Hers. While I pounded my head against concrete.

'Stay with me,' I said.

'If you got a new place, I would move in with you.'

I put down my sandwich. 'I don't know.'

'About me or a new place?'

'I've always known about you.'

'I need out of that house,' she said.

'What does your mom say?'

'She says to give my dad time. What does that even mean?'

When we left the restaurant, the hooker said to me, 'You treat that girl right.'

As we were walking back to the Cardinal, Judy Pollard called. Blood tests showed that Rocko was anemic. Since I had the truck, could I run by the veterinarian's office and pick up erythropoietin?

Others' problems.

'I need to bring my girlfriend along,' I said.

Judy banned outsiders from Safe Haven. 'We're not a zoo.'

'If you give her an ice cream cone, you can skip the balloon.'

'She stays in the truck.'

'Why do you want to insult her?' I asked.

'Don't push me.'

Two hours later, I pulled on to the gravel road at Safe Haven, a refrigerator pack with six ampoules of erythropoietin on the floor at Cynthia's feet.

Zemira came from the house as we rolled to a stop.

I lowered my window. 'Where's Judy?'

'By the new enclosure.' She looked in through the window. 'Is this the girlfriend?'

I introduced them. 'Cynthia, Zemira.'

'Hi,' Cynthia said.

Zemira said, 'Bring the meds.'

We got out and followed her across the lot.

Judy had freed the new tigers from the sensory-deprivation crates. Sorrel moved through her enclosure skittishly, as if worried she might step on a live wire. Lying under his sleep platform, Rocko panted heavily.

Judy stared at Cynthia, then me. 'What did I say about staying in the truck?'

'If I listened to everything people said, I would still be locked up at Raiford.'

She took the refrigerator pack. 'You can go.'

'How's Rocko doing?' I asked.

'What's it look like?' she said. 'He's dying.'

Cynthia asked, 'Will the medicine save him?'

Something in the way she asked made Judy soften. 'I can't rightly say. A tiger will surprise you every time.' She nodded at me. 'Go on, now.' Then at Zemira, 'You too.'

On our way to the truck, I took Cynthia to another enclosure and showed her a Javan black leopard.

'In the wild, she'd be dead by now,' I said. 'She's about twenty.'

'At least,' Zemira said.

Cynthia wandered to the next enclosure, which held the albino Zemira would feed with a wooden pole. In the late-morning sun, his fur looked ashy. Cynthia stood close to the fence and took out her phone to snap a photo.

'Uh-uh,' Zemira said, and moved us along.

I wondered if Judy had sent her with us to make sure we got back in the truck and left.

'Cool,' Cynthia said, as we drove out the gravel road.

'I'll show you something else.'

'Does it have claws and teeth?'

Because I couldn't stop myself, I drove north through the pine-woods and hooked on to the highway toward Chartein Farm. When we passed Clara Soto's house, the windows were dark, the driveway empty. We rounded the bend and, two miles later, turned into the drive at the sign with the pecking and neck-craning chickens.

'*This?*' Cynthia said. 'Didn't you hear what that woman told you about treating me well?'

'I think she said treating you *right*. That may be different.'

Everett Peters's German shepherd, lying at the top of the wooden steps to the singlewide, raised his head as we passed. The bay door to Chicken House Two was open, and a crew of a half dozen workers, in yellow plastic knee-high boots and heavy gloves, carted metal crates out to a flatbed truck. The stench of ammonia hung in the midday air.

'If this is right, I prefer wrong,' Cynthia said.

'C'mon,' I said, and got out as Mrs Chartein walked from the chicken house. She wore the same boots and gloves as the others, with her pants tucked into the boot tops.

She looked at me funny. 'We have nothing for you today, Franky.'

'I thought I would show my girlfriend the farm, if that's OK.'

'You should've asked first,' she said. But she pulled off her gloves and said, 'Come along.'

She took us to Chicken House Three, where thousands and thousands of week-old, lemon-yellow chicks stood on the sawdust-covered floor. 'Seven weeks from hatchling to broiler,' she said. 'They hardly have time to be cute.' She showed us the feed and watering systems. With the industrial fans, a breeze blew through, but the air still stunk.

'An acquired taste,' Mrs Chartein said, and led us outside.

When we were standing back by the pickup, her brother's Reclamation Painting van drove up the dirt road, cut across the lot, and sped out toward the highway.

'Why *Reclamation*?' I asked.

'It was the name of the business when my husband and I bought it for Harry. We liked it, and so we kept it. Harry designed the logo, though – and our sign out at the road too.'

And the painting of Peters's German shepherd in the singlewide, I figured.

She smiled at me. 'Your boss and I both take in the wounded.'

'Your brother seems tough enough.'

She tapped her chest. 'Broken heart. He ran off and married when he was twenty-one. A girl named Karine. It didn't last. He came back and we took him in.' She had a gentle smile. 'But which of us hasn't had trials?'

I thought about what she'd told me about her manager when she'd reprimanded me for going into his trailer. He too had faced hard times. 'Is that why you have Everett Peters?' I asked.

'Another man who needed shelter.'

'What happened with him?'

She shook her head as if I was stepping over another line. 'Some men hide because they've done wrong to others. Some because others have done wrong to them. He's in a third group – men who've done harm to themselves and no longer think they're fit for the world.'

'What happened?'

She said nothing.

'He doesn't seem like a good person,' I said.

She asked, gently, 'Are you any better?' Then she told Cynthia she'd enjoyed meeting her, and she walked back to the chicken house.

As we drove out to the highway, Cynthia said, 'She has a high opinion of herself, doesn't she?'

SEVENTEEN

Cynthia went home late in the evening, after her mom called and told her she needed to talk to her dad.

'Is he going to say he's sorry?' Cynthia asked.

'I think he expects an apology from you,' her mom said.

'Screw that.'

'Go easy on him,' her mom said.

'Isn't it supposed to work the other way around?'

'How much of life works the way it's supposed to?'

'I won't apologize,' Cynthia said.

'Just talk to him. Come to an understanding.'

I went back to Bar Deportivo alone at ten o'clock. On a Saturday night, the parking lot was full of pickup trucks, rusting SUVs, and a smattering of Corollas, Altimas, and Accords.

When I opened the door, a man was rapping in Spanish over Santana's 'No One to Depend On.' Couples crowded the dance floor under white strobe lights. The bank of large-screen TVs streamed kaleidoscopic patterns of green and yellow and purple. The bartenders in ruffled shirts worked the long bar. Servers in little black skirts carried drinks on trays. A black-haired woman with long eyelashes stood at a host station.

She said, 'No, no, no,' when I handed her the ten-dollar cover charge. 'This place is not for you. We don't want this.'

'What's *this*?'

'You don't belong here.'

I walked past her.

She signaled to a short, thick-chested bouncer, who crossed from the other side of the room.

I made it to the bar. But the bartender who'd pointed me toward Clara on my first visit said, 'Not tonight, my friend.'

I said, 'When I came last time, you told me you get outsiders looking to get laid and hassle people. On the night Antonia disappeared, did—?'

The bouncer put a fat hand on my shoulder. '*Señor*,' he said.

I shook free and asked the bartender, 'When Antonia disappeared, did—?'

The bouncer gripped my arm and spun me toward him. 'Please come with me,' he said. He had a kind face.

'I can't get a beer?'

'No, *señor*, no beer tonight.' He steered me back toward the entrance.

'Why?' I asked, but he gripped me harder, moving me through a crowd. So I shouted, 'Who here knew Antonia Soto?'

He stopped. 'What is your problem, *pendejo*? No one wants to listen to your questions.'

'Is the manager here? Your boss?'

'Not for you, no.'

As he pushed me toward the door, I broke his grip and started toward the bar again. I took two steps before his fist hammered the back of my head.

I barely hit the floor before he tugged me to my feet. 'Some men . . .' he said. He gripped me again, but instead of dragging me to the entrance, he took me toward the room with the pool tables, then into a hallway toward the men's and women's restrooms. Beyond the restrooms, we went through another door into a second hallway with three more doors.

He pushed me into an office where a thin man in his forties sat at a desk, working at a computer. The man wore a gray suit jacket over a red shirt, no tie. He had black-rimmed glasses, perched partway down his nose.

The bouncer spoke to him in rapid Spanish. I picked up Antonia's name.

The man opened a drawer, drew out a pistol, and laid it on top of the desk. 'I understand you want to talk to me?'

'Do you manage the bar?'

'I own it.'

'You don't let non-Mexicans in?'

'Sure, I let in Hondurans and Dominicans. We get a lot of Venezuelans.' He tapped a finger by the pistol. 'We let in most of the Americas. Everybody comes and has a good time. But not you—'

'Why?'

He pushed his glasses high on his nose. 'Last night, a bunch of you guys beat up six of my customers in the parking lot.'

'A bunch of *us* guys?'

'Yeah. Young white guys. *Pinches cabrones.* Three guys came inside and started fights.'

'Why?'

'You tell me. Why did they do the same thing three weeks ago? Why did they do it last summer?'

'I'm not like that,' I said.

'No?'

'I know Demetrius Jones.' He gave me a blank face. 'An immigration lawyer. And Clara Soto.'

He glanced at the bouncer, then at me again. 'You know Clara?'

'Sure – not well, but I know her.'

He nodded at the bouncer, who went out.

I asked, 'What did the guys who started the fights say?'

'The same thing they always say. You know about beaner hopping?'

'No.'

'It's a game they play – that's what they call it. They drive around looking for Mexicans. They hop out of their cars and trucks and beat the shit out of us. Up in New York, they killed an Ecuadorean named Marcelo Lucero. You know about Marcelo Lucero?'

I shook my head.

'Everyone out there – dancing and drinking – *they* know about Marcelo Lucero. They can't get him out of their heads. Luís Ramírez?'

'No.'

'Kicked to death in Pennsylvania. Beaner hoppers. Felipe Esparza? Mateo Gomez? Guadalupe Sanchez? Mauricío Florindo? Armando Martínez?'

'No.'

'Right up the road in Georgia. Six of them, all in one night, and *you've* never heard of them. But you have the nerve to ask me why you don't belong here?'

'Antonia Soto,' I said.

He frowned 'What about her?'

'I know who she is. I talked to her before she got killed. I know her mom and dad.'

His eyes showed nothing but scorn. 'Bravo. One of your best friends is Mexican.'

'My life is more complicated than that.'

'Don't tell me about it, OK?' His voice shook with contempt. Music from giant speakers in the main bar came through the walls. Hundreds of people were dancing, laughing, and partying fifty feet away. But he looked the way I must have when I was trapped in a cell at Raiford and everyone had an opinion about me and what was best for me. Back then, I'd wanted to hear none of it. I'd wanted them to shut the hell up and unlock my cell door.

The bouncer came back with Clara. When she looked at me, she drew in a sharp breath. She wore heavy eyeliner, above and below her eyes. She'd gelled her short blond hair and tucked a red-petaled flower over her ear.

She talked in Spanish with the man at the desk, and at first I thought she was denying she knew me. But she said Antonia's name again, then mine, and when they finished, the man opened his desk drawer and put away the pistol. Clara glared at me and walked out of the office.

The man folded his hands on top of the desk. 'Clara says you're a fool. Is that right?'

'I sometimes screw up.'

'She says you led the police to Carlos Medina.'

'I didn't mean to.'

'Great – a well-intentioned white man. Just what we need.'

'You prefer another beaner hopper?'

'No, I prefer you get out of my bar and leave me and my customers alone.'

'I don't know if the guys who came last night also killed Antonia, but whoever did it has killed another person.'

'What are you talking about?'

'A man named Kumar Mehta,' I said. 'Out for a walk a few nights ago.'

The look of scorn returned. 'He's not Mexican. The guys who did this hate Latinos.'

'He was visiting from India.'

'What does he have to do with Antonia Soto?'

'I don't know. That's why I came. To try to find out. Did you report the guys?'

The man exchanged a look with the bouncer, then said to me, 'Clara is right about you. A fool. If I tell the police that people are fighting, they won't turn on their sirens and chase after the guys. They'll check the identification cards of my customers. Maybe they'll arrest them. Then they'll threaten to take away my liquor license. No, no police. I take care of my own business.'

'You were here?' I asked the bouncer.

He shrugged.

'Show him,' the man at the desk said.

The bouncer pulled up his shirt. He'd taped a bandage over his belly.

I thought about the marks carved on Antonia's and Kumar Mehta's foreheads. 'A knife?'

'Box cutter,' the bouncer said. 'I broke his nose.'

'The world is full of idiots,' the man at the desk said. 'I just want to run my bar. That's what my customers want. People need to leave us alone.'

'I understand,' I said.

'Do you?' He looked doubtful.

'But I can't even leave myself alone most of the time.'

He rested his eyes on me. 'I believe you're trying to help,' he said. 'But do it somewhere else.'

That night I dreamed of a greyhound racetrack my dad liked when I was growing up. After my mom died but before I went to prison, he sometimes took me, as if he was doing me a favor. *I know dogs*, he would say. We would watch heat after heat of them chasing a lure at the end of a mechanical arm, until he was broke, sweating, and teary-eyed. For the next few weeks, he would study the Stat Force and tip sheets until he convinced himself he'd worked out his mistakes, and then we would go back to the track and he would blow more money.

In the dream, the mechanical arm disappeared. Instead, an enormous animal – which looked like a mix of Everett Peters's German shepherd and Judy's albino leopard – pursued the dogs around the dirt track. My dad cheered for a greyhound in a green jersey with a bright yellow number 7 on it – the slowest dog. As the other greyhounds sprinted ahead, the leopard-dog closed in on 7 and clamped enormous jaws over its belly. The leopard-dog tore the greyhound apart. The other dogs, no longer being chased, wandered from the track and grazed like sheep on the infield grass.

I woke up thinking about how I wouldn't give up even when I knew I should. I wondered how much I was my father's son.

EIGHTEEN

After stopping at Jenquist Meat, I drove toward the Sheriff's Office. At the processing company, a thick-armed man had wheeled out a cart of hog offal, topped with a goat carcass. We'd loaded the meat into the back of the pickup, and then he'd said, 'Hold on a minute,' and gone in through a steel door. He'd come back with a package. 'Lamb chops. From my boss to yours. Ollie's sweet on her.'

In late fall and winter in North Florida, the temperature some-times dropped to freezing around dawn, killing flowers and garden vegetables. Overnight, a front had blown in and frosted the grass on the highway side. The cold would keep the flies off the meat for an extra hour, so instead of going straight to Safe Haven, I exited at Adams Street. If Deborah Holt was working a regular day shift, I might catch her as she came into the police station.

At the information desk by the security checkpoint, I asked to talk to her.

The police clerk took my name, dialed a number, and pointed at a pillar by a garbage can. 'Wait over there.'

A minute later, he beckoned me. 'Detective Holt's in a meeting. You want to talk to someone else?'

'Can I leave her a message?'

He gave me a hard look.

'I'll try again later,' I said.

But as I started for the doors, Higby came in from outside.

He stopped. 'What are you doing here?' I stepped around him, and he blocked me. 'I asked you a question.'

'I'm going from one place I don't belong to another,' I said.

'Again, what are you doing here?' He was six inches taller than I was and carried sixty or seventy more pounds, mostly around the middle.

'I came to talk to someone else.' I tried to move past him.

'My partner?'

'Maybe.'

'What do you need?'

'Nothing from you.' Then I wondered why shouldn't I ask. 'Do you know about the guys who beat up Mexicans at the bar where Antonia Soto disappeared?'

'It's none of your business.' But he seemed to be processing the news.

'Yeah, that's what I thought.' I stepped around him and back out into the cold morning.

Whether the erythropoietin was helping or the effects of the trip from Louisiana were wearing off, Rocko was up on his feet at Safe Haven, his legs shaky under his gaunt body. He seemed suspicious about the meat Zemira slopped from a bucket, but we left him alone and when we came back, it was gone. We gave Sorrel one of the goat's hind-quarters, then the other. She would have eaten the whole animal if we'd let her.

'Easy, go easy,' Judy said. 'After all the abuse, too much love will kill her.'

At noon, as I pushed a wheelbarrow past the house, I smelled Ollie Jenquist's lamb chops frying. Then Judy and Diane sat on the porch, each with a plate in her lap.

In the afternoon, I trimmed the African tulip trees across from the house and mowed the big cat cemetery to ready it for winter. At four o'clock, I put the equipment in the work shed and drove from the refuge, dirty and hot.

I wanted to stand in my shower at the Cardinal Motel and come out raw. Instead, I sped past the Philips Highway turnoff and cruised through a series of subdivisions.

When I came to Mandarin Reach, I pulled up to the guard kiosk.

The man inside the service window was looking at his phone. 'What d'you got, buddy?'

'Work and more work.'

He looked me over lazily, and he must have been used to letting in sweaty lawn men and plumbers because he raised the gate and waved me through.

The Mandarin Reach community clubhouse stood two hundred yards beyond the kiosk. After the clubhouse, there were four tennis courts. Then the entrance road split in three directions, each winding past matching white stucco houses and branching further into little lanes with more white stucco houses.

I took the street to the right. I coasted past the houses, looking for signs that the Mehta family might live in one of them. The lawns were tidy, the bushes pruned close to the ground, hardly a tree in sight. When a teenage boy rode toward me on a bike, towing another boy on a skateboard, I pulled to the curb and rolled down my window. I called out, 'Can you tell me where the Mehtas live?' They passed without a glance.

At the cul-de-sac, there was an empty playground and, beyond it, a retention pond. I turned, drove out, and tried the next street.

Three houses in, standing at the end of a driveway, a dark-faced, high-foreheaded woman smoked a cigarette. She wore a long skirt and a too-big sweater. She looked as hunger-bitten as the Zooland tigers.

I pulled alongside and asked if she could point me to the Mehtas' house.

She shook her head – tiny shakes.

I drove.

At the end of the street, a man was washing his Lexus in front of his house. He wore shorts and a white sleeveless T-shirt in spite of the cold. I got out and waited for him to take earbuds from his ears. Could he tell me where the Mehtas lived? He didn't know, but he said Kumar Mehta's body was found on the next street over. 'It's a shame,' he said, and I believed the pain in his eyes. I asked if there'd been other attacks in the neighborhood – any guys pouring out of cars and trucks, looking for fights. 'No, no, it's quiet here. Safe.'

I drove up the third street. More white stucco houses. More tidy lawns and tightly clipped bushes. Now and then, a tiny tree. At a house on the corner of the first lane, a blond woman climbed from a Subaru Outback with a plastic bag looped over her wrist. She opened the back door and struggled to free a crying baby boy from a car seat. When she had the baby in her arms, I asked if she knew where the Mehta family lived. She nodded in the direction I'd been driving. 'Five houses up on the left. The nicest people.' Her baby grabbed at her. She held him away in both hands and said, *'No'* – then, 'So tragic.'

A boy who looked about fifteen sat on the front steps of the fifth house up the street. He wore jeans, green tennis shoes, and a green windbreaker.

I parked at the curb and went up the front walk.

I asked, 'Is this the Mehtas' house?'

He stared at me, silent and sullen, then stood and went inside. The lock clicked behind him.

I rang the bell. When no one came, I rang again.

A woman opened. She had a thin face and fierce dark eyes. 'Yes?' she said.

'Mrs Mehta?'

She nodded sharply. 'Aadhya Mehta, yes.'

'My name is Franky Dast,' I said. 'I'm sorry to bother you, but I'm hoping to talk to you about your father-in-law.'

She narrowed her eyes. 'Are you the police?'

'No.'

'Reporter?'

'No.'

'Who are you?'

'Did the police tell you about the connection between your father-in-law's death and the death of a girl named Antonia Soto?'

'I'm sorry – *who* are you?'

'Sort of a friend of the girl – of her family. I—'

'We have enough pain already,' she said, and she closed the door.
I touched the bell.

She opened again, fierce. 'What do you want?'

'Did you see your father-in-law's body before the police took
him away? If you did, he had a mark right here.' I touched my
forehead. 'Maybe the police told you to tell nobody about it.'

'*Who* are you?' she asked once more.

'The girl had the same mark. I'm not supposed to know. I told
her mother I would find out what happened. But to tell the truth,
I'm doing this for myself.'

'This was your girlfriend?'

'No, I hardly knew her. But I need to do something.'

'Why?'

'That's a really long story.'

She gazed at me with her hard eyes, then opened the door wider.
'Come in.'

The living room had a white rug, a brown Naugahyde couch, and
a large-screen TV, but no other furniture. The woman led me up a
hallway to a combination kitchen and dining room. 'Sit,' she said,
and gestured at a round table with five chairs. She went to the
refrigerator and brought me a glass of apple juice. She set out a
plate of Ritz crackers.

She sat. 'In Punjab state – in northern India – where my husband
and I come from – holidays were special. We ate together as a
family. We had a lot of conversation. I miss that. When my father-
in-law came, he brought that with him. For one month. One month
in a year.' She stared as if to see if I understood what she was
saying. 'Here, it's money, money, money. The new phone. The new
car. The big television. New, new, new. It's the land of opportunity,
but it isn't life. What I miss about India is you feel like you're at
home. You're used to things.'

A faint smile crossed her face. 'For my father-in-law, America
was paradise. He was very proud of my husband, very proud of our
son Pratul. He would sit on the couch. He would watch the big
television. He walked in the neighborhood like he was a king. He
talked to the lawn people, the garbage men. He talked to the neighbors. Everybody.'

'Did he have issues with any of them?'

'No, he never meddled with anybody. But this is a bad place –

too much discrimination. Every day, when I drive my car, somebody yells at me. In the stores, they look at me like I'm a bug.'

A voice spoke from the hallway. 'They're stupid. They say racist bullshit.' The kid who'd been sitting on the front step – Pratul, I guessed – came into the kitchen. He took a cracker from the plate.

His mom said, 'What are we going to do?'

'Fight back,' Pratul said.

She set her fierce eyes on him. 'With your skinny little hands, you'll fight back?'

'Uh-huh.' He took another cracker. He crushed it in his fist and dropped the pieces on the floor.

'Foolish,' his mom said. 'Don't be stupid like them.'

I asked him, 'Did you ever know a girl named Antonia Soto?' He was about the same age.

'Is that the Mexican kid who got killed?'

I nodded.

'I saw her on the news. Why would I know her?'

His mom told him, 'This man thinks her death has something to do with *dada*.'

Across the house, the front door opened.

'My husband,' she said. 'Saatvik.'

A bright-faced man came in through the hallway. He wore a pink button-down shirt with a brown tie. He carried an oversized briefcase.

His wife introduced us, and though his dad had just died, he seemed almost cheerful, eager to talk. He said he worked as a contract engineer for power plants in Florida and Georgia, overseeing special projects. For the past eight months, he'd been decommissioning a coal-fired generating station on the banks of the St Johns River. But mostly he worked at farther-away plants and returned home only for weekends. 'I came to America and never stopped traveling,' he said. 'But my family has a house, and my dad had a place to visit.'

'Did your dad ever tell you about someone bothering him here?' I asked.

'He was like me. He enjoyed people. He liked to hear gossip. He knew more of the neighbors than I do. No one bothered him.'

'Then, what happened?'

He came to the table and sat. His smile broke. He laid a hand on his wife's. 'Aadhya and I came here because the city in India where we lived still felt like an English colony. Do you want to know something funny? When we moved here, we rented with some other Indian families at Colony Point Apartments. Now we were the colonizers. I was an engineer, and Aadhya had a degree in chemistry. Doctor Naidu lived in the apartment next door. On the other side, Isha and Rajiv Singh owned World Grocery.' He looked me in the eyes. 'When I was a boy, I wanted nothing more than to leave India. I looked at America and thought, this is the place for me. My mom died when I was eleven years old, and the only reason Aadhya and I stayed was my dad and her parents. But my dad said, *Go* – because he wanted to leave too and he never did. So Aadhya and I left, and my dad visited, and now he's dead. You ask what happened. *He* hated no one. *I* hate no one. But I wonder who hates us.'

'I'm sorry,' I said.

'The city we came from, Patiala, is the same latitude as here. Thirty degrees north. This isn't a coincidence. Every day in Patiala, my dad went to the Kali Devi Temple – very famous in Punjab. He was punctual. I knew what time he would go. Wherever I was, I could imagine him there.'

His wife said, 'We thought we were safe here.'

Saatvik said, 'On this street, forty percent Indian, twenty percent Chinese, ten percent Korean, one Black family, one family from Venezuela, the others white. My boy' – he tipped his head at Pratul – 'he dates a Romanian girl. I don't hate her. I don't hate her parents. We like everybody. We tolerate. My dad was the same.'

When I left, he walked with me outside to my truck. We shook hands, and I asked, 'Do you mind telling me where your dad was killed?'

He pointed down the street toward the security kiosk. 'Near the clubhouse and tennis courts. Mr Seong – he owns the first house after the courts – he found him by Valencia Lane.'

'Your wife said your dad liked to walk in the neighborhood.'

'Every morning at eleven o'clock and every night again.' His smile flickered. 'He went to the ponds and sat on the benches. If there were people at the clubhouse or someone was swimming, he stopped to chat. He watched children at the playground. He might go to the development office and talk with the manager or the maintenance workers. He loved this place.'

As I drove out, I stopped at the corner of Valencia Lane.

There was no evidence that a man's body had lain on any of the lawns. The grass was short, the bushes trimmed low to the ground. The pavement was clean.

I walked down the street, past the Seongs' house, and along the tennis courts. The courts had been empty when I'd driven in. Now two women played.

I came to the clubhouse, which was bright yellow and had tinted floor-to-ceiling windows. Sawhorses stood at the four corners of the building, with two more on the sides of a path to the entrance. Yellow-and-black barrier tape stretched from each sawhorse to the next, with a gap for the front door.

I went up the path and inside. The all-weather carpet, the color of AstroTurf, smelled new. Picture frames, with images of tennis players, kids swimming, and tropical beaches, leaned against spotless walls. To one side, there was a kitchenette with a sink and refrigerator. Protective plastic coating covered new cabinets.

I poked my head through a door into a men's locker room with a shower stall, a toilet, a sink, a changing area, and a half dozen lockers.

I went out the other side on to a pool deck. Ten lounge chairs stood in a row, their tops folded over the seats, protecting them from dirt and sun. A pool hook hung on a chain-link fence next to a list of Pool Rules. The water was topped to the overflow gutters, glistening in the afternoon sunlight.

I stared at the pool and wondered what the hell I was doing.

I went back to my truck and drove to the Cardinal. I stood for an hour in the shower. When I got out, my skin was raw.

NINETEEN

While the TV and radio news didn't explicitly link the killings of Antonia Soto and Kumar Mehta, over the next three days the stories aired one after another.

The *Times-Union* covered developments side by side in the Metro section. Reporters quoted Holt on both cases. Even from lousy photographs, you could tell that the two victims had landed in North Florida from far away.

On Friday morning, after delivering a load of chicken, I left for another appointment with Dr Patel. The appointment was at noon, so I headed first for the county courthouse, where Demetrius Jones was holding an immigrant rights rally.

As lawyers, judges, jurors, and court employees climbed the steps, Demetrius gathered a couple dozen Mexicans, including Martin and Alejandra Soto and others from the poultry farm, and another dozen community activists. They carried signs that said *We Count!* and *¡Justicia Para Todos Los Trabajadores!* Two women in matching black berets held a banner that said *Cursed is anyone who withholds justice from the foreigner.* Uniformed cops watched from the sides. Passersby stopped in the courthouse plaza. A man in a gray suit and a woman in a blue skirt and jacket videoed the protesters on their phones. The grim-faced reporter who'd broken the story of Kumar Mehta's death stood with her camera crew on the side. Across from her, a group of Indians watched and waited. Aadhya Mehta and her son Pratul stood with them.

I went up the broad walkway and joined the two of them.

'What are you doing here?' I said.

Aadhya said, 'Pratul insisted.' Although the morning was warm, she wore a heavy jacket. She glanced at her son. 'He's angry.'

He glared at her. 'So are you.'

'My anger is different.'

Then, up on the courthouse steps, Demetrius spoke into a megaphone. 'This morning we're here to name the dead,' he said. 'Antonia Soto . . .'

Others on the steps repeated her name, some in hushed voices, some in shouts.

'Name the dead, and never forget them,' Demetrius said. He recited more names – ones the owner of Bar Deportivo had told me and other names too. 'Mateo and José Luís Tías Gomez,' he said, and the protesters repeated the names. 'Felipe Mauricio Esparza, Pedro Corzo, Mauricío Florindo, José Sucuzhañay.' The responding voices turned into a chant. He said, 'Armando Perez Martínez and Miguel Vega,' and waited for the echo. He went on and on, naming name after name, pausing for the men and women to call them back. Finally, he said Antonia's name again, and, after the others repeated her name, he gazed out at the growing crowd of listeners.

Then Pratul yelled, 'Kumar Mehta.' He stepped into the open, away from his mom and the other Indian demonstrators. Apart from them, he held himself as if he would fight anyone who objected to naming his grandfather.

Demetrius cocked his head. He spoke into the megaphone again. 'Name the dead. Name them all. There are too many names because *one* name is too many. We could build a monument with the names. These people died because a bullet made better sense to some hateful citizens than a roof and a plate of rice. A baseball bat made sense to them . . . or a knife . . . or steel-toed boots. Remember these names. Write them down. Carve them into your consciousness.'

Then another man called out, from behind me. 'Go home.'

I knew the voice – Randall Lehmann.

'You take our jobs,' Lehmann yelled. 'You take our welfare. You freeload on our taxes.' He pushed past the other listeners, shouting as he moved, as if his answer to Demetrius's call and response was to repeat every cliché he knew. 'Go home with your gangs and your guns and your drugs. No means no.' He climbed the steps toward the protesters. He tried to pull the banner from the hands of the women in the black berets. Then he turned to the crowd and seemed to preach. 'It's time to clean house. The apostle Paul took his men, and, the next day purifying himself with them, he entered the temple to signify the days of purification.'

Pratul stepped toward him, but then his mom was beside him, gripping his arm, holding him back. She hissed in his ear. '*No.*'

Demetrius mocked Lehmann through his megaphone. 'Are you a religious man, Councilman?'

Lehmann turned to him. 'I believe in purity, sir, yes I do.'

'And by purity, you mean yourself?'

'Purity is purity, man. Wash your hands after you do your filthy business.'

Demetrius looked amused.

'God's will,' Lehmann said. 'Live clean, live long—'

Someone in the crowd said, 'Crazy bastard.'

Then, weirdly, Lehmann started singing 'Amazing Grace.'

As the councilman finished the first verse, Martin Soto broke from the protesters, came down the steps, and faced him. Lehmann stopped singing.

'You disrespect me,' Martin Soto said.

Lehmann sneered at him. 'You've got to earn my respect. In what world do you think respect is a right? It's a privilege. You get it because you do something to deserve it. You accomplish something. You don't get it just because you're born. Creeping across the border won't do it either. What have you done that's worthy of my regard? What do you expect from me?'

'I expect dignity,' the other man said.

Lehmann said, 'Then act dignified.'

At Raiford, Lehmann's insult would get a man shanked. Outside of prison walls, it deserved at least a bloody lip.

Martin Soto said, 'I have enough dignity to walk away from you.' He turned and went back up the steps. The protesters clapped.

'You walk away?' Lehmann said. 'Only because there's no wall to tunnel under and no river to swim across.' He faced the crowd of onlookers. 'Lock your doors, my friends. That mariachi band is the drum and fife of an invading army. You can't dance to it. It's marching music, and they're coming to get you.' Then he walked down the steps and waved at the news cameras, before crossing the plaza to his car.

'That,' Demetrius said into his megaphone, 'is a sad excuse for a man.'

After more short speeches and more chanting, the rally ended. Demetrius came down, and I introduced him to Aadhya Mehta and Pratul. 'I mostly work with Mexicans and others from Central America,' he told Aadhya. 'Sometimes Nigerians and Somalians. But I would be happy to talk with you, or to set you up with someone else at Vanguard Reform.'

'What would you do?' she asked. 'What difference would it make?'

Demetrius gestured at the steps where he and the protesters had stood. 'As you see, we make ourselves heard. If we're heard, we're hard to ignore. We also give legal advice and, down the line, representation – pro bono or at a negotiated fee. At this point, we can pressure the police to thoroughly investigate what happened to your father-in-law.'

Pratul said, 'Someone killed him because he was Indian.'

Demetrius considered the boy. 'If that's true, we'll make that fact public. We'll do all we can to find the people who are responsible.'

'Someone should kill *them*,' Pratul said.

'Hush,' his mom said.

'We'll work for justice,' Demetrius said.

'All I want is peace,' Aadhya said.

Demetrius nodded. 'One of my heroes says peace can't exist without justice.'

'It's not true,' she said. 'You can lock your doors. You can bury injustice. I've seen it hundreds of times.'

'That's not peace, that's silence,' Demetrius said. He pulled out a wallet and gave her a business card. 'Look up Vanguard Reform online. If you think we can do anything for you, call me.' He smiled at her son and offered to shake hands. 'Good to meet you, Pratul. Take it easy, OK?' He glanced at me. 'Can we talk for a minute?'

As we stepped away, his smile dropped. 'Are you putting ideas in their heads?'

I said, 'Whoever killed Antonia also killed Kumar Mehta.'

'Did you tell them that?'

'I implied it.'

'Based on what?'

By talking to the Mehtas about the marks on Antonia's and the old man's foreheads, I'd already broken my promise to keep quiet, but Demetrius might go public with anything I said. What good would blowing up the secret do? 'Two foreigners were killed in a week.'

'One an undocumented immigrant, the other a legal visitor,' he said.

'No reason for either murder, except they weren't from here.'

'None you know of. Who was Kumar Mehta?'

'A proud dad and grandfather. Nothing else.'

'You *know* that?'

'It's my sense,' I said.

'Uh-huh. You need to back off. You've taken Kumar Mehta's grandson down a bad road.'

'He was there already.'

'Don't push him farther.'

'What are *you* doing, other than yelling names on the courthouse steps?'

He gave me the same amused look he'd given Lehmann. 'That's the first goal – making people aware.'

'How's Carlos Medina? Still in jail? Are you abandoning him?'

'The police are glad to hold him while they put together a case. If they let him go right now, ICE will grab him. So there's no rush. I've told him to sit tight and say nothing unless I'm there.'

'Could he have killed Antonia?'

He breathed out. 'I see no reason to think so.'

'But no reason to think he's innocent either?'

'After ten years of doing this, I've stopped assuming anything.'

At noon, I rode an elevator in the Baptist Hospital Medical Services Building. A harried-looking woman scurried out of Dr Patel's office, her eyes on the floor. I went in and sank into the plush couch.

I talked about Antonia. I talked about my visit to the Mehtas' house. I talked about my impulse to break through every locked door. I talked about my difficulty keeping secrets.

Dr Patel tapped his pen on his notebook. 'Yeah, you're really stretching your wings.'

'You say that like it might be a bad thing.'

'The question is where you fly when you stretch them – and what you leave behind. Reintegrating after prison involves a mix of returning to where you were before your conviction and moving forward. It's an issue of how to assimilate. For every ounce you gain, you lose a pound. How much of the new world do you absorb into yourself without losing the person you were?'

'I want to leave that person behind. That person weighs me down.'

'Is weighing down all bad? Sounds like an anchor. What would you do without that person? Drift away? Disappear into the clouds?'

'I would be free,' I said. 'No more Bill Higby judging me. All of the garbage that people have told me about how to behave, how to be good – all of the stuff that sent me to prison for something I didn't do – all of that would be gone. There'd be no doors locking me in or out.'

'We call locked doors civilized society.' He raised his eyebrows ironically. 'Are you done with civilization?'

'More or less, if that's what you want to call it.'

'But is it done with you?'

'Why should I worry about that?'

He set down the notebook. 'I was just reading a book about a slave. More than anything, he wanted to be free. So every chance he could, he collected a few pennies. After a long time, he saved enough to buy his own freedom from his master at the same price his master paid for him. Good for him, right?'

'Sure, good for him.'

'But that's the dilemma. Does the slave who buys his own freedom break the system that enslaved him or does he uphold it? Does he claim his humanity, or, by paying the price demanded by people who say they own him as an object, does he agree that you can count his value in dollars and cents? The answer, I think, is both. But the bigger, more important answer may be that he has no choice. Sometimes the only way to keep from getting chewed up by a machine is by climbing inside it and making sure the gears stay greased around you. We don't have to like it.'

'He could have run away.'

'Absolutely. And the man who owned him could have run after him. They both would've spent their lives running.'

I scratched my cheek. 'I like running.'

'I know you do.'

'He could've cut the owner's throat.'

'He could have,' Dr Patel said, 'but then he would have blood on his hands. Even if the owner deserved to bleed, that would have been a big stain. This slave lived in the world he was given – its past, its present, and its future. Maybe he could've lived better. But he did his best.'

'So you're saying a slave should pay the price of being a slave?'

'Anything but. I'm saying, do what you can. Don't hold yourself to more than that. Maybe you'll stretch your wings. Maybe you'll grow *new* wings. But don't be too hard on yourself if you don't fly too high. The world has a way of pulling men down.'

'All right,' I said.

He picked up the notebook again. 'And keep in mind that the world will have expectations of you, whether or not you want it to.'

'What do you mean?'

He looked at me over the notebook. 'How's Safe Haven?'

'Fine,' I said. 'Judy got a couple of new cats.'

'That's what I hear,' he said. 'She's concerned about your commitment. She says you're cutting out early.'

That kind of reminder was exactly what I wanted to break free from. 'I went to the rally.'

'Great. Stretch your wings. But did the rally sign your paycheck? Did it let you drive its pickup truck when you were off the clock? Did it give you an opportunity when others shot you down?'

My breath seemed to suck away. 'Sometimes I hate talking with you.'

He gave me an easy, maybe a forgiving smile. 'That's how I earn *my* paycheck.'

Screw Judy, I thought, as I drove out of the Medical Building garage. *Screw Dr Patel too. Screw Bill Higby and Deborah Holt. Screw my teachers and my dad, who made me the person I was and maybe always would be. Screw the prosecutor who charged me for the Bronson boys. Screw the judge who called me an outrage. Screw the Raiford guards with their Tasers and tear gas and, high in the watchtowers, their guns. Screw them all. Screw me for being myself – my screwed and screwed-up self.*

There *were* good people too – I knew that. Cynthia, who saved me day after day, night after night. Mrs and Mr Chartein, who gave without demanding. Maybe Demetrius Jones, full of himself but fighting the same forces that held me down and locked me up.

Could I be like them?

Cynthia said I saved her too.

Could I give without demanding?

I was pretty sure I couldn't.

Could I fight more selflessly than Demetrius?

Probably not.

I wanted to get out of the way of myself. But every direction I turned, there I was.

I turned on to Philips Highway and passed a CITGO station, a building supply business, Sahara Sandwiches, a smoke shop, a car wash, and other dingy motels, as worn and heartless as the Cardinal. What wrecks lay in the corners of each of them? What pockets of goodness?

I turned into the motel lot, cruised past the check-in office, and hit the brakes before the spot where I normally parked. In the bright light of the day – while I was delivering chickens to Safe Haven or standing at the rally or talking with my reintegration therapist – someone had spray-painted *Baby fucker* on my door, *Dirtbag* and *Pedo* on the wall, and *Cocksucker* on the window. There was also a hole in the window, as if the vandal had punched it with a hammer or a baseball bat.

Sweat broke from my neck, my back, between my legs. I eased the pickup into the parking space, cut the engine, and got out.

The afternoon had warmed, and sunlight glinted off the webs of fractured glass in the window. In Jimmy and Susan's room, a television played loudly.

I went to their door and pounded until it opened.

Jimmy, gripping a can of Miller High Life, looked at me wide-eyed. He wore torn jeans, without shoes or a shirt, his ribs showing through his skin. He looked stoned as well as drunk.

'The fuck, man?' he said.

I yelled at him. 'Did you see who did this?'

'Huh?'

'*This.*' I pointed at the wall.

He stepped outside and stared at the graffiti. He went to the hole in the window and stared into my room. He licked his lips, then looked at me with disgust, as if I'd done the damage to myself.

TWENTY

Hopper came from the reception office to see the damage. He blinked, then walked back to the office and returned with a roll of duct tape and a cardboard box. He taped a box flap over the hole in the window and said, 'I'll paint and order new glass next week.'

'I need it done now,' I said. 'I can't live like this.'

He looked weary. 'The toilet's backed up in number four, and the electric is shorting in twelve and thirteen. Does graffiti keep you from shitting? Does it smell like burning wires? Get in line.'

'I'll paint it myself,' I said.

'Not if you want to keep renting here,' he said, and walked back to the office.

When I'd first gotten out of prison and the story of my exoneration put my face on TV and in the paper, people at the grocery store and restaurants treated me with sympathy or, as often, suspicion. If I went to a bar, guys picked fights with me. When I sat at a stoplight or stood on a sidewalk, people rolled down their windows and shouted what they wanted to do to me or what they wished the other inmates had done to me at Raiford. After the *Times-Union* mentioned I was living at the Cardinal Motel, a man once climbed from an SUV and flung a paper bag of dog shit at me as I came out of my room. But for the past six months, people might look at me as if they thought we'd met before, but if I ignored them, they moved on.

Someone like the man with the dog shit could have written the graffiti and broken the window. But after tangling myself in Antonia Soto's and Kumar Mehta's killings, I might be pulling in new hate along with the old.

I went into my room and drew the shade over the patched-up window. I picked glass shards out of the carpet.

Then I called Cynthia at Bourne-Goff Storage.

'We've got to get you out of that place,' she said.

'It has nothing to do with the Cardinal – it's me.'

'Maybe it's both,' she said.

'Can you come over?' I asked.

'As soon as I get off work.'

That evening, Cynthia lay naked in my arms and we watched *Creature from the Black Lagoon*. Kay Lawrence, played by Julie Adams, was a scientist and a love interest too – desired by the men on an Amazon expedition and also by the Gill-man creature. When she swam in the Black Lagoon, the Gill-man did a sort of underwater ballet, swimming under her stroke for stroke, approaching as if he would touch her, drawing away, finally brushing against her ankle.

In the flickering light of the television, with the window shade closed, skin to skin with Cynthia, I could be anywhere – far away where people spoke other languages, where bullets and knives dropped as harmlessly to the ground as rain, where even monsters danced.

As the movie ended, with the Gill-man wounded, sinking into the lagoon, I touched my lips to Cynthia's. I said, 'You're all I want.'

'Fuck it,' she said.

'Huh?'

She pulled away. 'Hopper said he'll kick you out?'

'If I fix the wall.'

'You're supposed to live with a sign saying you're a baby fucker? That won't work.' She pulled on her pants.

We drove to a Lowes and bought a gallon of paint, two rollers, and a box of single-edge razor blades to scrape the window. As hookers walked along the highway side and the night cooled, we painted over the insults.

When we stepped into the parking lot to check our work, Cynthia slipped her fingers into mine. 'Better,' she said.

The smell of fresh paint hung in the still air.

That night, I dreamed that Higby held me against a wall. He said, *You did it, goddammit, you did it*, over and over again. I knew that his gaze and his muscular grip had no power over me. What terrified me – what I never could break free from, even if I struggled against my chains for thirty thousand years – was his belief, his absolute conviction, that I was guilty. I woke, sweating. I got up and went to the bathroom sink. I soaked my wrists in cold water. I splashed my face.

Then I went back to bed, where Cynthia breathed easy, away from my terror.

I dreamed again. I sat in a courtroom watching a marvelous man with intense blue eyes argue for the innocence of a skinny defendant against charges he'd killed a girl who may or may not have been Antonia Soto. The man's jaw was square and heavy, weighed down with the beginnings of jowls. His shoulders sloped. I believed he would free the defendant. But then the judge – a little man in enormous black robes – issued a death sentence. The defendant, like a magician, produced a shiv from his orange jumpsuit. He stabbed his brilliant-eyed lawyer in the throat. As a bailiff wrestled the defendant to the floor, the lawyer's eyes glistened with delight. With the blade sticking from his neck, he gazed at the judge, as if they shared a terrific joke. He said, 'I've never been more frightened in my life.' But his eyes seemed to tell a different story.

Then a glow intruded into the dream with a warmth and intensity that cast shadows over the brilliant-eyed lawyer, the thick-robed judge, the skinny defendant. A voice spoke over the scene. It told me to get out of the courtroom – *we need to get out* – and then it was Cynthia's voice, and other voices too – shouts of fear and excitement. Then I was awake. Cynthia sat on the bed beside me, struggling to put on her pants. 'We need to get out,' she said. A voice from the parking lot – Hopper's – shouted my name. The fresh-paint smell turned into the stink of chemical smoke. The electric wiring in units twelve and thirteen? The window shade glowed with the intense light of the dream.

Fists pounded on my door. I found my jeans and put on shoes and a shirt. Cynthia and I went out into the night. Flames licked up the outside walls, scarring the new paint. Acrid smoke snaked over the motel roof. Jimmy and Susan stood with a man who rented the room on the other side of theirs. A hooker in stilettos and a black vinyl jacket watched, grinning. Others – from the motel, or drawn by the fire from the late-night life of the highway side – watched too.

Hopper sprayed the flames with a fire extinguisher.

Broken glass glittered on the concrete walkway. A Molotov cocktail had smashed there. The fire extinguisher knocked down the blaze. If whoever had thrown the firebomb had gotten it into my room or on to the roof, it might have burned down the motel.

After Hopper doused the last flames, he stomped on the walkway as if he could grind the fire into the earth. Then he spun, furious. He came at me as if he would beat me with the steel extinguisher. 'Jesus Christ,' he said, 'what did you do?'

'Nothing,' I said. 'I did nothing.'

He was beyond hearing. 'I put up with just about anything – but I want you out of here.'

'I didn't—'

'Out,' he said. 'Two days.'

'I did nothing.'

TWENTY-ONE

'Let's get a place together,' I said the next morning.

'I can't,' Cynthia said.

'Sure you can. If I can move, you can.'

'My mom says it would kill my dad.'

'Kill him? He wanted to kick you out.'

'He's falling apart.'

'Seems like he wants to break you apart.'

'He wants to love me, that's what my mom says. But he hates himself for what happened to me—'

'What he *did* to you.'

'She says, when he sees my pain, it rips him apart. She thinks I shouldn't blame him. I asked her who I *should* blame? Myself? She says no one needs to be blamed. She says what happened happened, and that's all there is to it. But she still wants me to treat him like he's the one who needs something. He thinks I'm trying to get back at him by being with you.'

'Huh.'

'He says I don't belong with anyone who's been in prison. He thinks you're hardcore. He called me his little girl.'

'What did you say?'

'I told him I grew up fast. I stopped being a kid the night he dropped his cigarette in bed.'

'He must've loved that.'

'He made a fist.' She clenched a hand as if she would hit me. 'Then he said he was trying to keep me from getting hurt. I told him I feel safe with you. He got tears in his eyes. I felt bad. I can't move in with you.'

'He needs to let you live,' I said.

I brought a load of hog parts from Jenquist Meat to Safe Haven. When I pulled in, Zemira was slopping out the lynx enclosure with a shovel and hose. I grabbed a shovel and joined her. Then we fed the cats.

As she poured a bucket of meat on to a paver in one of the lion enclosures, she said, 'Your girlfriend, she's all right, isn't she?'

'Yeah, she's pretty good.'

'No explaining why some girls choose losers.' She walked to the albino leopard enclosure and picked up the feeding pole.

She prodded a whole chicken at the skittish cat. 'Why do you live here?' I said.

She acted like she didn't hear me, then said, 'You probably think I'm screwed-up.'

'Not necessarily.'

'Most people do. When the vet comes, he looks at me like I'm deranged. When we get deliveries, the drivers treat me like I'm either a wild child they want to drag into the woods and fuck or a sick animal they need to stay away from.'

'You can be quiet,' I said. 'You're sort of standoffish. They might treat you funny because you're hard to get to know.'

'I don't owe them anything.'

'I didn't say you did.'

'I don't owe *anyone*.'

'So why do you live here?'

'I like animals better than people.' The albino crept to the wooden pole, belly nearly touching the ground, and snatched the chicken, then retreated to eat it. 'If you think I sleep with Judy and Diane, I don't.'

'I didn't think you did.'

'The vet thinks so.'

'What does the vet know?'

During lunch break, I looked for apartments on my phone, narrowing the search to ones ready for immediate occupancy. I picked three, called about the first – at a complex called Riverview Apartments – and asked if a one-bedroom was available. The Riverview woman said I could move in that night if I wanted. I arranged to see it after work.

I was about to call the second when my phone rang.

Demetrius Jones.

'Tell me about Kumar Mehta,' he said.

'Why?' I said. 'Did Aadhya get in touch?'

'Uh-uh. Someone lit a fire outside Vanguard Reform last night.'

My stomach turned.

'It burned on the sidewalk and went out on its own,' he said. 'The fire department said it was an incendiary device. They think whoever set it meant to get our attention, not burn us down.'

I told him about the Molotov cocktail.

'Holy shit.'

I asked, 'What makes you think the fire had something to do with Kumar Mehta?'

'Vanguard got a call this morning. I don't know the details – our receptionist answered – but the caller said we were on the wrong side of things. He mentioned Antonia Soto *and* Kumar Mehta.'

'But you aren't working with the Mehtas.'

'Exactly. I met the family for the first and only time at the rally.'

I thought about that. 'Maybe the caller saw us talking at the courthouse?'

'Or saw the Mehtas in the crowd in the TV coverage.'

I could think of only one person who was a big enough bastard to light the fires – only one who would have seen Demetrius, Antonia's parents, the Mehtas, and me all together at the courthouse. 'Randall Lehmann?'

'He wants attention, and he likes to make a scene,' Demetrius said, 'but I don't see him doing this.'

'He's been hassling my girlfriend,' I said. 'And he might have hassled Kenyon Munro after she found Antonia's body. I see him doing anything he feels like.'

When we hung up, I breathed deep to try to calm down. It didn't work. I went to Judy's house and knocked.

I told her the Cardinal Motel had kicked me out. I said I'd lined up an apartment to check and asked if I could take the afternoon to see it.

Ten minutes later, I went out the gravel road and turned toward downtown. A half hour after that, I pulled into a parking garage a block from City Hall. The city council offices were on the fourth floor, upstairs from the council chamber. I rode the elevator and found Lehmann's door. A pale woman in a red dress and matching lipstick sat at a dark-wood desk in the front room. Behind her, framed pictures promoting the city covered the wall – a poster of the Main Street Bridge over the St Johns River, a large photograph of the downtown skyline, a pastel painting of a sailboat, and a chalk drawing of a live oak tree. Next to the oak tree, a large portrait captured a good likeness of Lehmann. There were doors to the left and the right of the pictures.

The woman asked if she could help me.

I said I needed to see the councilman.

'Concerning?'

'It's private,' I said.

She explained that she could put me on the calendar, but Lehmann's schedule was too tight for drop-ins.

I went to the door to the right of the desk.

She stood up. 'I'm sorry – you can't do that.'

I tried the knob.

Locked.

'You'll need to leave,' the woman said.

Then the other door opened, and Lehmann stepped out.

The woman said, 'Randy, this man—'

Seeing me, he jerked back and said to the woman, 'Call security.' He slipped behind the door and slammed it.

I went to the door and tried it.

Locked.

I spoke through it. 'I need to talk to you.'

'Last time, you punched me in the face.' He was standing on the other side.

I said, 'One question—'

'No questions. Call security, Kayla.'

She was already on the phone.

I talked through the door. 'Did you throw a Molotov cocktail at my room last night? Did you set a fire outside Vanguard Reform?'

The door opened again, and Lehmann peered out. 'What are you talking about?'

I could shoulder my way in. I could pin him to a wall the way Higby had pinned me. 'Two fires,' I said. 'Last night. One at the motel where I live, one at the organization representing Antonia Soto's family.'

He looked more angry than scared. 'What's that got to do with me?'

'Kumar Mehta.'

'Who?' It was hard to say if he was faking it.

I said, 'You're telling me a city councilman doesn't watch the local news?'

'I watch every night – and again in the morning. Who's Kumar Mehta?'

'A man from India? Killed at Mandarin Reach?'

'Yeah, yeah, I heard about that – visiting his son's family. What kind of name is that?'

'Kumar's daughter-in-law and grandson were at Demetrius Jones's courthouse rally. The person who lit the fires saw them with us.'

'Then talk to that person.'

'You're the only one I can think of who would do something like this.'

'You're accusing me of arson? Really? There were a few dozen protesters on the steps and about the same number of people watching – but you think *I* lit these fires? As opposed to the border jumpers up on those steps? As opposed to the degenerates listening to them?'

'You're a nasty man,' I said.

'I'm an elected representative in this city. You're an ex-con sticking up for a bunch of lowlifes. And you call *me* nasty? I'll tell you something – I hold this city together. I'm a principle of order. You? Disorder.'

'Your idea of order sucks.'

'You don't know better. It used to be different. When I was your age, if anything was out of place, we put it back where it belonged.'

'You mean anyone?'

'Anyone or anything,' he said. 'You wouldn't recognize that city now.'

The door from the corridor opened, and an ebony-faced security guard came in. His starched white shirt was tucked loosely into blue pants. He wore a pistol on his belt, but he seemed uninterested in using it.

He nodded at Lehmann. 'Councilman.' Then the receptionist. 'Kayla.'

'Hey, Grady,' Lehmann said. 'Would you be willing to see this gentleman out? He seems to have lost his way.'

Late that afternoon, I drove to the Riverview Apartments. Although the St Johns flowed through the middle of the city, and a tangle of streams and creeks snaked through the land on both sides, there was no river in view of the complex. The most that could be said was it was built in a low area that might flood in heavy rains.

When I pulled into a spot, a rental agent in a long-sleeved floral dress got out of an idling Volvo. She smiled and said, 'Franky?'

The apartment, the middle in a set of nine side-by-side units, had a combination kitchen-dining-living room. At the back, a sliding glass door looked out to a strip of concrete the agent said could be used as a barbeque patio. A narrow stairway went up to a bedroom and bathroom. 'Cozy,' the woman said. 'We do water and garbage. You cover electric. There's a swimming pool at the end of the complex, a laundry room next to the pool. That's the whole package.'

We went back to the rental office, and I signed an application. The agent seemed unperturbed that I'd lived in a motel room for the past year. She hesitated when I said I'd spent the eight years before that in prison but had been exonerated. She hesitated again when a tenant-screening company said I had no credit history.

'I was a kid when I got sent away,' I said.

Then Judy confirmed over the phone that I worked at Safe Haven.

The agent considered me. 'Will we have any complaints about you?'

'I just want a quiet place to live,' I said.

She countersigned the lease.

On my last night at the Cardinal, I packed my belongings into plastic bags. I'd slept for a long time on beds that weren't mine at the motel and at Raiford. I'd sat on chairs others could pull out from under me, breathed air they could stink up, walked across rooms I had no claim over beyond my weekly payments, or much less than that.

I stuffed a pair of jeans into a bag with gym shoes and socks, a couple of T-shirts on top of the socks. Then I sat on the bed. Living anywhere more permanent would mean having more that could be ripped away from me. Dr Patel had talked with me about my fear of commitment. 'Totally natural,' he'd said. 'Completely logical after what you've been through.'

But?

He'd set down his notebook as he did when he wanted me to think. 'But sooner or later, you need to inch back out on the ice. It may crack, or it may hold you. Either way, you need to trust it. You need to have faith in the world. You need to commit to its brittleness.'

The cost of committing seemed too high. A jury had decided I'd committed murder. A judge had committed me to prison. For a year after I left prison, putting my name on a lease would have felt like signing another confession the way I did after Higby broke me.

But now I had committed – and not just to an apartment. I'd committed to Cynthia. I'd committed, sort of, to working at Safe Haven. I'd committed to finding out what happened to Antonia, and maybe to Kumar Mehta too – whether or not anyone else wanted me to find out, even if someone chucked a flaming bottle of gasoline at my room. Maybe I'd committed to myself, the hardest commitment of all.

Around eight in the evening, Hopper came from the reception office. He apologized for kicking me out, and I said it was all right. But he looked worried, as if his evicting me might have wrecked me for good – most of us at the Cardinal hung on by a thread, and if that thread snapped, we would freefall.

I said, 'I found an apartment. You've been good to me.'

He glanced at the pile of plastic bags and said, 'Yeah, well, we'll miss you around here. It's been lively.'

'Sure,' I said.

'If you ever need a place – short term, a night or two – you can come back, all right?'

'I'll do that.'

'All right then,' he said and left.

At ten, Cynthia, who'd eaten dinner at home, came over. When we finished packing everything except the sheets, we climbed into bed. It was eleven, and we watched *First Coast News*. A motorcycle-semi accident had closed the northbound lanes of I-95. An eighty-one-year-old woman who'd wandered from her Galacia Road home had been found safe. Then the anchor warned that the following story might disturb sensitive viewers.

A reporter had interviewed Antonia Soto's mother at the house where the family lived.

Alejandra spoke in a soft, flat voice. She said, 'We walked through the desert for three days. There were fifteen people. Antonia was so little. I carried her in my arms and on my back. Then they put us on a truck. The men robbed us.' She seemed to hold her breath. 'They took off my pants. I could say nothing.'

The interviewer spoke over her, telling her she understood.

'I had no choice,' Alejandra said. 'Some people did not make it. They became weak. We are not bad people. We come here to survive.'

Later, with the TV off, Cynthia straddled me, her eyes inches from mine. She held my face in her hands and kissed me. We leaned into each other – our lips, our tongues, our bodies. She rose over me and lowered again. No place could bring us closer together than this room where we were spending a final night after dozens and dozens of other nights. No place could be farther from the city that had nearly destroyed us, each in our own time.

She said, 'I told my dad I want to move in with you.'

'You did?'

'Do you want me to?'

'You know I do.'

'I need to live,' she said.

The next afternoon after work, we loaded my bags into the back of the pickup.

Jimmy came out of his room and wanted to shake hands. He'd palmed a joint, and he grinned as he gave it to me. 'Smoke it with your girl and think about me and Susan,' he said. 'It's been a trip, bro. Remember where you came from.' He feigned a punch to my chin. 'If you ever need a pair of fists, you know where I am.'

When I took the keys to Hopper in the office, he said, 'Maybe it's for the best.'

'I guess so.'

He dropped the keys in a drawer. 'When I was a kid, my dad used to tell me, *Hold your head high.*'

'I'll keep that in mind,' I said.

'Thing is, if you're the kind of man who fights – like a soldier – that's how you get your brains blown out. Seems to me, you're the kind of man who fights. So keep your head down, OK? Stay safe.'

We shook hands too.

TWENTY-TWO

Late the next afternoon at Safe Haven, Judy came out of her house as I pushed a wheelbarrow past the front porch. 'Goddamned fools,' she said.

I stopped. 'What?'

'No one cares.' She was sweating, though, as far as I could tell, she hadn't been working.

'About?'

She narrowed her eyes. 'Aren't you paying attention? You don't watch the news?'

Before I could answer, she went back inside. I checked my phone.

The lead story on the *Action News* website knocked the breath from my chest. Naming juveniles because of the severity of the crime, it said Pratul Mehta had stolen a pistol from his dad's dresser drawer, then ridden around the city shooting from the passenger seat of his friend Rohit Bansal's Jeep Cherokee.

I yelled, 'Fuck,' and Judy came back out on the porch.

When a twenty-five-year-old man flipped him off, Pratul aimed the pistol at him and said, 'You're dead.' Then he and Rohit drove downtown. After a confrontation at a stoplight, a thirty-four-year-old Black man in a Honda Civic called them *Pakis*. Pratul shot four holes in his door. At the next light, he shot two more bullets into a Mazda. A half mile away, police cars boxed in the Jeep. Pratul threw the pistol from his window, and the boys climbed out and lay face down on the pavement.

'Holy shit,' I said.

'See?' Judy said.

Twenty minutes later, as I drove from Safe Haven toward my apartment, I called Demetrius. 'Did you see?'

'Yeah,' he said. 'It gets worse and worse. This is what happens when the cops do nothing. He's lucky he didn't kill someone.'

'I hate when people use the word *luck* for somebody like him,' I said. 'He lost his grandpa. Everywhere he goes, people treat him like garbage. Are you going to help him and his family?'

'I've got a friend, Janie, at Vanguard. She's smart. I'm hooking her up with them.' He took a breath. 'I also need a favor from you.'

'I thought you wanted me to stay out of the way,' I said.

'I've read the articles about you.'

'So?'

'So you do stuff you shouldn't, step in where you don't belong.'

'Yeah?'

'Vanguard needs to avoid bad publicity,' he said. 'Sometimes we push the rules almost to breaking, but never further – not if we want legislators to take meetings with us and judges to listen to our arguments, not if we want to be relevant.'

'You want me to break the rules for you?'

'I want you to do something we can't.'

'What's that?'

'I told you about this supremacist group, the Valknut. They get together every month or two. They come up from Palatka and down from southern Georgia. They meet at someone's house or go out in the woods and pretend they're training for a race war. Until now, they've seemed happy picking their noses with one hand and drinking beer with the other. Mostly, they're a bunch of inbreds with intelligence to match, but, believe it or not, they've got legal counsel, and the few times anyone has tried to bring a hammer down on them, their lawyers have yelled First Amendment. So when we learn where they're getting together, we send someone out to take pictures of license plates. We know who's who in case they get any big ideas in their shrunken heads.'

I said, 'You want me to watch who's coming to a meeting?'

'No, we can do that ourselves. But after we talked last time, I looked at what we had on these crazies. Turns out they met right before Antonia Soto was killed. It seems they had a guest speaker – a local big wheel who likes to mug his ugly face for cameras. Your friend and mine.'

'Randall Lehmann?'

'The very man,' he said.

'What do you want me to do?'

He sounded uneasy. 'Pressure him.'

'What does that mean?'

'He may have nothing to do with what happened to Antonia Soto and Kumar Mehta. He's probably just a loud mouth. But as you said, he saw us with Kumar's family and knows about our connection to Antonia. That's not much – it's hardly anything – but if he's linking himself to this group, it could be something.'

'Pressure him how?'

'Get in his face some more. See what he says. See what he does. Piss him off – push his buttons.'

'That's a weird request,' I said.

'It's a big part of what we do at Vanguard. We draw inside the lines – trying to change policy, representing people in court and all – but first we find out who we're dealing with. We hold a demonstration on the courthouse steps or picket outside a workplace. We flush out the opposition and get them to announce their intentions and, if possible, their strategies. We find out what's at stake.'

'It seems to me you've already done that with Lehmann.'

'A little. But if he's tied to these attacks, we need to know. Show up at his house. Knock on his door. Go to his office. Unsettle him.'

'I'm ahead of you,' I said. 'I went to his office the day after the fires at your building and my room.'

'Yeah? What did he say?'

'He denied he set them. Then he called security.'

'Good. Push him until he calls the cops – or decides not to. If he doesn't call, he's scared of what you might tell them.'

'Yeah, I'll skip the cops,' I said. 'Why don't you tell Deborah Holt or Bill Higby what you're thinking?'

'Vanguard and law enforcement don't get along so well either. Half of the chants at our protests name the police as an enemy, and we've signed on as a plaintiff in a couple of excessive force cases. Give them a choice between a city councilman and us, they'll side with the councilman every time, even a jagoff like Lehmann. What do you think? Can you help us out?'

He wanted me to take risks he wouldn't take himself. 'Tell me about Carlos Medina. Have you given up on him?'

'The cops are working on him. He was still free when Kumar Mehta died. But no one seems to have seen him at Mandarin Reach, and no one can work out a motive. He's the only one who makes any sense for Antonia, though. I figure he's best off where he is right now. If the cops let him out, Immigration would be happy to take him off their hands, and with half the city thinking he probably killed his pregnant girlfriend, he's as unsympathetic as they come.

He wouldn't have a chance. He has two choices – jail or ICE. If he's innocent, jail is better. Then we can show he's been treated unjustly. We might be able to turn that into a visa.'

'Maybe.'

'Anything I can do to persuade you?' he said.

'Can you get me the names of the people who go to these Valknut meetings?'

'Why?'

'Same reason you want them. So I know what I'm getting into.'

'Just focus on Lehmann, OK?'

'Never push me without giving me information. I spent eight years in prison when Higby did that to me.'

'I'm not Higby,' he said. 'We're fighting on the same side.'

'Before, you didn't want me fighting at all. Now, it seems like you want to march me around like a little foot soldier.'

'You know it's not like that.'

'I only know what I hear.'

He was silent a moment. 'I'll find out if I can share the names. If I can, you need to leave the people alone. We're watching them, that's all. Unless they act up, they can fantasize about whatever they want.'

'You're right about me doing stuff I shouldn't,' I said. 'I get ahead of myself. But I know how the world works.'

I drove to my apartment. Cynthia and I had bought a new mattress, and we'd found a fifty-buck couch at a Habitat for Humanity store. Then we'd gone to an art market that popped up each weekend under the Fuller Warren Bridge. I talked Cynthia out of a scented hand-dipped candle. We came to a booth where a man with a long gray braid sold pet portraits he did from photos or live at the market. To show off his work, he'd hung a painting of a Great Dane.

Cynthia asked him, 'How much?'

'It's a sample.'

'I don't have a dog,' she said. 'How much do you want?'

'Quit it,' I said.

'Two hundred,' the man said.

'I don't have two hundred either. Is it your dog?'

He shook his head. 'The woman who commissioned it refused to pay.'

'People can be rotten,' Cynthia said.

'You're telling me. A hundred and twenty-five.'

She shook her head. 'Fifty.'

'The canvas and paint cost that much. A hundred.'

'Fifty-five.'

'Cynthia . . .' I said.

'Sold,' the man said.

When we went back to the apartment, she hung it on the wall over the mattress. 'This feels like home,' she said.

Now I lay on the couch, which smelled of mildew from the resale store. But the couch was ours – one of the first pieces of furniture I owned. The thought that I owned something like it, something that said I had a place, pleased me and scared me. I breathed in deep, grinning because the smell was terrible, and breathed in deep again.

Then I thought about Demetrius's call – about what he was asking me to do. When I first got out of prison and was running wild, trying to figure out who'd killed the Bronson boys, furious because of the eight years I'd paid, I'd barged through doors I had no business going through. I'd broken into a judge's house looking for evidence that he was corrupt. I'd snuck up on a man sleeping in his sister's house and held a gun against his head. I'd even gone into Higby's house when he wasn't home and scared the hell out of his wife. I'd found evidence of corruption. I'd revealed to anyone who paid attention that Higby was a coward and a liar, more willing to jail me than turn against the powers that kept the city running and had made him a detective. I'd gotten in people's faces, pissed them off, pushed their buttons. I'd done what I needed to do to get the answers I wanted. And I'd almost died doing it. When I was done, I was as wiped out and ruptured as I was at Raiford.

Was it worth it?

That seemed like the wrong question. It was necessary. I'd barely lived through it, but I wouldn't have survived if I'd done less. To the degree that I had any identity or existence, I had it because I'd acted. I'd crashed through walls and come out the other side. I'd *needed* to come out the other side.

But what was I doing now? I'd already ridden up to the fourth floor at City Hall and shouldered into Lehmann's office. I'd charged into Clara Soto's house, twice. I'd broken into Everett Peters's trailer at Chartein Farm.

Dr Patel had warned me against ignoring limits. Taking away boundaries doesn't lead to freedom, he said. It leads to chaos, which leads to the imposition of more severe limits and so on and so on. Whether he was right or was just irritating, I felt no impulse to rush out and hassle Randall Lehmann. Not while I was lying on a couch – *my* couch – in *my* apartment.

I pulled a cushion down on my face and breathed the stink of the fabric. Dr Patel's voice rang in my head. *Autoerotic asphyxiation. Love and death – an odd couple, but they get along fine.*

I breathed deep – in, out, and in again. *No, Doctor*, I thought. *Not now. Not this time. Here, everything is simple – if only for a moment, if only in this one spot—*

Then a hand yanked the cushion from my face. Cynthia stared down at me. 'What are you doing?' she said.

I looked at her, confused. How had she come in without my hearing? 'The couch smells like mildew,' I said.

'Whatever. Want to see something weird?'

I sat up.

She had a cardboard box. 'It came at work today. A housewarming gift.'

She pulled out a tin of bathroom soaps from a company called Clearheart Soapworks. There were four bars – lavender, honey and cream, frankincense and myrrh, and sandalwood – each wrapped in waxed paper and nested in yellow-gold tissue.

A gift card, handwritten in block letters, said, *May your new home be blessed, serene, and joyous.*

'Did your mom send it?'

'Uh-uh. I called and asked.'

'Weird,' I said. 'Who else did you tell we were moving in together?'

'No one.' She held the lavender bar to her nose. 'It smells better than the couch.'

Then my sense of weirdness turned to fear. Because I'd also told no one Cynthia was moving in with me. Someone must have been watching us as we'd lugged the mattress and couch from the pickup into the apartment or as Cynthia had brought armloads of her clothes from the back seat of her car.

'Put it down,' I said.

'Why?'

'What's Clearheart Soapworks?'

She shrugged.

I Googled the name on my phone. The company operated out of a converted barn in an old cotton town near Huntsville, Alabama. They had slogans like *Farm to Bathroom* and *Pure America* and *Clean Hands and Clear Hearts*. They also sold essential oils, body butters, and loofah sponges. Their *About Us* link said Clearheart was a Christian business founded by a couple who wanted to remove harmful chemicals from their lives. The soaps were made from *The Purest Ingredients on God's Earth*. Customers could use them with an easy conscience and a clear heart. I read to the bottom.

'Fuck,' I said.

The last paragraph echoed words I'd heard before.

The Apostle Paul took the men, and the next day, having purified himself, he entered the temple with them, making public the completion of the days of purification when the sacrifice would be made for each of them.

As Lehmann had faced the crowd outside the courthouse, he'd also said something about Paul purifying himself and going into a temple for days of purification.

'What?' Cynthia said.

'Goddamned Lehmann.'

'You think he sent this?'

'I'm pretty sure.'

'That asshole.' She took the tin to the kitchen.

'Don't throw it out.'

'Why?'

'I'm taking it back,' I said.

It was already after six o'clock, and Lehmann would have left his office. I searched for him online. City government sites named him in council proceedings and in the records of policy meetings. TV links covered whatever spectacle he'd made of himself lately. A two-year-old *Times-Union* article introduced newly elected council members and included questions and answers about their reasons for serving and what they loved about the city. In the one on Lehmann, the reporter asked why he chose to live in a downtown high-rise residential tower, a building called the Northbank. He said that when he stood on his balcony, he could watch fireworks at the ballpark after every home run all summer and at the stadium after every touchdown in the fall. He said, 'Thirty stories above the city, I feel close to heaven.'

Ten minutes later, I drove out of the Riverview Apartments lot, the tin of soaps on the passenger seat.

TWENTY-THREE

At the Northbank, I parked in a guest space, waited for a short-haired woman to wave her pass card at the front door sensor, and slipped in behind her. The lobby had a high ceiling with two big glass chandeliers. The floor was tiled with red and gray granite. When the woman got in an elevator, I went into the mailroom. The mailboxes were numbered but unnamed.

I rode an elevator to the thirtieth floor.

I knocked on the first door to the left. When no one answered, I crossed the hall and knocked.

A short man in a white muscle T-shirt opened and peered at me.

I showed him Cynthia's box, as if I was delivering it. 'Randall Lehmann?'

He gave me a funny smile. 'Who?'

'Councilman Lehmann? Does he—?'

'Uh-uh.' He closed the door.

No one answered the next two doors. The woman at the following one knew who Lehmann was but didn't think he lived on the floor, though she'd seen him in the elevator.

At the final apartment on the right, a gray-headed woman answered, her husband standing behind her with a walker. 'He lives upstairs,' she said.

'Right upstairs?'

The man said, 'Day and night, he walks back and forth – *thump, thump, thump*.' His voice cracked when he spoke.

'That's not the worst of it,' the woman said. 'Have you heard what comes out of his mouth?'

'I have,' I said, and backed away.

I went into the stairwell and up to the thirty-first floor. I knocked at the door of the apartment above the old couple.

A dog barked inside, high-pitched. Footsteps approached, thumping.

Lehmann opened. He wore white cotton pants and a yellow button-down shirt. He held a glass of red wine. The dog, a Miniature Pinscher, barked from behind his ankles. Lehmann said, 'You're trespassing in my building. Do you know what can happen to you?'

'No more than has already happened.' I held the box to him.

'What's that?' He didn't touch it.

'Nothing I want.' I threw it past him, into the room. The dog barked.

'You're a stupid man,' he said.

'Where were you when Antonia Soto died?'

He set his wine glass on the floor and picked up the dog. 'What business is it of yours?'

I stepped toward him, pushing him back, and closed the door behind me.

'How about Kumar Mehta?'

An abrupt grin broke over his face. 'Are you accusing *me*? You think . . .' He burst into a laugh. It seemed genuine. He almost dropped the dog. 'Good God, you really *are* stupid.'

I crossed the room. In the middle, a sofa and armchair set surrounded a little Oriental rug. Paintings of ocean scenes hung on the walls. Tall windows and sliding glass doors faced a balcony looking east toward the ballpark and, beyond it, the football stadium.

One side of the room opened into a dining area and then a kitchen. On the other side, there were two closed doors.

I asked again, 'Where were you on the night Antonia Soto died?'

With a grin, 'In Tallahassee. A hundred fifty miles from here.'

'Prove it.'

His face hardened. 'No.' The dog whined and struggled in his arms.

'Where were you when Kumar Mehta was killed?'

'Watching TV – or sleeping.'

'Bullshit.'

Lehmann called, 'Erich?'

One of the doors opened, and an olive-skinned man came into the room. He looked about twenty years old.

Lehmann said, 'This idiot's name is Franky Dast. Tell him where I am every night if I'm not working.'

The younger man shrugged. 'Pretty much here.'

'Yeah?' I said. 'And who are you?'

He nodded at Lehmann. 'His son.'

Now I laughed. 'How about that?' This politician who was making his name as a bigot had a child who looked like the people he raged against. 'Where's his mother?'

'Your guess is as good as mine,' Lehmann said.

I asked Erich, 'How does it feel to be his kid? I had a messed-up dad, but nothing like him.'

Lehmann told him, 'Mr Dast is a troubled soul – and, as such, deserving of sympathy. But a troubled soul can also become dangerous. If that happens, the only option is to put him down.' The dog, seeming to read his hostility, barked again.

Erich said, 'Shhh, Bo.'

I gestured at the box on the floor and asked Lehmann, 'Why did you send that to Cynthia?'

He said to his son, 'Mr Dast's girlfriend is . . . what's the word we use for people like her now? Misshapen? The skin on her legs is like a lizard's. When I was a young boy, circuses exhibited folks like her.'

'Disabled?' his son said.

'That's not quite right either.' The dog whined.

Furious, with a pit in my stomach, I said, 'Why did you send it?'

He gazed at me. 'I did no such thing.'

'You've been watching – and following . . .'

He glanced at Erich, then turned to me. 'I'll take you apart. Piece by piece.' The dog barked again. Lehmann held him to his son. 'Will you get Bo out of here?'

Erich took the dog and asked his father, 'You'll be all right?'

Lehmann smiled. 'With Mr Dast? I should think so.'

His son got a leash from the kitchen and went out with the dog.

Lehmann set his eyes on me. 'My son's smart. He's had rocky times, but they've made him sharper. It's a shame when they have the opposite effect.'

I held the gaze. '*The Apostle Paul purified himself and went into a temple for days of purification.* You said that at the rally for Antonia, and it's on the soap company website.'

'Yeah? From the Bible. Common knowledge.'

'I don't think so.'

'There's probably a lot of good stuff you don't know. Ever hear the story of Nehemiah?'

'No.'

'No wonder. A guy like you, ignorant of the scripture. Nehemiah built a wall around Jerusalem and separated the mixed multitude from Israel. He got rid of the riffraff – the Moabites and Ammonites and the rest. You like that?'

'Not much.'

'No wonder – and you might burn for it. How do you do with Romans, chapter thirteen? *Render to all their dues?*'

'If you bother Cynthia or me, I'll come after you,' I said.

'That would be dumb,' he said. 'Just mind your own business. Why bother with stuff you don't understand? Stop listening to people who fill your head with garbage. That Demetrius Jones – you aren't like him. I believe you're good at heart. Your girlfriend too.'

'I'm warning you,' I said.

'And I'm telling you that you don't want to do that. Now, pick up your box and get out of my home.'

'Keep it,' I said, and left him alone.

The elevator took me down to an empty lobby. The glass crystals on the chandeliers shined like ice. I pushed through the door to the sidewalk.

Lehmann's son stood with the Miniature Pinscher by a crepe myrtle tree between the sidewalk and the street. He and the dog considered me with the same curious expression.

I walked to the pickup, and they followed me over. 'You asked what it's like to be his kid.'

I fumbled the key into the door lock. 'Yeah, never mind.'

With the dog calm on a slack leash, he said, 'My dad loves me. I've never questioned that.'

I hadn't touched Lehmann, and he hadn't touched me, but I felt as if we'd wrestled on his floor. 'Good for you.'

'I would never hurt him. I couldn't. But he'll fuck you up. Then he'll deny he's done anything. I've seen it. He'll deny and deny until he has you questioning yourself, though you'll feel him on your skin.' His mouth twitched. 'When he said he'll take you apart, he meant it. If he thinks people are wrong, he wants to see them suffer.'

'Why are you telling me this?' I asked.

'I don't think he knows what he's doing. I was six when my mom left. The man she went with was a worship leader at their church. To tell the truth, I don't remember much. Whatever my dad says or does, he has always protected me.'

'You shouldn't make excuses for him.'

'Maybe not. I know what he says. I know what he does. I see him and hear him. I'm just telling you who he is to me.'

I drove back to my new apartment. I considered Lehmann's denial that he sent Cynthia the box of soap and his laugh when I implied he had something to do with Antonia Soto's and Kumar Mehta's deaths. I considered his threats against me. I considered his son Erich and how some prisoners learn to love their cells.

TWENTY-FOUR

The next morning, as Cynthia slept upstairs, I called Demetrius Jones. If my call woke him, he didn't complain.

I told him about the soap and the website echoing Lehmann's words from the rally. I said, 'I pushed him. I threw the box at him, and he held his mini Doberman like a weapon. The funny thing is, the more I pushed, the calmer he got. He laughed when I asked about Antonia Soto and Kumar Mehta. When I was in prison, a lot of men said they were innocent. Some I knew right away were lying, some I couldn't tell, and a few I sort of believed. I sort of believed Lehmann. I didn't want to.'

'What else did he say?'

'He preached at me and threatened me. I threatened him too. What do you know about his son?'

'I didn't realize he had one.'

'He's about twenty,' I said. 'The mother left when he was six. From the look of him, she might've been Mexican or Guatemalan.'

'Huh. Wouldn't be the first time a man learned to hate what he once loved.'

'What are you hearing about Pratul Mehta?' I asked.

He sighed. 'Yeah, *him*. He'll stay in juvenile detention for now. The friend who drove the Jeep is seventeen and goes over to county jail later today.'

'Anything you can do for them?'

'No way – and I wouldn't if I could. Everyone's safer with them locked up right now.'

'Pratul lost his grandfather,' I said. 'Now his mom and dad have lost their son.'

'That won't get him very far with a judge.'

When I went out to the pickup, the sky was still dark, and I traced the stars in Orion's belt and shield. The air smelled like the rotting grasses in the lowland marshes that clung to rivers and creeks near the apartment complex. In the last minutes of night, peace seemed to settle into this part of the city.

Why shouldn't I have this?

Despite Pratul Mehta's suffering, despite the Randall Lehmanns of the world, despite the deaths of a fourteen-year-old girl and a man visiting his son from nine thousand miles away, despite my jagged past, in a place and time like this, I could imagine being happy.

Had I earned happiness? Did people ever earn the good that came to them? Did we deserve more than cold and hunger? After our first sparks of life, we took what wasn't ours. Any warmth we felt, any food we ate, we got by cheating the world of it. We burned, butchered, cut at the roots, and ripped from the stem. Maybe we didn't need to feel guilty about that – it was how life worked – but we shouldn't be smug. Even the air we breathed – rich with decay, stinking of engine exhaust – we sucked away from the world. What did we give back? Maybe a little warmth to someone else who was cold.

I drove out and hooked on to the highway, then shot toward Chartein Farm. When I passed Clara Soto's house, the lights were on, but the driveway was empty. I rounded the bend, drove another two miles, and turned in at the Chartein sign. In the first light, the chickens on the sign seemed to glow – the one eating corn from the ground, the other craning its neck as if it would snatch clouds from the sky.

Everett Peters stood on the wooden porch outside his singlewide, drinking a cup of coffee, his German Shepherd at his feet. When I got out of the truck, he tossed me the keys to the cold shed. I drove toward the chicken houses.

As I pulled on to the dirt lot, Clara was talking with the Charteins and Harry in front of the first chicken house. Clara's Ford Taurus idled beside them, the headlights on. She looked upset and seemed to be chewing out Mr Chartein.

I tapped the horn and drove to the shed. There were forty chickens in the freezer, half the number of a normal morning. I loaded them on to the truck bed and tied the tarp.

As I drove out, Clara's car was still idling. Now she was yelling at Mrs Chartein.

I cut toward them to ask if more birds would be available later in the day.

The hum of Clara's engine and the churning industrial fans might have drowned out the sound of my tires on the dirt. Or maybe Clara was so caught up in whatever angered her that she lost sense of everything else. But as I pulled behind her, she spun away from the others and stepped into my path.

It happened so fast that I had no time to turn or stop.

But Harry – pale, soft-bellied Harry – leaped at her. He was standing in gray coveralls, his arms loose at his sides, squinting at her, and then he was tackling her.

I screamed as the truck skidded. I jumped out, breathless. Harry was on top of Clara. He'd taken her to the ground, away from the tires. He looked up at me, blinking. Then he got to his feet.

I helped Clara up.

Her eyes shined with fury and fear. 'What the living fuck?' she said. She looked herself over. Her slacks and blouse were streaked with dirt. 'You people,' she said, and she seemed to mean all of us. She went to her car, then faced us again. She had tears in her eyes. 'I thought you were better than this,' she said. She got in and drove across the lot and out toward the highway.

I could hardly breathe.

'It's all right,' Mr Chartein said.

Mrs Chartein said to her brother, 'You saved her life.'

'I don't know,' Harry said.

'What just happened?' I said.

Mrs Chartein closed her eyes, opened them again. 'She's distressed.'

'I saw *that*.'

'She's upset about Carlos Medina. She wants us to help pay for a new lawyer – a better one.'

'Demetrius Jones thinks jail is safer than ICE detention,' I said.

She hesitated. 'Carlos called Clara yesterday afternoon. One of the other prisoners attacked him. He's OK this time, but everyone apparently knows he got Antonia pregnant, and there are rumors about him killing her. He might not be safe out of jail, but he definitely isn't safe there.'

Demetrius had mentioned nothing about the attack when we talked. 'You can't help pay for a new lawyer?'

She glanced at Mr Chartein.

He said, 'Won't.'

Harry said, 'Carlos Medina killed the girl.'

'You don't know that,' his sister said.

'He killed her,' Harry said, 'and Clara's in love with him.'

She pursed her lips. 'That may or may not be the case.'

Harry glanced at his hands. He wiped them on his coveralls. 'She hid him. She gave him a bed. You saw her. She's in love.'

'Poor Antonia,' Mrs Chartein said.

TWENTY-FIVE

As I pulled on to the gravel road at Safe Haven, my phone rang.

It was Demetrius Jones. 'I have another angle,' he said.

'A what?'

'What do you know about the old Sugar Hill neighborhood?'

I needed to start work. 'Clara Soto wants to fire you,' I said.

'Huh?'

'She thinks you're screwing around with Carlos Medina.'

'Where did you hear this?'

'It's been a busy morning. Did you hear that an inmate attacked him?'

'Yeah . . . a couple of stitches in his back and a couple in his shoulder. You know better than I do that this kind of thing happens.'

'It happens, but it shouldn't,' I said. 'You're leaving him to it.'

'I've asked for the jail to isolate him.'

'What did they say?'

'The jail is overcrowded. They'll do what they can.'

'That's never enough.'

'I know,' he said.

'Then *you* should do something.'

'The best we can do is show that someone else killed Antonia Soto and Kumar Mehta. That's why I'm asking for your help.'

'Clara's right. This is too much for you.'

He repeated himself. 'Sugar Hill.'

'What about it?'

'I asked an intern to look into Lehmann's past – the stuff that doesn't appear in the City Council bio. He spent his teenage years in Sugar Hill. He was one of the brightest of a mentally challenged crew. The official story is he went to Rollins College for two years on scholarship before dropping out to help run his dad's car lot. The real story sounds more like he was kicked out. Sugar Hill was always a rough neighborhood. The old joke was there was no sugar and there was no hill. The Chinese lived there. Then the Greeks and Syrians came. Then it turned mostly African American, though a bunch of Chinese, Greeks, and Syrians held on, along with old white Florida families like the Lehmanns who were either too poor or too mixed up to live anywhere else. Eventually, the government knocked it down and laid the expressway through. It was an easy target.'

'So what?' I'd pulled up in front of Judy's house with my half load of chickens.

'So Sugar Hill was a hard place to be a kid. Not a lot of guns, but plenty of rocks, knives, and sticks. Lehmann seems to have liked it, though. He ran with a gang of kids like him who didn't fit in with the other ethnic groups. When he was sixteen, he and another boy held a blade to the neck of a Syrian girl. A news article named both boys. It said nothing about rape, but it wouldn't back then.'

'He didn't get locked up?'

'The intern hunted for more information. But after the one article, the story went away. Maybe Lehmann and the other boy – or some of their friends – threatened the girl and she dropped the accusation. Maybe everyone decided she should disappear. Lehmann finished high school and went to college. There's no word on what led to him getting kicked out, but maybe the story of the girl followed him.'

'He's lived his whole life this way,' I said.

'Seems like it. But I've got something else too, and I don't know what to do with it. The other boy who got arrested with Lehmann? His name was Bruce Chartein.'

A twist in my stomach. '*The* Charteins? Chartein Farm?'

'Douglas Chartein's cousin, as far as I can tell,' he said. 'Younger than Douglas and worlds apart, but still.'

'Where's Bruce Chartein now?'

'Dead. Twelve years ago, in a car wreck. DUI. It's possible the Charteins don't know about the connection between him and Lehmann, but that seems unlikely. Maybe they're just embarrassed by it. Anyway, it was a long time ago.'

'No, that's messed up,' I said.

'I agree. You want to go back to Lehmann and hit him with it?'

I considered what the information meant. 'Whatever he's up to, I don't think he personally touched Antonia. He says he was in Tallahassee on the night she went missing.'

'You believe him?'

'Get your intern to check.'

'So you won't go after him?'

The twist in my stomach. 'I didn't say that.'

When Judy came out and I showed her under the tarp, she lit into me for bringing so few chickens. I turned and walked away.

Judy yelled after me, 'You want to explain to the cats where their food is? Excuses won't cut it.'

Sorrel and Rocko were on their feet, gaining weight, and hungry – eating as much as two or three healthy tigers. As the weather cooled, the other cats were eating more too. We'd gone through the spare meat in one of the freezer cases and started into a second.

'One slip wrecks everything,' Judy yelled. '*Everything.*'

I found Zemira in the refrigerator shed, bleaching the empty freezer. She glanced at me, returned to scrubbing, and glanced again. 'What's wrong?'

I told her about the half load and about Judy's reaction.

'Yeah, there's no room to fuck up,' Zemira said.

'I'm not fucking up.'

'Could fool me.'

'I can quit,' I said.

'We'll celebrate.'

Twenty minutes later, as Zemira and I carried food to the enclosures, Judy came out of the house again. She waited for me to slop a bucket on to a paver for a lion, then said, 'Go back to the farm. They were dealing with a family crisis and hadn't prepared all the chickens. If you'd asked, they would've told you.'

When I pulled back into Chartein Farm in the cool mid-morning, a dozen Mexican workers were loading crated chickens into box trucks, driving forklifts in and out of the chicken houses, or busying themselves with other parts of the operation.

I found Everett Peters supervising the installation of a new feed hopper.

When I told him why I'd come, he shook his head as if he also thought I was fucking up. 'Help yourself,' he said.

There were sixty more chickens in the freezer, enough to replace the back-up meat. I loaded them and tied the tarp. I started to drive out to the highway, then hit the brakes.

I steered back toward the Charteins' house. It was a clapboard two-story, gray with blue shutters. A wide porch stretched across the front.

I parked in the yard. Harry was putting cans of house paint into his van. I waved, and he waved back.

When I knocked on the Charteins' door, Mr Chartein opened. He'd changed out of his work shirt and into a brick-red cardigan.

He had a kind smile. 'Franky?'

'Sorry to bother you, Mr Chartein,' I said.

'No, no – come in. Bella's gone downtown . . .' He led me into a living room, furnished with a heavy yellow sofa, floral armchairs, a dark-wood credenza, and a curio cabinet of horse figurines. At the far end of the room, a painting of a black bull hung above a fireplace. The bull was muscular, its shaggy coat glistening as if someone had hosed it down. The background was white, radiant, as though a brilliant light had flashed behind the big animal. The painting had the same effect as the chicken sign by the highway and the picture of the German shepherd on Everett Peters's wall. 'Did your wife's brother paint it?'

Mr Chartein gave it a wry grin. 'I tell Harry he should set up a booth at an art fair.'

'He's better than that,' I said.

'I wouldn't know. Bella likes it, so we hang it. What can I do for you?'

'I'm hoping you can explain something.'

'Our conversation with Clara? That was regrettable. But you understand, there's only so much we can do for a man the police seem to think is guilty of murder.'

'That's not it,' I said. 'What can you tell me about your cousin Bruce?'

He looked surprised, then confused. Then the kind smile returned. 'A man I haven't thought about in a while. Where'd you get his name?'

'From the lawyer Clara wants to fire. Were you close?'

'My dad had a falling out with his brother, Bruce's father,' he said. 'My grandparents had three kids, all boys. The oldest didn't want the farm, which was much smaller then. Bruce's dad wanted it, but when my grandparents died, they left the place to my dad. I met Bruce for the first time at my dad's funeral – him and his sister Katherine. Bruce died a while back. Car crash. He drank, you know.'

'He was friends with Randall Lehmann,' I said.

'Was he? Well, I don't doubt it. My uncle tried to start a chicken operation a mile west of here. But if he didn't find trouble, it found him. He lost the place, and the family moved downtown. That would've put Bruce in the right place to get to know Randy.'

'You ever hear about the two of them and a Syrian girl?'

The kind smile. 'I never heard about them with or without anyone else. This was how long ago? Forty years?'

'At least.'

'No, I can't say I know much about Bruce or that part of the family. If Bella was here, you could ask her. Her dad ran a business and owned some property downtown where Randy grew up. She knows more of the people and history.'

I thanked him and asked him to mention Bruce's friendship with Lehmann to Mrs Chartein. 'I would be interested in anything she remembers,' I said.

'It was a long time ago.'

'Sure,' I said.

I went back outside. Harry had finished loading his equipment and was getting into his van. When I crossed the yard, he rolled down his window.

I said, 'Thanks for earlier. I couldn't stop. It scared the hell out of me. I don't think Clara knows how close I came to hitting her.'

He scratched a pale cheek. 'Yeah, next time, watch where you're going.'

I tried to smile. 'You made an impressive catch.'

He shrugged.

I nodded toward the Charteins' house. 'I like your painting of the bull.'

For a moment, he eyed me as though he might have misjudged me. 'It's a Heck,' he said.

'A what?'

'A Heck bull. Handsome but mean. As close as you come to wild cattle. They're bred that way.'

'Beautiful,' I said. 'You're a good painter.'

He shook his head. 'I gotta go.'

I stepped back from the van.

He pulled forward, then stopped again. He leaned out of his window a little. 'Word of advice. Don't bother my sister and Douglas. They do a lot of good. But people take advantage.'

'I'll keep that in mind,' I said.

That evening, I was lying on the couch when Cynthia came in.

'Give me a hand,' she said.

She'd bought a big-screen TV from Walmart during her lunch break, cramming it into the back seat of her car. 'Screw Lehmann and his soap,' she said. 'A housewarming gift, from me to us.'

We set up the TV in the living room, and, after dinner, Cynthia found the 1931 black-and-white *Frankenstein*.

An actor in a tuxedo gave a *friendly word of warning* that the movie might shock and horrify us, and then the title and credits appeared. We stripped to our underwear and held each other on the couch.

The body of the monster rose on a pulley system into a lightning storm and came back down alive. He floated flowers on a mountain lake with a little girl and, knowing no better, threw the girl into the water too. He drank wine and smoked a cigar with a blind man.

But nothing lasts forever. While fleeing from a raging mob, he climbed to the top of a giant windmill. The mob set fire to the building, and flames flared up the sides. The monster screeched – a high-pitched, tortured screech – and waved his arms in a pathetic attempt to save himself. He never really had a chance. Anyone who knew the story knew that much.

As the windmill burned with the monster inside, the camera pulled back as if the director couldn't bear to watch. Then the mob's torches flickered on the screen like pretty candles.

TWENTY-SIX

I pulled into Jenquist Meat in the pre-dawn dark, forty minutes before the factory whistle. The morning was cold, the sky clear, and the stars brilliant. The thick-armed man in the front office said, 'Ollie's got something special for you.' He carted out three goat carcasses. He went in again and came back with a platform hand-truck loaded with a half cow, broken into six sections.

'What's the occasion?' I said.

'I guess your boss called with a sob story. Ollie's got it bad for her.'

We lifted the meat into the truck. I said, 'He knows she's gay, doesn't he?'

'Who can explain love?'

I drove out of the processing plant, passed a strip of warehouses and factories, and cut on to the expressway toward Safe Haven.

Why shouldn't Ollie love Judy? Little would come of it, other than a lamb lunch and well-fed cats, but he would go home at the end of each day, his thoughts sticky with the blood of the animals he'd slaughtered, knowing he'd given her something valuable. She would never repay it. She wouldn't reciprocate even with kindness.

Maybe Ollie's knowledge that he would get no more back from her than if he put the meat in an incinerator was the whole point. His gifts might be a kind of self-indulgent sacrifice.

Sacrifice.

Clara Soto said that the Spanish word *sacrificar* also meant *butcher*. The threatening note Antonia received before she died said *she* would be sacrificed like an animal. And Dr Patel had come up with one of his endless examples – of a cancer doctor sacrificing cells to cure a patient, killing to save. Even the Bible passage Lehmann quoted had something to do with sacrifice – the Apostle Paul purifying men for a sacrifice.

Ollie's sacrifices for Judy seemed most like the ones Dr Patel described. The healing ones. Or maybe Ollie was just blindly in love. Maybe he just had it bad.

How about my love for Cynthia? How about her love for me? As I exited the expressway on to the wooded road to Safe Haven, I let myself smile. There was no sacrifice between Cynthia and me – at least none on my side. It was all gain.

How about Lehmann and his son – the love Lehmann gave him, if that's what it was, and the love his son returned to him? I believed that Lehmann's feelings, whatever they were, must be selfish. His son's love for him? A delusion. The love a beaten dog has for its owner, a prisoner for the warden. Sympathy for the devil.

Maybe that was—

I jerked from my thoughts. Behind me, a truck or SUV – something jacked high enough off the road for its headlights to shine through my back window – flashed its brights as if the driver wanted to pass. It might have turned off the expressway with me – I wasn't paying attention – but now, a mile from Safe Haven, it closed the gap. The high beams glared in my rearview mirror. I moved to the side, hugging the edge of the road where the shoulder sloped into a drainage ditch and then an old pine forest.

'Asshole,' I said, and I waved at the driver to go around.

The vehicle accelerated and came within five or seven feet of the tail of my pickup. I yelled over my shoulder, 'What're you doing?'

The vehicle moved closer, three feet, two, metal nearly touching metal.

I took my foot off the gas and coasted. My pickup slowed from seventy to sixty, sixty to fifty, fifty to forty, the lights of the other vehicle brilliant in the cab.

Then I hit the gas and opened the distance between us. In another half mile, the gravel drive into Safe Haven would branch from the road.

The pickup cab went black. The driver behind me had turned off the headlights – or had stopped. I checked the rearview, checked again. The road was dark. I eased the gas and checked the mirror.

In the moment before the other vehicle rammed me, I felt its rushing. Then its high beams went on again, exploding light into the cab. It crashed into my back. The pickup pitched from the road – lurching, flying – and landed on the passenger side. It rolled, bounced into the air again, tumbled, and rolled again. Every twist. Every blow and glance. The crushing metal and glass. I felt and saw it all. I thought about Cynthia, skin to skin in my arms, and about the Bronson boys, who'd died violently and whose death nearly led to my own, and about Bill Higby, who'd seemed intent on locking me up forever, if not killing me. Then I thought about meat – the three goats and the half cow, flinging from the truck bed, scattering through the weedy roadside ditch, lofting into the branches of the pine trees.

The truck came to a rest, wheels up, on a triangle of grass where Judy had hired a service to clear the trees. I hung from the seatbelt, my shoulder crammed against the door. One headlight shined on the grass. The air smelled of oil and copper and vaguely of smoke. The bent truck ticked. An engine hose hissed. If the cab caught fire, would I screech like Frankenstein's monster?

Then the hissing stopped, and the only sound was ticking. I worked my fingers along the seatbelt strap and, after some time, forced the buckle open. I crawled out through the broken windshield and lay in the grass and weeds until the sun came up.

TWENTY-SEVEN

'Jesus Christ,' Judy said, when I knocked on her door.

'Someone ran me off the road.' I felt like crying. I thought she would blame me. I thought I should blame myself.

'Jesus Christ almighty,' she said. 'Get in here.'

'I'm bleeding.'

'*Get in here.*'

'I'll—'

'Dammit, boy, I won't tell you again.'

I stepped inside.

The house was dim and smelled like frying bacon. I wanted to lie on the floor and sleep. I followed Judy down a hall. Diane, naked, stuck her head out of a bedroom door.

Judy took me into a bathroom. Except for my eyes, I didn't know the man who looked at me in the mirror. Glass from the windshield had cut my forehead. My face was stained with blood. I had a gash on my wrist.

'You're a goddamned tragedy,' Judy said, and she ran the sink.

She mopped my face with a washcloth. She rinsed and sopped blood from under my eyes. She touched the cloth to my forehead.

She said, 'Hold still.'

She pulled a glass splinter from my eyebrow.

She said, 'Heads bleed – that's all there is to it.'

She swabbed the skin. Blood welled up. The more she washed, the more it came. She held the cloth firm against my head.

She said, 'You know I don't have insurance, right?'

'Right.'

She yelled into the house, 'Diane . . . Zemira . . .'

The women came to the bathroom doorway. Diane had put on clothes. Zemira clutched a piece of bacon.

Judy said, 'Get me a T-shirt.'

Diane went to find one.

'And get Rocko's salve,' Judy said to Zemira.

Then she said, 'Hold the cloth,' and while I pressed it to my head, she cleaned the gash on my wrist.

When Diane brought a shirt, Judy had her rip it into strips. Zemira came back with a container labeled *Veterinary Antibacterial and Antifungal Care Cream with Insect Barrier*.

Judy slathered the cream on my forehead. She said, 'I used it when I cut myself with the chop saw. Gave me a taste for deer liver.'

It was the first joke I'd ever heard her tell. No one laughed.

She bandaged my head and arm. She said, 'Come.' She took me to the kitchen, had me sit at the table, and poured me a glass of water. 'Tell me what happened.'

I told her about driving toward Safe Haven from the expressway, the high beams, the impact, the rollover. I told her I'd crawled out through the broken windshield, and, after lying in the grass and weeds, unsure if I was alive or dead, I'd stumbled up the gravel road to the house.

Judy frowned. 'Tell it again.'

I told it all, filling in what I'd left out the first time. When I mentioned the meat Ollie had sent from the processing plant, she stopped me and said to Zemira, 'Get it.'

Zemira went out the side door, where there was a utility vehicle with a dump trailer.

When I finished retelling the story, Judy said, 'The truck?'

'Totaled.'

I thought she would blame me then, accuse me of carelessness, argue I should have done something – anything – to avoid getting run off the road. She said, 'When we opened the refuge, a couple of the neighbors let us know they objected. Nothing like this and not for a long time.' Then she phoned the police.

Two sheriff's deputies came in a car, a bald man in his forties and a young, serious-faced woman with a black ponytail. They looked over the wrecked pickup as Judy told them about the unhappy neighbors.

The woman deputy took pictures.

Then the man eyed me the way a lot of older cops did. 'Have I seen you before?'

'I don't know.'

He seemed to shake off the feeling. 'Well, you had every chance of smashing into a tree. Every reason to die. You're a lucky man – a lucky, lucky man. Can you describe the vehicle that hit you?'

'It was dark out,' I said. 'The driver blinded me with the brights.'

'That's regrettable,' he said. He glanced at Judy. 'I'll take down the names of your neighbors if you want, but there's not much we can do without a description.'

'I'll take care of them myself,' she said. 'As long as you have a record of who threw the first stone.'

He said, 'You don't want to be threatening anyone.'

'The neighbors shouldn't threaten *me*.' She walked away.

'It wasn't a neighbor,' I told the bald cop.

'No?'

'No, and it wasn't about her animals.'

'What was it, then?' he said.

'Do you know Randall Lehmann on the City Council?'

'Of course.'

'Talk to Detective Holt in your homicide unit,' I said. 'Ask her about him. Ask her about Antonia Soto and Kumar Mehta.'

'Why would I do that?'

'Because I upset Lehmann when I asked him about them.'

He looked doubtful. 'And you think the city councilman ran you off the road?'

'Talk to Holt,' I said.

When we went back to the house, Judy asked, 'You up to working?'

My forehead throbbed. 'I think so.'

Zemira had salvaged the goat carcasses and most of the cow from the roadside. After breaking the pieces down with saws and hatchets, we brought the meat to the enclosures. As we laid it on the pavers for Rocko and Sorrel, Zemira eyed me. She looked at the cats, then at me again.

'What?' I said.

'They smell the blood on you.'

'They're just hungry because we're late.'

By early afternoon, my head ached. I knocked on Judy's door and said, 'I'm going to call Cynthia and ask her to pick me up.'

Judy said, 'How are we supposed to get food for the cats?'

'I don't know.'

She beckoned me inside. We went through the house and out the back to where her old GMC Sierra Grande was tucked halfway under a carport. She popped the tailgate and swept dirt, leaves, and sticks on to the ground. 'It's been a while, but it got us through our first years here.' She rattled the driver's door until it loosened and opened. 'Stick to back roads, and stay under fifty, you should be all right. We'll put on new tires in a week or two if it's still running.' She climbed in and tried the engine.

It coughed and died.

She tried again. It caught, and the tailpipe spat black smoke. She gave the truck gas, then more, and the engine made noises you don't want an engine to make. She eased the gas and pumped it, and the engine calmed to a rough purr.

She got out. 'I knew she had it in her. Call if you break down.' Her voice was almost tender. 'Drive safe.'

A wrecker had hauled the destroyed pickup from the side of the road. Broken glass sparkled in the grass and weeds. I turned from Safe Haven and hit the gas. The engine missed, then surged. I eased the accelerator and pulled over. Other than the rough engine, all was quiet. Peace was here, if it was anywhere. But panic surged in my belly. I made myself breathe – in deep, hard out, over and over. Then I pulled back on to the road.

I passed the expressway and turned north on Philips Highway. If I stayed on the road for twenty miles, I could return to the Cardinal Motel and demand that Hopper give me my old room. I could do a thousand pushups, a thousand sit-ups. I could lie on my bed, a pillow over my face.

Or I could exit after ten miles and drive to the apartment I shared with Cynthia. When she came in, she might cry at the sight of me. I might cry too.

My phone rang.

It was Deborah Holt. 'Come to the station and talk with me,' she said.

'Why?'

'Why do you think? I hear you got in a fender bender this morning.'

'Is that what the bald cop called it?'

'Deputy Christensen. He said you talked a lot of nonsense about one of our council members . . . and about a couple of homicide investigations. He said you asked him to get in touch with me.'

'Carlos Medina is innocent,' I said.

'Is that what you think?'

'Someone else is involved – other people. Someone who's worried enough about me to try to kill me.'

'No offense,' she said, 'but I don't see anyone worrying too much about you. You might have questionable intentions, but no one would see you as a threat.'

'Maybe I angered them.'

'That I could see.'

I said, 'You should let Carlos go.'

'Too late.'

'Huh?'

'His lawyer bailed him out this morning.'

'Demetrius Jones?'

'Nope – a fancy guy in pinstripes. Jerry Dickerson.'

'Oh.'

'I'm telling you, Medina's our guy. We're building the case. Then, if Medina doesn't scramble for the border before we grab him, he'll never go free again.'

'You're wrong,' I said, and I hung up.

I turned from the highway on to the street to my apartment. I wanted to split my skin and crawl out wet and new. I wanted to hold a pillow to my face until my lungs burst.

I pulled into the parking lot, steered the old pickup into a spot, and went in. The living room was dark, the kitchen dark. I went upstairs. The bedroom was dark. I hit the bathroom light.

I knew the face in the mirror.

I knew the crazy bandages around my head.

I knew the gashed wrist.

I knew myself as well as I knew anything in the world.

I turned on the faucet and peeled the bloody cotton strips from my forehead, dropping them in the sink. The wound bled. I put on clean bandages with medical tape Cynthia sometimes used to strap ice packs to her legs.

I went into the bedroom and stared at the picture of the Great Dane that Cynthia had hung over the mattress. I lifted it from its nail. If I smashed it against the wall – if I shredded the canvas – I would be calling a lie a lie. I would be doing something *real*. I held the dog to my face, gazed at it eye to eye. Then I hung it back on the nail.

I went down and sat on the couch. The refrigerator hummed in the kitchen. Outside, a car rolled across the parking lot grit and then was silent. The refrigerator cycled off. Upstairs, the showerhead dripped. When the sky darkened, I turned on a lamp. I sat.

Then a key turned in the front-door lock, and Cynthia came in. When she saw me, she cried.

TWENTY-EIGHT

I stayed home the next morning. When I got out of bed, my vision narrowed, and I sat back down. My head throbbed.

'You all right?' Cynthia said.

'Yeah.' I got up again and went into the bathroom.

She followed me and watched as I peeled away the bandages, which had soaked through while we slept. The cut bled when I tamped it with a washcloth.

'You need a doctor,' Cynthia said.

'I'm fine.'

'Or not.'

I held the cloth to staunch the blood.

She handed me a roll of gauze. 'Call in sick at least.'

'OK.'

'Really?'

'Yeah.'

When Cynthia left for Bourne-Goff, I watched the morning news. Ten minutes into the local report, they did a segment on Antonia Soto's and Kumar Mehta's killings, which they continued to pair, though the police had barely implied a connection.

The anchor said, 'Carlos Medina, who the police have described as a person of interest in Antonia Soto's death, posted bail on enticement charges.' After a little more background, a correspondent talked with Carlos's new lawyer.

Jerry Dickerson sat behind a heavy wooden desk in an office lined with law books and bound case files. His face was jowly, his shoulders narrow. He wore a blue pinstripe suit and a white shirt. He spoke so quietly that the reporter leaned across the desk to hear him.

He calmly condemned the rush to judgment, as if he was embarrassed to be discussing the case.

The reporter asked, 'Where is Carlos Medina now?'

Dickerson crossed his fingers on his desk and seemed about to pray. 'He's where he's safe from those who would hurt him.'

'There's some concern he will flee to Mexico.'

'Why would he do that? He took enormous risks to be here.'

The reporter asked, 'What do you say to people who think his explanations of his relationship with Antonia Soto and his behavior after her death are troubling?'

'I say Mr Medina has nothing to answer for. I say that under our system of justice, the accounting is always to be done by the police and prosecution.' He leaned in too, and his voice hardened. 'We have questions for the police. They've implied that Mr Medina harmed the woman he loved—'

'The *girl*,' said the reporter.

'They've insinuated, but they haven't produced evidence. If they have it, they need to bring it forth.'

'The police say—'

Dickerson shook his head to silence the reporter. 'They can say whatever they want, but our courts require evidence.' His voice hardened further. 'Show the goods or shut up. The police have also implied, without substantiation, that Mr Medina may have committed a second crime – the murder of Kumar Mehta. What possible reason would my client have for killing this man? Not only have the police failed to produce a rationale for treating Mr Medina as a violent criminal, they've suppressed evidence that shows, first, that the killings are linked and, second, that the killer has a different agenda from any my client might have. I ask the police – on behalf of my client and of the families of the victims – to come clean with information they have about matching wounds left on the faces of Antonia Soto and Kumar Mehta.'

'Huh,' I said.

'What kind of wounds?' the reporter asked.

'I'll leave that to the police,' Dickerson said. 'And I ask them to come forth with any information they have that these murders were hate crimes, perpetrated by an individual or individuals targeting people born outside the United States.'

'What kind of information?' the reporter asked.

'Messages the police – or the victims' families – have received indicating as much.'

'Holy shit,' I said, when the news cut back to the anchor. Jerry Dickerson also must have gotten to the couple who'd seen the mark on Antonia's forehead as she floated in Clapboard Creek – or he had a source in the Sheriff's Office. He'd been working for Carlos Medina only one day, and he was already blasting apart anything the police had put together. I went into places I didn't belong and often got thrown back out. With his expensive suit and office, speaking calmly until he needed to raise his voice, Dickerson pulled down walls from inside.

His services must cost a lot of money. But the Charteins had refused to chip in. Who was paying him? And what was he up to? Demetrius Jones made a good argument for keeping Carlos in county jail and out of the hands of ICE. Dickerson didn't identify the people who would hurt him, though they would include law enforcement along with bigoted vigilantes. Could Dickerson protect him?

By mid-morning, the throbbing in my head weakened to a dull ache. But when I tried running in place, the pain roared back. So I turned on the TV, sat on the couch, and watched *The Today Show*. After ten minutes, I went upstairs and put on jeans and a sweatshirt. Cynthia was supposed to wear a Bourne-Goff baseball hat at work but never did. I found it in the closet, loosened the back strap, and eased it on to my head.

I went out to the Sierra Grande. The engine caught on my second try. I crossed the parking lot, edged on to the road, and drove back toward Philips Highway.

The guard at the Mandarin Reach security kiosk glanced at me and said, 'What d'you got, buddy?'

'Franky Dast – here to see the Mehtas,' I said.

He called their house, hung up, and raised the gate. I drove in past the clubhouse, the pool, and the tennis courts, and parked in the Mehtas' driveway.

Saatvik answered the door. He wore a white T-shirt and white pants that ballooned around his legs and ended above his ankles. He looked exhausted, his chin unshaved, the skin around his eyes tender, as if he'd been crying.

He stared at my hat and face and asked, 'What happened to you?'

'That's why I'm here.'

He walked up the hall, and I went in and closed the door.

In the kitchen, he said, 'Sit.' He went to the refrigerator.

'I don't need anything,' I said.

He brought a glass of apple juice to the table and set it in front of me.

'How's Pratul?' I asked.

He sat down across from me. 'They've locked him up. They've destroyed my family.'

'I'm sorry,' I said, because what else could I say to a man whose son had driven through the city shooting at strangers?

'What happened to you?' he asked again.

I told him about heading to Safe Haven in the early-morning dark, about the vehicle ramming me, about crawling out through the broken windshield.

'Did this happen because of my dad?'

'I don't know,' I said. 'Maybe. What are the police telling you about him?'

'Nothing. I call three or four times a day. They say the investigation is active. I ask what that means. The woman detective – Detective Holt – says it means they know who killed my dad but they can't prove it.'

'Carlos Medina.'

'She won't tell me how they know. Then, last night, Medina's lawyer called and said he would like to represent Pratul.'

'Jerry Dickerson?'

'Yes.'

'I don't know what he's up to,' I said.

'I told him no. I don't trust him.'

'You're going to need someone good – someone who can outmaneuver a prosecutor.'

'My wife's heart is broken. She wants Pratul to come home. He didn't mean to hurt anyone. He was angry about his *dada* – his grandfather.'

'I'm sorry,' I said again. 'This morning, I saw Dickerson on TV. He talked about connections between your dad's killing and Antonia Soto's.'

'That's what he said when he called.'

'Did your dad ever receive threatening messages – hate mail, or a note stuck under the windshield wiper, or graffiti, anything?'

'No, nothing like that,' Saatvik said.

'How about you or your wife?'

'Nothing.'

Aadhya drifted in from the hallway, where she seemed to have been listening. 'Pratul did,' she said. She wore a long olive-green dress, and she'd painted a red bindi on her forehead – as thick as lipstick, as bright as blood. Other than the bindi, her face was blank, ghostlike. 'A bully message. From children at school.'

'Do you have it?' I asked.

'No, we threw it away,' she said. 'Pratul insisted. He wanted to be tough. He wanted to do it his way. But what does a fifteen-year-old know?'

'Do you remember what the message said?'

'A lot of stupidity,' Saatvik said.

'Ugliness,' Aadhya said. 'They threatened to cut him like a dirty pig.'

Clara Soto had told me that the notes to Antonia had said something similar – calling her a pig, an animal, threatening to tie her down and slaughter her. 'What else?'

'I don't know,' Aadhya said. She seemed as drained as her husband. 'We are used to these things.'

'Did you tell the police about the message?' I asked.

'Yes,' Saatvik said. 'Detective Holt.'

'Kids gave it to him at school? Bullies?'

'Yes,' Aadhya said.

'Not exactly,' Saatvik said.

'It had to be,' she said.

Saatvik looked down. 'Pratul came home from school with the note, but he wouldn't let us talk to the principal. He said it wasn't one of the kids.'

'He wants to be tough,' Aadhya said.

I asked, 'If it wasn't a kid, did he say who?'

'No,' Saatvik said.

Aadhya said, 'We need to bring Pratul home.'

'It wasn't his fault,' Saatvik said. 'He couldn't take any more, you know? His *dada* is dead. Why shouldn't he be angry?'

At the Mandarin Reach exit, I pulled to the side and went to talk to the guard in the security kiosk.

'How're the Mehtas?' he asked.

'Having a hard time.'

'It's bad all over.'

'How do people get along in the neighborhood?' I asked.

He squinted at me, letting his gaze hang on my hat and bandages. He must have decided I was harmless. 'We get the normal kinds of things. A neighbor doesn't like another neighbor's loud music. Someone cakes up the clubhouse grill with garlic or turmeric or whatever. Maybe a boy pays attention to a girl whose family says she's off limits to anyone who's different from them. Until Mr Mehta's dad, nothing terrible.'

'How do the kids get along?'

'Kids are kids. Some of them hang out together. Some of them fight.'

'Does anyone fight with Pratul Mehta?'

'Not that I ever saw. But I'm in this booth eight hours at a stretch – I don't see much.'

I drove to Chartein Farm. In the late morning, workers were loading trucks with crated chickens. Men stood by the open doors, drinking from water bottles and smoking cigarettes. Everett Peters stood with a group of them, grinning.

I pulled alongside and got out. Peters eyed my bandaged head. His grin dropped. 'What?' he said.

'Is it too late for a pickup?'

He narrowed his eyes. 'Sure, come over whenever you like. Anytime at all – I'm at your disposal.'

'Sorry,' I said.

He scratched his neck and nodded at the old Sierra Grande. 'What the hell is that?'

'The other truck had issues.'

He shrugged. 'C'mon, then.' We went to the cold shed, where eighty-five chickens were piled on wooden pallets.

As we finished loading them into the truck bed, Mr Chartein walked out of Chicken House Three. He came over and patted a rusting side panel. 'I remember this from back in the day,' he said. Then he looked at me with vague concern. 'What happened to you?'

'The same thing that happened to the other truck,' I said.

'Well, be careful.'

'Yes, sir.'

He started back toward the chicken houses, but I asked, 'Did you decide to pay for Dickerson after all?'

He gave me a bemused look. 'The owner of El Jimador is paying. I suppose Carlos was a valued employee. Clara says her friends also set up a fund. I wish them well.' He walked away.

Peters said, 'They take care of their own, that's all. Like the rest of us.' He followed Mr Chartein across the lot.

Forty minutes later, I turned on to the gravel road to Safe Haven. The grass and weeds would soon grow over the scars from the wrecked pickup. Already, the glitter of shattered glass was gone.

I stopped in front of Judy's house and tried the horn. It made a mournful sound.

Judy came out to the porch. When she saw the load of chickens, she smiled almost lovingly.

TWENTY-NINE

That night, Cynthia and I watched Mel Brooks's *Young Frankenstein*. Right after the monster sat on a seesaw, catapulting a girl through an open window into the safety of her bed, Jerry Dickerson called me.

'Huh,' I said, when he identified himself.

'Can you come to my office to talk tomorrow?' he asked.

'I work.'

'At the end of the day, then.'

'Can we talk on the phone?'

'I like face to face, but fair enough. I have a couple of quick questions.'

I realized he probably never preferred to meet in person and now he'd gotten me to agree to talk to him. 'How did you get my number?'

'What good would I be as a lawyer if I couldn't find a phone number?'

'From Clara Soto?'

'Of course.'

'I'm surprised she would want you to talk to me.'

'She doesn't – not after you tipped the police to Carlos Medina.'

'I didn't mean to.'

'Uh-huh. I understand you've involved yourself in the investigation into Antonia Soto's murder. Might I ask why?' He was using the soft voice.

'My job takes me to Chartein Farm, where her family works. When she first went missing, before her body was found, her mom asked me to look for her. I turned her down. Then she was dead. I have a complicated background with dead people. I spent eight years in prison for killing two boys I never touched.'

'Yes, I know who you are,' he said.

'What good would you be as a lawyer if you didn't?'

'Exactly. I also understand that you attacked Randall Lehmann.'

'You understand, or you saw me on the news?'

'Both. Would you explain why you did it?'

'He's a prick.'

'The world is full of pricks,' he said.

'Honestly, I was angry that Antonia was dead – and that I'd done nothing to help her or her family. Then Lehmann showed up and started spitting garbage about how Antonia was responsible for her own death. He seemed like a good person to punch.'

'Uh-huh. You know you could get yourself arrested for that.'

'Are you offering to represent me?'

He laughed. 'I have my hands full.'

'But not so full you didn't reach out to Saatvik and Aadhya Mehta.'

'You know more than you might,' he said. 'That brings me to my real question.' His voice hardened. 'Some people might say you're overinvested in Antonia Soto's killing – and I suppose Kumar

Mehta's too. I believe Carlos Medina is innocent. I say that not only
as a lawyer who's representing a client, but because I really believe
it. That makes me wonder, who did kill this girl and this man? I
would like to be able to answer that question for a jury. I've defended
enough people for a long enough time to recognize certain patterns.
Do you understand what I'm saying?'

Bill Higby had started into me about the Bronson boys with a
similar line nine years earlier. 'I told you why I'm doing this.'

'You did, but not persuasively. Are you sure you don't want to
come in to talk to me in my office?'

'I have nothing to say to you.'

He softened again. 'Well, then, thank you for your help.'

'But I have a question for you. What do *you* think connects
Antonia Soto's and Kumar Mehta's killings?'

'Other than that you're interested in both?'

'Tell me about the threatening notes,' I said. 'The stuff about
gutting Antonia and Pratul like pigs.'

'Ah, you know about that too.'

'What good would I be if I didn't?'

'OK . . .'

'You should talk to Pratul Mehta,' I said. 'Ask who gave him the
message.'

He hesitated. 'And yet I can't, not unless his parents hire me.'

I hesitated too. 'I can.'

'You won't be allowed to see him. Only family—'

'I can if the Mehtas allow it, and Pratul agrees.'

'Why do you think they would do that?'

'Why do you think they wouldn't?'

'No,' he said, 'I don't think that will be necessary.'

'Too much mess getting me involved?'

'Exactly.'

'But, as you said, I've already stuck myself in the middle.'

'And, as I implied, that raises questions.'

'OK,' I said.

'Whatever your reasons, you've already harmed Carlos Medina.
If you continue, you might harm others – including yourself.'

'OK.'

He seemed to read my voice too. Even if he didn't like what he
heard, he was smart enough to use what he picked up. 'But if you

do happen to talk to Pratul, I would appreciate hearing what he says.'

'Right.' I hung up.

Cynthia had paused the movie when my phone rang. I filled her in. Then she nodded at the TV. 'Ready?'

'Two more quick calls.'

I dialed the Mehtas. I told Saatvik I wanted to meet with his son at the juvenile detention center. He held the phone and talked with his wife, who said no.

He asked me, 'What good would it do?'

'He shot at people. No one's saying he didn't. But he's a kid. They'll lock him up, but they'll also decide if he's worth saving. If he drove around shooting a gun only because he was angry, he'll have a hard time of it. If he was also scared, then maybe a judge will put him in a program where he gets help.'

'Of course he was scared. His grandfather was killed.'

'If he felt a *personal* threat – if he thought whoever killed your dad would also hurt him – a judge might see him differently. He didn't shoot in self-defense, but maybe he shot because he was terrified.'

Saatvik talked with his wife again. Then he told me, 'We will let you see him.'

Next, I called Demetrius Jones.

'What happened?' I said.

'What do you mean?'

'Jerry Dickerson.'

'Carlos decided another lawyer could do a better job for him, that's all. It happens.'

'I just talked with Dickerson,' I said. 'He seems smart, but you would fight harder.'

'I can only fight if people want me to. There's a lot of injustice. I don't waste energy where it's unwelcome.'

He passed off Carlos's firing him coolly, but the hurt came through. 'Antonia's still dead,' I said. 'So is Kumar Mehta. Did you get me the names from the supremacist group?'

'I can't give them to you. Vanguard has been watching the Valknut for a couple of years. We understand the way they operate. My boss is worried that you – or anyone else who disrupts them – will muddy up what we know and make us miss risks.'

'I'm going to talk to Pratul Mehta,' I said. 'He got the same kind of threat that Antonia did before she died. His mom and dad can't agree if kids at school harassed him or someone else did. If an adult did, I want to show him pictures of faces. I need the names.'

'Get descriptions from Pratul,' he said. 'We'll compare them to our files.'

'That's not enough.'

'It's all I have.' He sounded as weary as the Mehtas. 'I'm doing all I can.'

'I know.'

'Is that it, then?' he asked.

'That's it. But for what it's worth, I think Carlos made a mistake by switching to Dickerson.'

He sighed. 'Yeah, but you're also the guy who spent eight years in prison for a crime you didn't commit.'

'I'm not a fool,' I said.

'I would never mistake you for one. But you don't always make the wisest choices.'

By the time we hung up, Cynthia had gone upstairs to bed.

THIRTY

The Regional Juvenile Detention Center looked like a big elementary school, except coils of barbed wire topped the fences around the playing fields and the roofs of most of the buildings. There were dormitories on one side, classrooms and auditoriums on the other, offices in between.

Forty minutes after driving from Safe Haven, I filled out paperwork at a security desk.

Then a uniformed guard with a Taser on his belt led me through two heavy, locked doors into the residential quarters.

The kids wore khakis and pale blue shirts, laceless sneakers. But a jail is a jail, no matter the age of the inmates and no matter the uniforms, and the sweat and bleach smell of the hallways turned my stomach. After walking out of Raiford, I'd never wanted to breathe that stink again.

The guard put me in a carpeted, windowless conference room. Pratul was sitting on a round stool at a round table – school furniture, except that it was bolted to the floor.

'You all right?' the guard asked him.

Pratul looked sullen. He had a welt shaped like a crescent moon under his left eye. His shirt was a size too big.

The guard left the room, and I sat down.

'Thanks for letting me come,' I said.

Pratul stared at the table.

'I was a couple of years older than you when I got locked up. I hated every minute of it – and I had a lot of minutes.'

Without raising his eyes, he said, 'They say it gets easier.'

'No,' I said. 'It doesn't.'

Then he looked up, with fear or defiance, or both. 'They say you get used to it.'

'Maybe some people do, but don't let yourself. Every day you're in here is a day away from where you should be. Don't ever let this become normal.'

His eyes teared. 'I want to go home.'

'Yeah,' I said. 'Keep wanting that. Even if it's impossible for a while – even if wanting it rips you apart – always want to go home.'

He wiped his eyes with the back of a hand.

I gestured at the welt on his cheek. 'Who did that?'

He shrugged and pointed at my bandages. 'Who did *that*?'

'My best friend in prison was a big guy named Stuart. He protected me. The guards hated him. Every chance they got, they jabbed him in the ribs or beat him with a stick. But he took it without complaining, and that frightened the guards and the other inmates. It's good to have a friend like him. Find one.'

Pratul held his fingers over the welt, as if afraid to touch it. 'A big guy hit me. The guards like him.' He pointed at the door that the guard had led me through. 'Except that one.'

'Then stay close to him . . . but never trust him.'

'I can handle myself.'

'Bullshit,' I said.

He teared up again.

I said, 'Why did you do it? You must've known you would end up in a place like this.'

'I thought the police would shoot me.'

'You wanted that?'

'I'm sick of everything. People treat us like shit, and then they're surprised when we act like shit.'

'Who treats you like shit?'

'They don't want us living here. Why shouldn't I do what I did? They want us dead.'

'*Who* wants you dead?'

His eyes shined with anger. 'Everyone. Whoever killed my grandpa.'

'I know about the note.'

'It said they would kill *me*. But they killed him. Why not me?'

'Your mom thinks a kid gave you the note at school. Some asswipe bully. But I don't think that's who gave it to you.'

He looked at me – hard or pretending to be hard.

'Maybe you're scared,' I said. 'Maybe you shot that gun because you thought it would stop you from feeling scared. Maybe you think talking to me – or anyone else – will do no good. Maybe you have your own reasons for keeping quiet. The truth is, I might not be able to do anything. Maybe no one can. But if whoever gave you the note also killed your grandpa—'

He blurted, as if against his will, 'He said he would kill my family.'

'Who?'

He closed his eyes, opened them. He looked miserable. 'A guy in a pickup truck. Rohit and I were walking home from the bus—'

'The kid who drove you around with the gun?'

He nodded, a single tip of the head. 'We were smoking cigarettes. I flicked mine at the truck, and it bounced off the windshield. I didn't mean anything by it. We didn't see the guy inside.'

'This was in Mandarin Reach?'

'By the clubhouse.'

'Then what happened?'

He screwed his mouth. 'The next day, I was walking home alone. The guy was in his truck again. He called me over. He gave me the note. He said he would kill me like a pig. He said he would kill my family if I told them. I thought he was just trying to scare me. I showed the note to my mom and dad. Then my grandpa got killed.'

'This guy doesn't live in the neighborhood?'

He shook his head. 'Security lets everyone in – UPS, Amazon, FedEx, the lawn people. The guard is supposed to check where they're going, but he hardly ever does.'

I thought about my first time at the gated community and how the guard waved me through. 'Can you describe the guy?'

'He was white.'

'Tall or short?'

He shook his head again. 'He was in the truck . . .'

'Fat? Skinny?'

He shrugged. 'I don't know.'

'What did his face look like? How old?'

'Old. Older than my dad. Not as old as my grandpa. I don't—'

'Randall Lehmann?'

'Who?'

'The guy on the courthouse steps during the immigration rally.'

'No, not him.'

'If I showed you a picture, would you recognize him?'

'I don't know.'

'Can you describe the truck?'

'A red Silverado, with a camper shell.'

'Good. Jacked up high?'

'No. It was a two-seater. Clean, but sort of banged-up.'

'OK.'

'You can't tell anyone I told you about the guy,' he said.

'If I bring back photos, would you look?'

He seemed to fear he'd already told me too much, but he said I could return.

'You're in a bad place,' I said. 'I won't lie to you. Everyone else in here will, and so will a lot of lawyers and judges and social workers. They might not even know they're lying. Listen hard. Watch everything. When you're locked up, you've got only one job. To find your way out as soon as you can.'

He nodded.

I stood up. 'Stay safe.'

'What happened to your friend? The one who protected you in jail.'

'Stuart? He died. He had a heart attack, and the guards ignored it.'

'Oh.'

'I won't lie,' I said.

I walked out of the detention center into the evening dark. In twenty minutes, back at the apartment, Cynthia and I could turn on a movie and drown out the noise of the rest of the world. I could be as close to freedom as I expected I would ever get.

But instead of heading south to the Riverview, I drove toward the western edge of the city and cut on to the highway toward Chartein Farm. As I neared Clara's house, I slowed. Her Ford Taurus stood in front. I turned in and parked behind it.

Before going to the door, I walked behind the house. When Carlos was first hiding, he'd parked his truck there. He was young and brown-skinned, not old and white. He drove a Ranger, not a Silverado – brown, not red. But like the pickup Pratul described, his had a camper shell, was a little banged up, and seated two. I didn't expect the truck to be there. It wasn't.

When I knocked, Clara answered in jeans and a loose sweater. 'What do you want?' She looked at my bandages. 'And what happened to you?' She sounded like she'd been drinking.

'An accident,' I said. 'Can we talk?'

'About what?'

'I just met with a kid named Pratul Mehta,' I said. 'A year older than Antonia. You might have seen him in the news. His grandfather was Kumar Mehta, who was killed after your cousin.'

'So what?'

'So the first time we talked, you said Antonia got a note threatening to kill her and telling her how it would happen. Pratul got a note like that too. He says an old guy gave it to him. At the bar, you said you thought Antonia knew who wrote the note to her. I need to find out who that was.'

Her mouth hardened. 'I also said Antonia didn't tell me.'

'Nothing at all? Did she act different around anyone at the farm? Anyone somewhere else?'

'Asking me the same question a different way doesn't change my answer.' She started to close the door.

I said, 'Why were you fighting with Mr and Mrs Chartein the other morning?'

'Why is that any of your business?'

'You found money for Dickerson anyway. Why did you think the Charteins would pay for a lawyer to defend a man accused of killing the daughter of two of their workers?'

She held me with her eyes, then said, 'I thought they would want to get the person who killed her, not the first person the police thought was convenient.'

'Have you heard from Carlos since he's been out?'

She frowned. 'You don't understand how this works,' she said.

'Are you in love with him?'

Then she did close the door.

'One more thing,' I yelled.

The door stayed closed.

I spoke through it. 'What color would you say Carlos's truck is?'

She opened again. She looked bewildered. 'Brown.'

'Reddish?'

'Why?'

'I think he probably didn't kill Antonia.'

'Probably?'

'That's the best I can do.'

I walked back to the driveway, leaving her at the door.

A little after nine o'clock, I pulled into a parking spot outside my apartment. When I went inside, Cynthia was watching the end of *Young Frankenstein*.

I found a carton of fried rice in the refrigerator, and I sat with her on the couch. Dr Frankenstein went into a room in his castle, where Teri Garr, playing his lab assistant Inga, waited for him in bed.

'Who says you can't improve on a classic?' I said.

As the credits rolled, I told Cynthia about Pratul and Clara. She told me about a woman who wanted to rent four thousand square feet of climate-controlled storage at Bourne-Goff but refused to say what for.

Then I took the carton to the garbage, and she turned on the news.

As I settled back on to the couch, the anchor cut to a story on San Jose Boulevard, in a neighborhood of riverfront mansions. A young couple, returning to one of the houses, had been forced off the road and shot. Few details were known, the reporter said, but the confrontation apparently began a mile away in a Publix Supermarket parking lot.

I asked Cynthia, 'Want to go upstairs?'

But she pointed at the screen. 'Isn't that—?'

The reporter stood in front of a police cordon. Behind her, Bill Higby walked past a silver Acura. He shouldn't be there. With Kumar Mehta's and Antonia Soto's murders already in his and Holt's hands, a double killing should go to another detective. Then Holt appeared on the screen, walking around the car to the shoulder of the road.

'What the hell?' I said.

Then I knew. Whatever had happened on San Jose Boulevard must tie to the earlier killings.

'Are you OK?' Cynthia said.

I fumbled with my phone and dialed Jerry Dickerson. When he answered, I said, 'Where's Carlos Medina?'

He said, 'You know I won't tell you that.'

'You won't or you can't? Do you know where he is?'

His voice broke a little. 'He might have slipped away.'

THIRTY-ONE

More came out about the victims the next morning. A twenty-three-year-old named Dominick Durant was driving the Acura. He was the son of Dr Henry Durant, who owned four gastroenterology clinics throughout North Florida. Arlenis Canó, riding beside Dominick, was an eighteen-year-old nanny from the Dominican Republic. She cared for the young twins of Dr Durant and his second wife, Sheila. Pictures of the victims showed a blond, wavy-haired boy and a thin, brown-skinned girl with an afro.

The confrontation started inside the Publix, where witnesses said a man insulted Arlenis. It escalated in the parking lot and along the road into the San Jose neighborhood.

Publix released a twenty-five-second video clip of the parking lot altercation. In it, a dark pickup truck with a camper shell shot out of a parking aisle and cut off Dominick's Acura. The Acura jerked to a stop, barely missing the front end of the truck. To move past each other, one would need to back up. Neither did. The passenger window on the Acura rolled down, and Arlenis leaned out and seemed to shout at the pickup. A hand emerged from the driver's side window on the pickup. It held a gun. The Acura flew backward, almost hitting a woman with a shopping cart. Then it cut wide around the pickup and vanished from view. The pickup slowly turned and followed it.

The police were asking anyone who recognized the truck to call a hotline. Their statement made no mention of Deborah Holt or Bill Higby. It also said nothing about why a rich boy and his family's nanny were out shopping together on a November night.

Before going to Jenquist Meat, I left a voicemail message for Holt at the Sheriff's Office. I said, 'I saw you on TV last night. Did the guy who killed Dominick Durant and Arlenis Canó cut their foreheads too?' I figured that would get me a return call. I added, 'I know something about the pickup truck at Publix.'

An hour later, as I drove toward Safe Haven with a load of pig heads, feet, tails, and innards in the back, a radio reporter said the police were searching for Carlos Medina again. The terms of his release had required him to wear an ankle monitor. He'd cut it and was gone from a relative's house where he'd been staying.

I called Holt again and left another message. 'You know it's not Medina.' I could think of a lot of reasons he might run from the police – fear, a sense of being trapped, a burning desire to be anywhere but where he was. But I hedged. 'At least not him alone.'

When I got to Safe Haven, Judy said Zemira was sick and I would work on my own for the day. 'Can you handle that?' She didn't stare at my bandages the way everyone else did, but my head injury seemed to have made me part of her little family.

I slopped meat on to the pavers for the lions and tigers, smaller portions for the lynx and panthers. I stuck the wooden pole, with a piglet's head on it, into the albino leopard's enclosure and waited for him to approach, retreat, and approach again. Through the rest of the morning, I repaired a tilting section of fence back by the cat cemetery.

At noon, Diane brought me a bowl of tomato soup.

'How's Zemira?' I said.

She raised an eyebrow. 'Some of them you never put down no matter how bad they get. You coax them along and coax them along.'

After lunch, I firmed up the rest of the cemetery fence and checked on the cat enclosures. At three, I drove the old pickup back out the gravel road and turned toward my apartment.

When I pulled into the lot, Holt was walking from my door to her Grand Marquis. Higby sat in the passenger seat, reading his phone.

I got out, and Holt said, 'Franky.' She eyed the bandages. 'Handsome as ever.'

I pointed a thumb at Higby. 'Did you lock him in the car?'

'We have different opinions about the value of talking to you.'

'His opinion is he should stick a fist in my mouth whenever I open it.'

'I expect he's not alone,' she said.

'You got my messages?' I asked.

'I did. What's the idea of leaving that kind of garbage?'

'Am I wrong?'

'You're dangerously close to getting yourself locked up for impeding the investigation.'

'Is that what I'm doing?'

'Yep. What do you know about the truck at Publix?'

'It was also at Mandarin Reach.'

'I know.'

'You do?'

'Do you think Publix is the only place with video cameras? The Mandarin Reach security booth recorded the truck coming into the neighborhood at least twice. Lousy quality but good enough to know it's the same vehicle.'

'Good. Get a description of the driver from the guard.'

'Yeah, you're a genius. The guard paid no attention to the driver. He waved the truck through.'

If I sent her to Pratul, the chances were he would tell her nothing. And then he would refuse to see me again. 'Is the truck all that connects the San Jose killings to Kumar Mehta?'

'You never stop, do you?'

'I know someone who talked to the truck driver,' I said. 'He won't talk to you, though. He wouldn't talk to me if he knew I told you this much. But if you want, I—'

'Screw you, Franky,' she said.

We went back and forth for a while longer, and then she walked to her car, and she and Higby drove away.

'Want to go for a ride?' I asked Cynthia when she came in.

'Probably not,' she said. 'Where to?'

'I need to see it.'

'Yeah, probably not.'

But she went upstairs and changed from her Bourne-Goff clothes, and then we went outside to the truck.

The sun was setting as we pulled on to San Jose Boulevard. On the side of the road away from the river, there were a bunch of small businesses, a Baptist church, an animal clinic, and a few houses. On the other side, driveways crossed through woods and over huge lawns to riverfront mansions. At the head of one of the cobblestone driveways, neighbors and friends of Dominick and Arlenis had set up a memorial – a cluster of votive candles, a ragged teddy bear, a wooden cross decorated with yellow beads, little bunches of flowers, and framed photos. In the dimming light, two gray-haired women, one with her fingers pressed to her mouth, gazed at the memorial. So did a man and a red-haired woman in their twenties, their arms around each other's waist. A Prius was parked on the other side of the driveway. I pulled beyond it, on to the grass.

The others were silent when Cynthia and I joined them.

Then the man said, 'Goddamn.' Then everyone was silent again.

There were flower shop arrangements, along with handpicked mixes from late-fall gardens. The photos of Dominick included him as a six- or seven-year-old, a young teenager on a bike, and the blond, wavy-haired boy who'd appeared on the news. A large photo of Arlenis looked like a yearbook headshot. Then there were pictures of them together, laughing at a restaurant table, gazing at a camera so serenely they must have been drunk or stoned, and side by side with their arms around each other like the couple who'd come to mourn them.

'They were together,' Cynthia said. '*Together* together.'

'I guess so,' I said.

The red-haired woman said, 'For a year. They were perfect.' Her voice blended grief and anger.

'They look it,' Cynthia said.

'It pissed off Dom's stepmom,' the woman said.

'Shh,' the man said.

'Fuck it,' the woman said.

I glanced up the driveway. A hundred or so feet in, it curved through woods into the dark. If anyone was at the Durant house, the bordering trees shielded them from sight.

I walked in.

'What are you doing?' Cynthia said.

I kept going.

The trees and the palm and fern undergrowth were cleaned of dead branches, the ground under them raked to the bare soil.

I walked around the bend. Another hundred feet in, the woods opened on to a broad lawn, with a large live oak and flowerbeds on either side of a front path leading to an enormous white shingle-sided house. Landscape lighting shined into the oak branches and up the walls to a dormered roof. The windows on the ground floor were bright, the rest of the house dark. A wing with a three-car garage extended from the right side.

Cynthia caught up with me. 'Don't,' she said.

'What?'

'You need to leave them alone.'

'I know,' I said.

We stood on the driveway.

'That's a hell of a house,' I said.

That evening, the police looked for Carlos again. The news liked the story of a rich boy and his family's nanny even more than the stories about Antonia Soto and Kumar Mehta. I dialed Jerry Dickerson. When my call bumped to voicemail, I hung up. I tried Demetrius Jones. Same thing.

I dialed Clara, and she picked up. She was staying at a Hampton Inn by the airport, she said. Cops had kicked down her front door in the afternoon while she was meeting with a parent at Callahan Middle School. 'Do you know how screwed-up this is?' she said.

'Have you heard from Carlos?'

'Would I tell you if I had?'

'When cops start kicking down doors, they also have their fingers on their triggers,' I said. 'He might be safer turning himself in.'

'He'll take his chances on his own.'

'I don't blame him, as long as he knows what could happen. The truck at Publix looks a lot like his.'

'It was a different truck,' she said.

'The video's rotten. It's hard to tell.'

'It's different,' she said. 'The guy who insulted that girl in the store was different too. Older than Carlos and shorter.'

I said, 'If you talk to Carlos, tell him to keep his head down.'

'Do you believe him?'

'I don't know what to believe,' I said.

THIRTY-TWO

After work the next day, I drove to El Jimador. The staff was setting tables for the dinner crowd. Two men in suits and ties sat in a back booth. They'd pushed empty plates aside and laid out business papers. The sequined party sombrero hung on a high hook behind the checkout counter. The air smelled of grease.

I went to the counter, and, after a while, a wide-eyed woman came and asked if I wanted to order takeout. She looked away from my bandages.

'Can I talk to one of the owners?' I said.

'Maybe,' she said. 'What about?'

'Carlos.'

She made a face, crossed the restaurant, and went through a swinging kitchen door.

A minute later, the heavy man I'd talked to before came out. He was sweating.

'You again?' he said.

We went to a table and sat. 'How do you feel about losing your bail money?' I asked.

'Who says I lost it?'

'That's the way it works. Carlos ran, you forfeit.'

'Unless it works different,' he said. 'If they have the wrong man, they'll settle. The lawyer will make them.' He mopped his forehead with a paper napkin.

'Is that what Jerry Dickerson told you?'

'Faith is best, don't you think? If I'm wrong, I lose everything.
I prefer to be right.'

'I hope you are. Why would you risk it all on Carlos?'

'When you came in, you talked to Leticia. If she was in trouble,
I would risk it for her. And him?' – he pointed at a little man wiping
a table with a wet rag – 'Ricardo. I would risk it for him. Why not?
The restaurant wouldn't be here without them. They trust me, and
I trust them.'

'You think Carlos is innocent?'

'Some people plan, and some people act without thinking. I plan.
I need to for the restaurant. When Carlos left Mexico, he had no
money, no extra clothes, no direction. Maybe he and Antonia would
be all right in Mexico. Not here. But he didn't think about it. I hired
him after he came in and paid for lunch with nickels and dimes.
Do you think a man like that could do what the police say?'

'Do you know where he is now?'

'No,' he said.

'For a man who doesn't think, he does a good job of hiding.'

'How difficult is it? We had a mouse here for two months last
summer. Every morning, we saw it had been on the tables. Every
night, we set traps. But the dumb animal hid. Finally, it died or it
left on its own. We never found it.'

When I drove from El Jimador, I went to the Publix where the
faceoff between the pickup and Dominick Durant's Acura began. I
went up and down the parking lot aisles, got out, and looked at the
spot where the two vehicles had stood inches apart – a blank area
of concrete.

Then I drove a mile to San Jose Boulevard. The memorial had
doubled in size since the previous night. Two girls in their mid-teens
sat cross-legged by the votive candles, their bikes lying in the grass.
A dark-skinned woman in green hospital scrubs and white tennis
shoes stood apart. Her close-cut afro looked like Arlenis's.

I pulled past the cobblestone driveway and parked behind a yellow
Jetta.

Then I walked up the driveway to the bend – and stopped.

I went back to the road and approached the woman. I said, 'Excuse
me . . .'

She was in her late thirties, no older than forty. Brilliant pain showed in her eyes.

'Did you know Arlenis and Dominick?' I asked.

She turned away and walked to the Jetta.

I tried to imagine what she'd seen in the stuffed animals, the flowers, the empty Stella Artois bottles, the full bottle of Ketel One Vodka, and the candles. Whatever she saw must have corkscrewed into her like a wire, my question another twist.

I went back to the driveway and walked to the house.

When I rang the bell, a Filipino woman in a brown skirt and pink blouse answered.

'Yes?'

'Are you – or is Mr or Mrs Durant here?'

She shook her head, her eyes hard.

'My name is Franky Dast,' I said. 'I'm here to . . .' I wasn't sure what I was there to do. 'I'm trying to understand.'

'What is there to understand?'

'Will Mr and Mrs Durant be back later?'

'Later, yes.'

'Do you know when?'

A little shake of the head. 'They didn't say.'

'But you knew Dominick . . . and Arlenis.'

'Yes.'

'You knew them well?'

Her lips tightened. 'I've worked for Mr Durant for many years.'

'And Mrs Durant.'

'Since they married.'

'I'm helping . . . another girl died. Antonia Soto. And an older man . . .' Her gaze told me nothing. 'It's brutal,' I said. 'What have the police said to the Durants?'

She gazed at me. She said, 'The two of them clung to each other.' As if she'd been holding the words inside her. 'I worried for Arlenis.'

'Why?'

The head shake. 'She was too much in love. That kind of love is unbearable. Someone gets hurt, too often the girl – especially in a situation like this, with a boy from a family like his.' Then she smiled gently. 'He seemed to love her too. It was too much – too good to last.'

'Did she live here?'

'No, with her mom.'

'I think I saw her out by the street with the candles and flowers.'

'She's a nurse at St Vincent's Hospital.'

'Yeah.'

The woman sighed. 'Is that all?'

It wasn't, but I thanked her and turned away.

She said, 'She stole.' I turned back, and she looked embarrassed. 'From Mrs Durant. Dominick caught her. That's how it started between them.'

'Oh,' I said.

'Small thefts. A pair of earrings. A bottle of perfume. Lipstick.'

I waited.

'I walked in on them' – again the gentle smile – 'in the sun room, last August, after Dominick finished college. Arlenis would read Mrs Durant's magazines while the twins napped. They kissed. I watched them. I said nothing.'

'I suppose Dominick's parents found out.'

She nodded. 'I suppose they did.'

'But they didn't fire her?'

'Dominick wouldn't hear of it, and he was Mr Durant's only child from before his divorce. Mr Durant thought Dominick would tire of Arlenis. He was mistaken.'

I asked, 'Do you know where Arlenis lived? Her address?'

She hesitated. 'Mrs Durant has it in the kitchen.'

As I waited, a breeze blew through the live oak branches. The sun was dipping behind the house, and the afternoon was cooling. The air smelled of pool chlorine.

She came back with a sheet from a notepad, and I thanked her again.

She shook her head once more. 'Yes, it's brutal,' she said. 'But they died in love. How many of us can say that?'

I drove into Springfield, a neighborhood of big old houses that landlords had split into apartment units. Paint peeled from the outside walls, baring gray weathered wood.

The yellow Jetta was parked at the curb in front of a pink two-story with a porch extending across the front of each floor. I left my truck behind the car again and climbed concrete steps to the front door. I rang a buzzer for an upstairs apartment.

For a minute, there was silence.

I rang again.

Above me, the porch doors opened, and a woman called out. 'What?'

I went out to the front path.

The woman in green scrubs stood at the porch rail.

'Ms Canó?'

'What?'

'My name's Franky Dast – I'm sorry for . . .'

She looked bewildered.

'I've been through it too,' I said.

'Through what?' Her voice was thick with the Caribbean.

I couldn't tell her all that had happened to me over the past nine years, not there, not then. 'If the police haven't told you that Arlenis's and Dominick's deaths are connected to two other killings, they will.'

'They told me,' she said.

'Let me in,' I said.

'Why?'

What good would talking to this woman do? What could she possibly tell me that would help me understand what happened to Antonia and the others? What could she do to help me sort myself out? 'I knew one of the others. Antonia Soto. But she's not why I'm here – not completely. Maybe it means nothing to you – maybe it means nothing to anyone – but when I was Arlenis's age, I got arrested. I went to prison for eight years before they realized they had me wrong. For most of that time, I thought I would never get out. I would die there. I was still breathing, but a lot of me was gone. Maybe it sounds stupid to you – maybe it *is* stupid – but I need to do this. Coming to talk to you, working out what happened, is the only way I can figure out if I'm still here.'

She stared down at me.

'You owe me nothing,' I said. 'I owe you nothing.'

She said, 'What did they arrest you for?'

'Killing two boys.'

She bit her lip. 'You didn't kill them?'

'No.'

'What do you want from me?'

'Just to talk.'

She seemed to struggle. 'What happened to your head?'

'I was asking too many questions. I didn't know when to stop.'

She said, 'Come in then.'

In the front room of the apartment, the old plaster walls bulged, and a leak from the roof spotted the high ceiling. Bright red and blue throw rugs covered sections of a wood floor.

She tipped her head toward a fabric couch. 'I can't give you anything.'

I sat. 'I don't need it.'

She pulled up a wooden chair.

I started over. 'I'm Franky Dast.'

'Karelyn Canó.'

'The other two victims – Antonia Soto and Kumar Mehta – make no sense,' I said. 'They didn't know each other. Antonia was fourteen and lived way out on the northwest side with her family. Kumar Mehta was visiting, staying with his son's family in Mandarin Reach. They had quiet lives.'

'Not Arlenis.' Her mother gripped her hands in her lap. 'She was mouthy. I couldn't shut her up. I said she'd get hurt someday. She wanted too much.'

'Too much of what?'

'Everything. Her dad died when she was nine. That's when we came here. We struggled. But I told her, maybe we didn't have money for Disney, and maybe we didn't have new phones – maybe we didn't even have a new dress – but we had food and a roof, and that was enough as long as we were together.' She gripped her hands so tight the bones showed through her skin.

'Did the Durants treat her well?'

She shrugged. 'They paid her on time.'

'That bad?'

'Mostly Mrs Durant. Some people like to remind you they have power. Arlenis hardly saw the father until she started dating Dominick.'

'I hear he didn't like them together.'

'To tell the truth, I didn't either – not at first. Dominick was an over-educated boy who thought he needed to save someone unfortunate. When *you* came to the door, I thought you might be like that too. You aren't, are you?'

'No one ever called me over-educated, or overly smart either. And I'm more and more convinced no one can be saved.'

'Then you are cynical. That's worse. Dominick had all the words he learned at school. All the theories. I want to break the arm of a kid like that. I want to open his eyes. But I'll tell you something real. Dominick loved Arlenis. He wasn't playing at that. I can't hate him for it. When Arlenis came into a room, the kid couldn't hide what he was feeling.'

'Antonia Soto was like that with her boyfriend.'

'The one the police are looking for?'

'I think the police are wrong,' I said.

'How about the Indian man? Was he in love too?'

'Not that I know of. He loved his grandson – that's about it.'

'The detective said Arlenis and Dominick seem like an unplanned killing. She thinks the man hunted for the other two, but he went after my girl because of what happened at the store.'

'Was that Deborah Holt?' I asked.

'Uh-huh.'

'Holt's OK. She tries.'

Arlenis's mother seemed to be holding herself together by gripping her hands. 'What else?'

'Can I see Arlenis's room?'

'Why would you want to do that?'

'I honestly don't know.'

'Detective Holt says it was random.'

'Even if it was unplanned, it wasn't random,' I said. 'Antonia Soto was Mexican, Kumar Mehta Indian. This guy went after Arlenis.'

She worked her mouth as if she was biting something inside. Then she got up and walked to a bedroom door. I went and stood beside her. The bed was unmade, a striped blanket piled at the bottom. An empty water glass was perched at the edge of a night-stand. A pair of jeans, a purple T-shirt, and a bra lay on the floor. Maybe Arlenis's mother hadn't entered the room since she got the bad news. Maybe she would never go in again.

I stepped past her.

'Don't,' she said.

But I went to a table Arlenis had set up as a desk. On it, there were sketchpads, cups of colored pens and pencils, a box of pastels, and loose sheets of paper. On some of the sheets, Arlenis had drawn action poses of a big-eyed, dark-skinned girl in black leotards. On some, she'd drawn round-faced characters who looked like they belonged in old comic strips. On some, she'd sketched portraits of Dominick.

'She was pretty good,' I said.

'She wanted to go to Savannah College of Art and Design. They gave her a scholarship, but not enough.'

I walked around the room, peering into the closet, looking at a collection of books on a shelf, and picking up a framed picture of a dark-skinned man from the dresser. 'Her dad?'

'Uh-huh.'

I went back to the table and opened a sketchpad. Arlenis had drawn outdoor scenes from around the city. One showed men unloading produce trucks at a farmers' market. A series showed people sitting on benches or playing chess in the park across from City Hall. Another series showed men and women lingering by a fountain. The back pages were empty. A loose piece of paper stuck from between them. I pulled it out and unfolded it.

It was another picture – a full-body portrait of Arlenis – but by a different hand. The black-ink lines were so precise they could have been etched with a blade. Arlenis was naked, her feet big and bony, her legs skinny, her knees turned inward, a patch of pubic hair clinging to her pelvis, her nipples erect. Her neck stretched and strained as if she was trying to hold her head above rising water. Her mouth . . . her mouth was wide and twisted, her teeth enormous, her gums protruding, her tongue black and curling like an eel. She might be screaming in pain – might be beyond pain, silent in her agony. But her almond-shaped eyes looked full of pleasure. Around her, the white-inked background was stark, blank, a gulf of empti-ness. Arlenis seemed to be falling into it.

I'd seen other pictures like it – the one of Everett Peters's German shepherd, hanging on the wall of his singlewide trailer, the one of the black bull, hanging in the Charteins' house. Harry had painted them.

'Where did—?' I cut myself off. I couldn't show the drawing to Arlenis's mother. I looked at the back of the paper. There was a doodle of three interlocking triangles, like a puzzle.

'What?' Arlenis's mom said.

I tucked the paper into the pages and set the sketchpad on the others. 'Did Arlenis ever talk about someone bothering her?'

'You mean besides the grief every pretty girl gets – especially brown girls with an accent? The *Hey, baby, I love the way you talk?* The hand that brushes against you in a crowd? The man who stands too close?'

'I mean threats. Anything scary.'

'Not that she told me. But she told me only what she thought I needed to know, and that was a small piece of her. She wanted to escape. I couldn't hold her here, and I couldn't help her go – and now she's gone.'

We walked back to the living room. I still had the hardest question to ask. Had the killer marked Arlenis's forehead with a blade?

I said, 'Did the police let you see her?'

She flinched. 'I didn't want to. I don't want that to be my last sight of her. I want my laughing, loud, obnoxious girl. Looking at her now would kill me.' She trembled. 'I'm doing what I can. I worked this morning. The day after my daughter died, I stuck a catheter in an eighty-year-old man. I drew blood from a girl. I handed out enough pain medication to kill a cow. If I'd sat here all day alone, my heart would have stopped.'

Nothing good would ever come of Arlenis's death. I wanted to hold her mother close and tell her the pain would ease, but she already knew the truth. So I listened to her for a while longer as she remembered the child Arlenis had been and the woman she was becoming.

Then I left her alone.

I sat out front in the truck. What had I seen in the picture of Arlenis in her sketchbook? Beauty with an obscene face. A mouth like a split side of beef. An abyss. On the back of the drawing, a symbol. What else? What had her mother told me?

I turned the key in the ignition but stayed at the curb.

I called Demetrius Jones. 'I need you to check the list of the group you're watching.'

'Yeah, when I can,' he said.

'Do it now. Look for anyone with the first name Harry or Harold.'

'Who is he?' He sounded impatient.

'He's at Chartein Farm. What do you know about three interlocking triangles?'

His voice changed. 'Where did you see that?'

'What's it mean?'

'It's the Valknut symbol. Some medieval thing they're into. Where
was it?'

'Where it shouldn't have been,' I said. 'I need to know if you
have that name.'

'Where was it?' he asked again.

'I'll tell you when you check the list.' I hung up.

THIRTY-THREE

I called Cynthia as she was leaving Bourne-Goff and told her I
needed to go to Chartein Farm. 'I might be late,' I said.

'Lehmann came in again,' she said.

'That asshole.'

'He apologized.'

'Huh?'

'He said he'd been rude. He was sorry. I got the feeling he wanted
something.'

'What happened?'

'I told him it was all right. It was only words – I would get
over them. But he stood at the desk until I asked if he needed
anything else. He said, sometimes things get out of hand. He
doesn't mean for them to, but people get hurt. I asked if he was
threatening me. I sort of meant it as a joke, but it didn't come
out that way, and he freaked out a little. He said he would never
hurt me. Never. That scared me more than the rest of it, because
it seemed as if he'd been thinking about it. I told him to stop
acting like a creep. He said he was a lot of things but he wasn't
a creep. I told him if he really was sorry, he should leave. He
left.'

'Watch out for him. He's worse than a creep.'

'Yeah, I worked that out a while ago.'

* * *

The sky was dark when I stopped on the narrow highway in front of Chartein Farm. My headlights shined on the sign with the two chickens – the one pecking corn, the other craning its neck to the clouds.

I turned into the drive, passed Peters's singlewide, crossed the lot by the chicken houses, and hooked on to the dirt road toward the Charteins' house. I pulled around the side to the cottage where Harry lived.

The lights were out, and no one answered when I knocked. I peered in through a front window to a shadowy room, then walked around to the back. Harry's van was parked by a metal shed nearly as big as the cottage.

I went back around to the Charteins' house. When I knocked, Mrs Chartein came to the door. 'Yes?'

'I'm looking for Harry,'

She gave me a confused smile. 'He lives in the back.'

'He didn't answer. I think he's out.'

She showed her hands as if to say she couldn't help me. 'Why do you need him?'

I said, 'Can you tell me about the painting over your fireplace?'

She squinted. 'I'm sorry?'

'The bull over the mantel.'

She sighed. 'What's to tell? Harry painted it. He does animals.'

'The sign by the highway? Everett Peters's dog?'

She nodded. 'He could populate a barnyard with his pictures.'

'Pigs?'

She looked bewildered. 'I don't know. What's this about?'

'Does he do pictures of people?'

'He used to, when he was younger. But not in a long, long time.'

'Why?' I asked.

She shook her head. 'Why do you care?'

'What if I wanted to pay him to do one of my girlfriend?'

'Is that what this is about?' She softened, hesitated, then said, 'When Harry was twenty, he traveled. He was very different then. He thought he needed to follow the steps of artists he read about or heard about in school. He went to Europe and, afterward, to Martinique. He thought he would be the next Gauguin. So he went to some islands in the Pacific. On Huahine, he fell in love with a girl named Karine. He married her when he was twenty-three, and a year later, she broke his heart. I don't know the details. I only know he came back here and burned his paintings. He said he would never paint another person. After a few months, he began painting houses for a living. He wasn't bitter – just changed. When Karine hurt him, he dropped one life and started another. Ten years passed before he painted anything more than walls and ceilings – and then it was only the animals. He won't do your girlfriend. I'm sorry.'

'Do you know when he'll be back?'

She shook her head.

'What's his last name?'

The bewilderment returned. 'Summers. We're both Summers.'

I went back out the dirt road and past the chicken houses. When I came to the singlewide, I pulled over. I knocked, and Peters's German shepherd barked. A porchlight went on, and Peters opened the door.

'What are you doing here?'

'I want to apologize for walking into your home when you weren't here,' I said. 'And for being a jerk.' If Lehmann could do it, I could.

Peters gazed at me. 'Is that all?'

'That's it.'

'All right.' He started to close the door.

I said, 'How long have you worked here?'

He opened again. 'What business is that of yours?'

'Just a friendly question.'

'Now you want to be my friend? Ain't going to happen.'

'The Charteins take in a lot of broken people, don't they?'

'If you mean me, I work harder than anyone else here.'

'I'm not saying you don't. Some broken people do – it's the only way they can keep moving.'

'You know that for a fact?'

'I do.'

'Well, I don't need your understanding, and I sure as hell don't need your pity.'

'Who's the girl in the pictures – in your dresser drawer?'

His expression made me think he might slug me. 'That's my daughter.'

I swallowed hard. 'You don't get to see her much?'

'I can visit her plot whenever I want.'

'I'm sorry,' I said.

'No need. You didn't do it.' He was almost trembling.

'Are you friends with Harry?'

He stared at me hard. 'I'm going to get back now. You have a good night.' He closed the door.

I pulled on to the highway toward Clara Soto's house. But before I reached the bend, I turned around and drove to the farm again. I cut the headlights, steered in, and rolled past Peters's trailer. At the chicken houses, I cut on to the dirt road. The Charteins' house was quiet as I went around the side to Harry's cottage.

I left my truck in the dark and circled to the back. The single window at the rear of the house was black. I tried the back door. It was unlocked.

I stepped into a kitchen and touched a light switch. An old oven stood beside a new refrigerator. Next to the sink, a single white plate and a drinking glass were perched on a drying rack. The white vinyl floor was grimy. I went through a hall past two closed doors to the shadowy room I'd looked into earlier from the front. There was a sofa and an easy chair, a TV on top of a cabinet.

I went back down the hall and checked the first door. It opened to a bedroom with a twin bed, a tall dresser, and a night table.

I checked the second room. Buckets of paintbrushes stood on tables. A heavy drop cloth lay under an easel. Tubes and cans of paint were stacked on a long set of shelves. Paint-spattered scissors, measuring tapes, and X-Acto knives were heaped in an aluminum bucket. Rolled canvases leaned in a corner.

A single painting, nearly six feet high and almost as wide, hung on one of the walls. It was of a woman's face. Her skin was golden brown. A sheen rose from her cheeks. Her lips were so deep pink they were almost purple. Her silvery blue eyes shined with pleasure. Streaks of bright white paint emanated from her head – or a spot behind her head – like a radiating halo.

Dozens of pictures of other women and girls, painted over brilliant white backgrounds, hung on the other three walls.

'Holy shit,' I said.

Everything about the portraits was precise and lifelike, all but the eyes, which gleamed, ecstatic, and the mouths, which contorted as if the women's and girls' jaws had been wrenched or crushed. Everything beside or behind the portraits was a void.

There were two paintings of Antonia. Harry had hung them side by side. In them, her eyes sparked with childish joy. Her mouth hung open in a wide *O*, as toothless as a hole in the ground, as though her insides had sucked into the gravity of the surrounding canvases. She looked no older than twelve or thirteen. Had she posed for the paintings? Had Harry made her open her mouth like that?

I looked at another portrait, and my stomach twisted. It was a full-body pencil sketch of Arlenis. In it, she leaned forward, a pencil in her hand, her eyes intent on the gleaming white space to the side. Harry had gotten the fingers wrong. They looked as knotty and arthritic as an old woman's.

I took a photo of the sketch on my phone. I took another of the portraits of Antonia.

Then I went out to the hallway and back to the bedroom. Three pairs of coveralls hung in the closet and, next to them, three long-sleeved work shirts. Boots and shoes lined the floor under them. The shelf above was stacked with boxes, metal cases, and wooden crates.

In the top dresser drawer, there were socks and underwear. Nested among them was a revolver.

A half dozen T-shirts lay in the second drawer, a pair of pajama pants in the third.

The fourth drawer, at the bottom, was empty except for a single glossy photo.

It was an old, overexposed picture of the woman in the large painting that hung alone on the wall in the other room. She wore a white lace top and looked at the camera with eyes obscured by the light. Her lips were parted as if she meant to speak. A pin or needle – or the point of an X-Acto blade – had scratched an *X* into the photo.

I realized I wasn't breathing. I sucked air into my chest, but it didn't seem enough.

I put the photo back in the drawer and slammed it shut. Then I ran out through the kitchen and into the night.

I sucked air.

I rounded the house and got into the truck. The engine coughed and caught. I knew to go slowly – to be quiet – but I shot out past the Charteins' house to the dirt road. When I reached the chicken houses, I braked, then hit the gas again. I eased off at Peters's singlewide, then swung on to the highway and sped into the night.

I rounded the bend before Clara Soto's driveway, then shot past the house. I rolled down my window, and the cool wind blasted against my face. I sucked at the air. Still, I could hardly breathe.

THIRTY-FOUR

I showed Cynthia the pictures on my phone.

'Damn,' she said.

'I know.'

'You need to show the police.'

Every part of me resisted. 'I know.'

I called Holt at the Sheriff's Office. 'I need to see you,' I said.

'I'm out of here in ten minutes,' she said.

'I have something for you.'

'What?'

'No,' I said. 'You need to look at it. It's messed up.'

'What is?'

'I'll be there in a half hour.'

'I don't play games, Franky. Tell me what you have.'

'A half hour.'

She sighed. 'I've been on since five this morning. I'll stick around for twenty.'

Twenty-five minutes later, I parked at the curb and ran into the station. Before I opened my mouth, the man at the security checkpoint said, 'Calm down, son.'

'Deborah Holt,' I said. 'She's waiting for me.'

He dialed the homicide room, asked me my name, and repeated it for the person on the other end. He hung up and scribbled on a pass. 'You know the way?'

Holt shared a cubicle with Bill Higby. His chair was pushed tight to his desk, his desktop clear except for an empty coffee cup and a stack of green binders. Holt caught me looking. 'Gone,' she said.

I said, 'I went out to Chartein Farm this evening. Bella Chartein's brother – Harry Summers – lives in a cottage behind her house. He's a painter.' I pulled up the picture of Antonia's portraits and gave her my phone.

She expanded the image. 'Yeah, that's some messed-up art.' She handed me the phone. 'She looks young. When did he do the paintings?'

'I don't know. I'm guessing a year or two ago.' I swiped to the sketch of Arlenis and gave her the phone again.

She considered it a while. 'When did he do this one?'

'Does it matter? How would he know what she looked like? She just died.'

Holt gave me the phone. 'She and her boyfriend are all over the Internet now. A few hours ago, *Action News* talked with her high school art teacher and one of her friends. You would've thought she was Rembrandt.'

'Harry didn't draw this in the last few hours.'

'Do you know that?'

'I saw a sketch like it at Arlenis's house too. Not exactly the same but close.'

Holt narrowed her eyes. 'How close?'

'Same wrecked mouth. Less detail, but—'

'Did Harry Summers sign it?'

'Did he *what*?'

'Arlenis drew too. I'll bet a lot of her friends did. How sure are you that Harry Summers did the sketch at her house?'

'Positive.'

She gestured at my phone. 'Let's see the picture of it.'

'I don't have it.'

She breathed out. 'Look, it's been a long day . . .'

'Come *on*.'

'I'm not saying what you have isn't important. I'm not even asking you how you got inside Harry Summers's place to take the snapshots. But we have every reason to think Carlos Medina is—'

'Beyond his relationship with Antonia?'

'And the timing – Arlenis Canó and Dominick Durant got killed right after Medina's friends bailed him out. And he cut his anklet and ran. And he has a history with knives in Mexico. And his truck looks like the one in the Publix lot.

'No, it doesn't.'

'That's open to debate. The video is lousy.'

'Does Carlos look anything like the man Arlenis argued with in the store?' I said.

'Are you sure that man was the same as the one in the truck?'

'Harry Summers is almost seventy. *He* looks like him.'

'So do all the other almost-seventy-year-olds in the city.'

'Show the people who were in the store a picture of him. See if they recognize him.'

'Now you're telling me how to do my job?'

'It doesn't seem to me like you're doing it.'

'Go to hell, Franky,' she said. 'I make a special effort with you. I don't know why. Maybe I try to compensate for Higby. But you come in here so sure of yourself, insulting me, full of whatever new ideas have lit your pants on fire, and I begin to understand why Higby dislikes you. You aren't the only person in the world. You aren't the only one bringing us information about the killings. You definitely aren't the most persuasive.'

I started to argue, but she cut me off.

'I'm going home,' she said. 'I'm going to make dinner, pour a glass of wine, and try to forget you. Will you let me do that?'

I walked out.

Late that night, as I lay in bed with Cynthia, Demetrius Jones called.

'All right,' he said, 'The Valknut have only about thirty guys, but two of them are Harolds. A Harold DeSmitt, who comes in for meetings from Baldwin. Forty-seven years old – a pipe fitter – no wife or kids.'

'And the other one?' I said.

'A new guy. He's been to two of the monthly meetings – we're just starting a file. Harold Summers.'

THIRTY-FIVE

I called in sick again the next morning. Judy already knew I had a noon appointment with Dr Patel, but I told her I needed extra time.

'Keep your head together,' she said.

I did two hundred sit-ups on the bedroom carpet. Two hundred pushups. I laced on my shoes, went outside, and ran east on the road from the apartment. After years of running in place in my Raiford cell and then in my room at the Cardinal Motel, I let loose on the open pavement. After a mile, exhausted, I turned and walked back.

I showered, fried an egg, and, a few minutes before eight, drove to the Durants' riverfront house.

The Filipino housekeeper answered the door again. She looked like she expected me. 'Mr Durant is already gone,' she said.

'Mrs Durant?'

'What should I tell her you want?'

'Tell her I have information about Arlenis.'

She shut the door. A leaf blower whined in a nearby yard. A cool breeze bent the palms and tree branches.

When the housekeeper returned, she led me down a wide, slate-tiled hallway toward an enormous window facing a swimming pool, a long lawn, and then the river. We passed a living room with pastel paintings of beach scenes and a den with dark-wood walls and an anchor-patterned rug. Off to the side of the big window, there was a bright sunroom – the one where the housekeeper must have spied Dominick and Arlenis kissing.

Sheila Durant sat on a white fabric chair, her feet kicked up on an ottoman. She wore beige linen pants, a pink blouse, pink lipstick, pink fingernail polish. Like me, she was in her late twenties. Two boys with fine blond hair played with plastic blocks inside a yellow playpen just far enough from her that they couldn't reach her.

She gazed up at me as I came in. 'Who are you?'

I looked at the housekeeper.

Sheila Durant said, 'Nina is discreet. Discreet and reticent, aren't you, Nina?'

'Yes, ma'am.'

I repeated what I'd told the housekeeper when I'd first come. 'I'm helping the families of two others who were killed – Antonia Soto and Kumar Mehta. I'm sorry about Dominick and Arlenis.'

She pursed her lips. 'Thank you. But why are you here?'

'The police told you about the connection between the deaths?'

'Yes.'

'Dominick is the strange one. Everyone else came from other countries. Immigrants or visitors.'

Again, the pursed lips. 'Not so strange. He wanted to fix the world. If there was an organization, he joined it. I'm sure one of them fought for immigrant rights, along with climate change, gun control, prison reform, you name it.'

'He sounds like a good person.'

'He was naïve,' she said. 'My husband thought he did it to stick a finger in his eye.'

'Was Arlenis into all of that too?'

She looked out of the window toward the river. At the end of a long dock, a white motor boat glistened in the sun. 'I don't know. She was just eighteen. Dominick was twenty-three. But she seemed more mature – and more realistic. He was so much softer than she was. So soft.' She turned her gaze back to me. 'I liked Arlenis. She was good with the twins.'

'Did she or Dominick ever mention a man named Harry Summers?'

'No, no one like that. But we rarely talked. My relationship with Dominick was strained, and my husband had little patience for what he was doing. They fought, but he loved Dominick.'

'But he's not here now?'

'He's at his Lake Butler clinic.' She let her eyes rest on mine. 'He grieves by working. I don't pretend to understand. But I don't judge.'

When I left, I drove to Jerry Dickerson's law office. It was on the eighth floor of a thirteen-story glass-sided building on Pearl Street. The elevator rose so smoothly that it seemed never to leave the lobby. The door opened to a circular mahogany reception desk. The air smelled like it was filtered through cedar chips.

A receptionist with a black ponytail and a navy blue skirt and jacket asked if she could help.

I told her my name and asked to see Dickerson.

She spoke quietly into a phone, then took me through a door to a suite of offices and conference rooms.

Dickerson met us outside the office where he'd posed in his website pictures. His suit was a shade lighter than the receptionist's, his shirt white and starched.

He grinned and said, 'Franky.'

'You look like you've stopped worrying about Carlos,' I said.

He led me inside. 'We control the pieces we can and respond to the others as they come. That's what makes the game exciting.'

'It's not a game,' I said.

'You're wrong.' He sat down in a black leather chair. 'If you treat it as anything else, men like me – who keep our eyes on the game board – will win every time.'

'How's the game working out right now?'

He smiled. 'I'm taking it as it comes.'

'Maybe you'll know what to do with this, then,' I said. I showed him the pictures from Harry's cottage.

'Wow,' he said. 'Uh-huh, I know exactly what to do with them. Send me copies?'

'What's your thought?' I asked.

'Show them to the media. Create turbulence. Remove pressure from Carlos.'

'How about getting Harry Summers if he's the killer?'

Dickerson said, 'That's not my job, and it's not yours. That's for the police to sort out.'

'What if they sort it out wrong?'

'Then it does become my job.'

I considered him. If I'd had a lawyer like him when Higby arrested me for the Bronson boys, I might have avoided eight years in prison. But I wondered if he would have done more than point a light at anything shiny enough to distract the investigators. A bright enough light might also blind them to the truth, though. 'I'm going to hold on to the pictures,' I said. 'If the cops grab Carlos, I'll let you have them.'

He considered me too, with a frown. 'You're one of the wild cards,' he said. 'You make the game more challenging, but you also make it more interesting.'

I kept my appointment with Dr Patel.

I said, 'You know that feeling when you're looking down from a roof and something tugs at you? You're afraid you might let yourself fall – you kind of want to – and so you back away? But then you lean close again?'

'Sure, a lot of people get that,' he said.

'I feel like I'm living my life that way,' I said. 'Pulled to the edge.'

'The pull comes from the same part of the brain as a fear of heights,' he said. 'Fear and temptation are close cousins. We're drawn by what scares us.'

'What am I supposed to do with that?'

'Be wise and cheerful?' he said.

'Fat chance.' I told him about going into Harry's cottage and what I found there.

As he listened, he wrote in his notebook. Then he said, 'This is twice you've broken into someone's home in the past month, am I right?'

'Three times, if you count when I barged into Clara Soto's house to talk with Carlos Medina.'

He pressed his lips. 'Thank you for your candor. But you can't do this kind of thing. You're giving in to your impulses. You'll hurt yourself, or you'll hurt someone else. Most likely both. How convinced are you that Harry Summers is behind the killings?'

'I'm pretty sure.'

'OK,' he said, setting down the notebook. 'How convinced was Bill Higby that you'd killed the Bronson brothers?'

'That's different, and it's not fair.'

'If you had the power, would you arrest Harry Summers?'

'I don't have the power.'

'*If.*'

'I would ask him about the paintings. I would find out what he's doing with this hate group.'

'Fair enough,' Dr Patel said. 'In the meantime, we need to talk about respecting limits.'

THIRTY-SIX

The next morning, Harry was standing with his sister outside Chicken House Three when I pulled into Chartein Farm. I rolled past, heading to the cold shed, then stopped and circled back.

Respecting limits . . .

I got out.

Mrs Chartein nodded to me. 'Hello again.'

Harry gave me an elfish grin. 'You wanted to see me?'

The morning was cool, but sweat slicked my back. A forklift drove past and disappeared into the chicken house. 'I did, but I hear you stopped painting portraits.'

'Unless you like animals.' Broken veins spread like red threads across his cheeks. 'You can't get them to pose, so you don't ask.'

Mrs Chartein told him, 'Franky wanted a picture of his girlfriend. He's in love.'

Harry grinned. 'That so?'

'I guess so,' I said. 'Were *you* in love with Antonia Soto?'

His grin broke. 'What kind of question is that?'

'She had great eyes,' I said. 'An interesting mouth. I could see you painting her.'

'Not me,' he said. 'Not in a long time.'

'Or Arlenis Canó.'

'Who?'

Mrs Chartein eyed me strangely but said, 'She's that girl who was shot – the nanny.'

Harry tried his grin. 'I'm a bit old for a nanny.'

I felt a burning. 'What happened to you in Huahine?' I said. 'What did Karine do to you?'

His face reddened. 'What do you know about her?'

'Sounds as if she hurt you bad,' I said.

Mrs Chartein looked stricken.

'What did you do to Antonia?' I said.

Harry lunged at me. He was as light and quick as when he'd tackled Clara to keep my truck from hitting her. But after eight years at Raiford, I'd learned to dodge men like him.

Mrs Chartein yelled, 'Stop.' She stepped between us.

'What do you know about anything?' Harry said to me.

'More than you want me to know.'

Mrs Chartein glared at me. 'Leave.'

'Why?'

'Leave *now*. You've taken advantage of our generosity. You've insulted us. Why in the world would you think that's OK?'

Harry looked furious.

I was breathing hard again. 'Fine.' I started to climb into the truck. 'What about the chickens?'

'Not today,' she said.

'I missed yesterday's pickup.'

'Then you can explain to Judy why you're empty-handed today.'

I left. I was no better than Dickerson, stirring up garbage to see what crawled out of it.

Forty minutes later, I told Judy, 'I had a good reason for fighting with him.'

'Tell it to the cats. Then explain why you're feeding them half portions.'

'We have plenty of meat in the freezers.'

She gave me a blank face. 'Define plenty.'

'We have enough for—'

She stepped toward me. 'Do you *really* think I want you to define it? Do you think I care what your judgment of *enough* is? Do you think you can come into a place I've been running for twenty years and tell me how it works?'

'I'm sorry,' I said.

'Go find Zemira,' she said. 'Tell her to put you somewhere I won't see you.'

I stood there.

'What?' she said.

'I work hard. If I screw up, I admit my mistakes. But I do good work.'

'Define good work,' she said.

I went to the tool shed, then carried a hammer and saw out to the cemetery behind the enclosures. I cut new fence posts. I pounded nails into loose sections of fence. As if wild hogs would dig up old bones. As if the dead cats would claw from the sandy soil and escape into the surrounding woods.

I resisted an impulse to knock down the fence. Most of the buried cats had spent their lives in cages. What good did penning them in now do?

Zemira found me while I was eating lunch. She sat down beside me and ate a sandwich. Then she said, 'You pissed off Judy this time.'

'I explained what happened,' I said.

'I guess she called Mrs Chartein, who explained it differently. Judy wants to fire you. Diane and I told her you're all right and she should keep you on.'

'You didn't need to do that.'

'I don't *need* to do anything,' she said. 'I did it because it's true. You come off as sort of a shithead, but who doesn't?'

'Thanks, I guess.'

'Speaking of shit, Judy told me to have you turn the compost tank.' When we mucked out the enclosures, we put the waste in a big blue metal vat. Now and then, we stirred in hay and sawdust to break the waste down. Afterward, the stink clung to our skin even after we soaped and scrubbed ourselves.

'She wants to rub my nose in it?'

'I'll help with the hay.'

At five o'clock, Judy stood on her front porch and watched as I drove out on the gravel road. I half raised a hand to wave, and she returned the gesture. She'd devoted her life to caring for big cats that would have suffered without her. But she made me question whether anyone was *fully* good or bad. There were forgivable people and unforgivable people. I supposed she was one of the forgivable ones. I wondered if I was too.

As I reached the exit from Safe Haven, my phone rang.

It was Demetrius Jones.

'Checking in,' he said.

I told him what I'd found in the cottage behind the Charteins' house. I told him how I'd confronted Harry and he'd lunged at me.

'Holy shit,' he said.

I asked if he'd found out anything since we'd last talked.

'Nothing we can act on,' he said. 'But we're holding another rally at the courthouse. This time with about a hundred people. We're going to let the public see what a crowd of undocumented families looks like – see if they have the heart to criticize them. Day after tomorrow. Three p.m. Join us.'

We hung up. Before I could put my phone down, it rang again. Deborah Holt.

She said, 'Higby thinks there's something to Harry Summers' paintings.'

'Higby does?'

'Yeah. We ran Summers' name, and it turns out he's in the system from twenty-five years ago. The arrest involved a seventeen-year-old girl and a razor blade. She refused to testify, but he cut her up pretty good.'

'Mexican?'

'Honduran. No papers.'

'Then she would've been afraid to testify,' I said.

'He also drives a truck with a topper,' she said.

'Why are you telling me this?'

'We don't have probable cause yet. Your pictures are no good if you broke in to take them.'

'The paintings are in a back bedroom – next to the kitchen. He turned the room into a studio. Get a warrant. It's full of all the probable cause you could want.'

'No warrant without cause. The Charteins own the cottage, but they won't let us search it.'

'You asked?'

'Not in so many words. I told them we need access to the whole farm. They said no. They're more suspicious of us than worried about catching Antonia Soto's killer.'

'That's because the first time you looked at Antonia's family, you saw criminals.'

'That's because they're illegal.'

'The Charteins see something else. For them, the Sotos are personal.'

'Then the Charteins have their priorities wrong.'

'You still haven't said why you're telling me all this.'

She said, 'How well have you gotten to know Harry Summers?'

'He tried to punch me this morning.'

She was silent for a moment. 'Higby wants to draw him out. We need someone close to him to do that – close but not a friend.'

'He gets together with a hate group, a couple of dozen crazies who drink beer and shoot guns in the woods. You might be able to use that for a warrant.'

'How do you know this?'

I gave her Demetrius Jones's phone number and said, 'Before Dominick Durant died, his dad also got angry with him for fighting for things like immigrant rights.'

Again, she hesitated. 'Let's focus on one thing at a time, OK?'

My phone clicked with an incoming call. Cynthia. I let the call go to voicemail. 'Also, Randall Lehmann gave a talk to Harry Summers' group right before Antonia's murder.'

Silence.

'I don't know that this is just one person,' I said.

She sighed. 'Until we have strong reason to think it's more than one, it's one.'

'Are you giving up on Carlos Medina?'

'Uh-uh,' she said. 'Higby has his person. I have mine.'

'It seems like you're stuck on him.'

'Forgive me for suspecting a man who screws a fourteen-year-old, freaks out when she gets pregnant, and takes a runner when he's out on bail.'

'Except for the sex with Antonia, everything he's done is logical,' I said. 'At least it's understandable.'

'*Except* for the sex?'

When we hung up, I listened to Cynthia's message.

She was leaving the storage facility, she said, walking into the parking garage. 'Guess who came in today?' she said. 'Creep number two. Maybe Lehmann belongs to an old trolls club.' Her voice was light, but I sensed unease. 'This new guy went straight to it. He told me what he likes to do to a girl. I said he could leave or I would call the cops. He left, but he kept walking by outside and staring in through the window.' She sort of laughed, but I knew she didn't mean it. Then she said, 'See you at home,' and hung up.

I dialed her number. The call bounced to voicemail. Too little time had passed for her to drive to the Riverview. 'Are you all right?' I said. 'Call me when you get this.'

I drove back to our apartment – our *home*, Cynthia had just called it. *Home*. The word terrified me. I hadn't had a home in almost ten years. Was that what I had now with Cynthia? The thought seemed too good and too much. I checked my phone each time traffic slowed.

When I pulled into the parking lot, the spot where Cynthia usually parked was empty. I went inside and called her phone again.

It rang and rang and went to voicemail.

I sat on the couch and turned on the TV. Faces flashed on the screen. Mouths talked and laughed.

I called again.

An hour later, she still wasn't back, and she still didn't answer her phone.

I put water on the stove. But I left off the heat.

I called her number six more times before ten o'clock. Then I called her parents' house. When her dad answered, I asked if Cynthia was there.

'What do you mean? Isn't she with you?' He sounded more annoyed than concerned.

'No,' I said. 'No, she's not,' and I hung up.

I drove downtown to the parking garage. Cynthia's car was there, alone on the third level.

I walked to the storage facility. Lights were on for anyone who needed twenty-four-hour access, but there was no attendant, and the door to the sidewalk required a customer passcode. A sign advertising locker rates hung on the wall behind the counter where Cynthia usually sat. A display of packing boxes, tape, and bubble wrap stood to the side.

I pounded on the window.

No one came.

I yelled.

No one answered – not even a homeless man lying wide-eyed on the sidewalk two storefronts away.

I drove back to the apartment, hoping . . . hoping.

She wasn't there.

I stayed awake through the night.

At four a.m., three hours before sunrise, I went outside. The air was clear, a few degrees above freezing. I got in the truck and turned the engine over until it coughed and caught.

Then I shot out over the dark streets and highways to Chartein Farm.

THIRTY-SEVEN

Everett Peters's singlewide and the chicken houses were dark as I went up the drive and cut on to the dirt road to the Charteins' house. The house was dark too. I rounded to the back and stopped at Harry's cottage. Dark.

I went to the porch and pounded on his front door.

No lights. No answer.

I pounded again and yelled Harry's name.

Nothing.

I tried the door handle.

Locked.

I went to the back of the cottage. The van stood where it had been the last time I'd come. The metal shed looked heavy in the dark. I tried the door into the cottage.

Locked.

I kicked it.

It didn't give.

I kicked again.

Solid on its hinges.

I yelled, 'Harry,' and kicked again.

The frame split.

I threw my shoulder against the door, and the latch bolt ripped away.

I kicked again and stepped inside.

When I switched on the kitchen light, the old oven and the new refrigerator looked as they did before, but the plate, which had been in the drying rack, lay in the sink, thick and yellow with dried egg yolk.

I went up the hall and turned on the light in the room Harry used as a studio. Nothing had changed. The golden-brown woman with silver-blue eyes stared at me from one wall. Girls and women with skewed jaws stared at me from the other three. Antonia's mouth opened in a bent oval, as if she would scream. Arlenis stared to the side, gripping a pencil in fingers that looked as if the bones had broken and healed wrong.

I went to Harry's bedroom. The bed was neat, a brown cotton cover tucked around the sides. I pulled the case from the pillow, pulled off the cover and sheets, and piled them on the floor. I lifted the mattress and checked under the bedframe.

Nothing.

I opened the top dresser drawer. The revolver was gone. I dumped the drawer on the pile of bed linens. I dumped T-shirts from the second drawer, pajamas from the third. I looked under the dresser, pulled it from the wall.

Nothing.

I went to the closet. The painter's coveralls hung from the bar next to the work shirts. Under them were three pairs of work boots and a pair of black dress shoes. I pulled a cardboard box from a shelf above the clothes and emptied it on the floor.

A mix of dusty tools, brushes, and old electronics. A watch with a broken face. Crusted batteries.

I lifted down a metal fire-retardant case, a couple of feet long, a couple of feet wide. A key lock had once fixed the lid to the case, but it had been drilled or punched out.

I took the case to the mattress.

A metal divider split the interior in two. At one end, there was a paperclipped stack of ten one-hundred-dollar bills, an expired passport, a jar of foreign coins, a cowry shell pendant on a brown leather lace, a ring of ten or twelve keys, and a bone-handled folding knife with the initials *H S* etched into one side and the image of an eagle etched into the other.

At the other end of the case, there were a birth certificate, an old bank register, Harry's will, and his parents' death certificates. In a folder, there was a stamped document titled *Apostille*, another called a *Certificat de Celibat*, and a marriage license, written in French, issued to Harold Summers and Karine Tamarii. Below the folder, a skinny album held photographs of Harry as a short, broad-shouldered, muscular man with a shock of blond hair, and Karine as a golden-skinned woman, two or three inches taller than Harry, staring at the camera with eyes as brilliant as the ones in Harry's portrait of her. In the final photograph, she stood alone instead of by his side. On it, Harry had drawn a red *X* over her forehead.

At the bottom of the box, in a yellow legal-size envelope folded over on itself, there was a black leather-bound notebook. Inside the front cover, Harry had written the words *Deus Vult* in thick black letters. On the opening pages, he'd penned various symbols and signs, geometric shapes, and fists and faces as square as machine parts. On the next two pages, he'd drawn simple side-by-side bolts of lightning, mostly in black, some in red or yellow. Then, for five pages, he'd drawn a mix of crosses and *X*-es – plain Christian crosses, ankhs, crosses with arms of equal lengths, *X*-es with the top bars reaching up to form diamonds, *X*-es and crosses enclosed in perfect circles.

I Googled the words from the front cover. *Deus Vult*. The translation – *God Wills*. Before I could consider what Harry might mean, steps came into the cottage through the kitchen.

If Harry had come back . . . If he had his revolver . . .

I grabbed the bone-handled knife.

Mr Chartein appeared in the doorway. He wore gray pajamas, and he held a shotgun, which he pointed at my chest. Mrs Chartein came to the doorway beside him – in jeans, tennis shoes, a green sweatshirt.

Mrs Chartein eyed the mess on the floor with as much amazement as anger. 'What in the world . . .?'

Mr Chartein aimed the shotgun at my face.

I dropped the knife.

'Where's Harry?' I said.

Mrs Chartein glanced around the room. 'Why?' she said.

'He has Cynthia.'

'Who?'

'My girlfriend.'

'Why would he have her?'

I gestured at the metal box. 'Do you know who he is? Do you know what he does?'

'I should say so,' she said. 'I've known him all my life.'

I glared at her. 'You don't know a damn thing.'

Mr Chartein tightened his grip on the gun and said to her, 'Call the police.'

'Uh-uh,' I said. 'I'm leaving.'

Mr Chartein drove the shotgun barrel at me. 'Hell no, you're not. Not on your two feet.'

'Please,' I said.

Keeping his eyes on me, he said to his wife again, 'Call the police.'

Twenty-five minutes later, I told my story to a wide-faced uniformed cop. We stood in front of the Charteins' house. Mr Chartein had lowered the shotgun only when the cop cuffed me. A group of farmworkers watched from the shadows.

'He has my girlfriend,' I said.

The cop said, 'Mr Summers does? How do you know this?'

'She left a message as she came out of work. She said a guy

who looked like him was hassling her. Call Deborah Holt. She's a homicide detective. She knows who I am.'

He had the wry smile of a man who has seen too much craziness. 'Sure, we all know who you are,' he said. 'You're Franky Dast. You convinced a judge you didn't kill those two boys a long time ago.'

'Because I didn't,' I said.

'I guess there's mixed opinions about that,' he said. 'But there's no question you kicked in a man's door here, right?'

'Because he has Cynthia,' I said. 'He's killing people. You need to let me go.'

'No, son, that's not what I need to do at all. *You* need to calm down and climb in the back seat of my car. Unless you prefer I put you there myself.'

Forty minutes later, in a detention center intake room that smelled of sweat and urine, he and a sleepy desk officer booked me on charges of breaking and entering. A third cop asked me if I wanted a public defender.

I could call either Demetrius or Dickerson. Demetrius seemed to care about the people he represented, while Dickerson seemed to care mostly about Dickerson. But Demetrius had let Carlos Medina sit in jail. I called Dickerson.

'You know what I'll want for getting you out, don't you?' he said.

'The photos from the cottage.'

'That's right.'

'I would give them to you anyway. But I can't do that if I'm here.'

'Hold tight for a couple of hours,' he said.

At three o'clock that afternoon, a clerk gave me my wallet, phone, and keys, along with an information sheet on a towing company the city contracted to impound vehicles from crime scenes. I checked my phone as I walked out of the detention center. Cynthia hadn't called. I sent the pictures of Harry's paintings to Dickerson. At three thirty, I bailed out Judy's old Sierra Grande.

I went back to the apartment and showered. I turned the water so hot my skin reddened and stung. When I could take no more, I turned the water cold. I thought about Cynthia and the pleasure she took from ice. I stood until I shivered and my skin ached.

After I got dressed, I listened to two messages Judy had left while I was locked up. A few minutes after nine, she'd called to see where I was and how soon I would bring the chickens from Chartein Farm. At eleven, she'd called again. She had just talked with Mrs Chartein. I should return the pickup truck to her as soon as I got out of jail. After that, she would consider me a trespasser if I stepped on Safe Haven land.

She had good reason to be angry. I destroyed all I touched. But I didn't feel wrong – and I didn't plan to do what she told me to do. If she wanted her truck, she could come get it. I would drive it so hard the engine rasped and hacked. If I wrecked it, as I'd wrecked the other pickup, I would just confirm her worst thoughts about me.

I was nauseous with hunger and exhaustion. I went to the kitchen and toasted two pieces of bread. Then I went to the couch and sat. I closed my eyes – opened them. When my phone rang on the kitchen counter, I leaped for it.

The screen identified the caller as Demetrius.

I let the call bounce to voicemail.

At five, I turned on the news. Dickerson had wasted no time. Harry's paintings of Antonia and Arlenis appeared over a *Breaking Story* banner. Without naming Harry Summers, the woman reporter said a man with connections to Antonia Soto had painted the images of her and Arlenis Canó before their murders. The police weren't commenting, she said, though I knew that Holt would have plenty to say to me. In the meantime, the search for Carlos Medina continued.

I went upstairs to the bathroom. I ripped the bandages from my forehead. The wound had scabbed. I leaned over the toilet and tried to vomit. Nothing came.

I went back down to the couch.

Five minutes later, my phone rang again.

A local number without a name.

I answered.

Harry spoke. 'You goddamned fool,' he said.

I hardly breathed. 'Where's Cynthia?'

'Do you know what you've done?'

'Let me talk to her,' I said.

'You're kidding, right? You think because you've been through a few trials you're better than the rest of us. Guess what? The rest of us have been through them too. Personally, I find yours boring.'

'Please. Let me talk—'

'I'm going to hang up,' he said.

'No – no – I'm here. I'm listening.'

'What the hell were you thinking?'

I said, 'You watched the news?'

'How hard was this to understand?' he said. 'All you needed to do was shut your mouth. I've got nothing against your girlfriend. I *didn't* have anything against you. You couldn't let it go?'

'I'll make it right,' I said.

'Too late.'

'Don't hurt her.'

'I like her more than you – a hell of a lot more. She knows what it means to hurt. I don't need to teach her that.'

'You don't need to teach either of us anything,' I said. 'Just let her go.'

'Sorry, I'm busy with her right now.'

'If you touch her . . .'

'Now, you're being stupid again. I'll tell you a secret I learned a long time ago. They're stronger than we are, much stronger.'

'Who?'

'Women. Girls,' he said. 'The weakest of them can break a man's back.'

'Antonia was stronger?'

'Do you know what she needed to do to get to this country?' he said. 'She should've drowned when she crossed the Rio Grande. A normal person would've. I'd've never had a problem with her then. But she skipped across the border and kept skipping. She was too happy. Too, too happy, man. I couldn't have that.'

'So you dumped her body in the creek – where you thought she belonged.'

'Ashes to ashes, dust to dust.'

'What did Karine do to you?'

'Ah, that's better. Now you're thinking. Karine taught me about unfair advantages. You can have all the power in the world, but you can't make them love you. They're stubborn old beasts.'

'Cynthia has nothing to do with Karine. Let her go.'

'Stop whimpering.'

'Let her—'

He yelled into the phone. 'I'm trying to tell you something.'

'OK,' I said.

'I'm telling you about love – something a man like you should understand.'

'I'm listening,' I said again.

'I've thought about it. Studied it. Romantic love. Familial love. Religious love. They're all different, but *true* love is always the same. You know how?'

'Tell me.'

'True love always means killing yourself or killing the people closest to you – one way or another.'

'You're insane.'

'Abraham and Isaac. Romeo and Juliet. God and Jesus. It's a long list. Tell me I'm wrong.'

'Yeah, you're wrong.'

'What would *you* do to get Cynthia back? Would you die for her? Would you kill?'

'I would kill *you*.'

'The question is, when push comes to shove – when people can choose between saving themselves or saving another person – what will they do? Is their love for themselves or their love for the other person stronger?'

'What made you this way?'

'You've got to admit it's an interesting question. It might be the only question that matters.'

'What did Karine do to you?'

'It's what she didn't do. She was like you. She didn't listen. If a man is willing to give up everything – if he's willing to sacrifice himself – doesn't that count for something? Do you understand what I'm telling you?'

I understood he was so fixed on himself the rest of the world didn't matter. 'Sure.'

'Really?'

'What do I need to do for you to let Cynthia go?'

He laughed, bitter. 'You aren't fooling anyone. You want to see her? From what I hear, there'll be another rally at the courthouse tomorrow. You know about it?'

'Yeah.' Demetrius's immigrant families rally. 'Three p.m. A lot of people.'

'That's what I hear. Sounds like a good time. Why don't you go? Maybe I'll be there. I might bring some friends. Your girlfriend might even come along.'

I felt like I had a hole in my stomach. 'What's going to happen?'

'If you want to see her, you need to shut up and keep your head down. No more talking to the news. No talking to the police. Stomp that thought. Show restraint. Call it what you want – sacrifice yourself a little.'

'What are you going to do?' I asked.

'Someone needs to sacrifice,' he said. 'It's a matter of love.'

THIRTY-EIGHT

I called Holt.

She picked up, sharp. 'What?'

I said Harry Summers had Cynthia. I told her what he'd told me, word for word.

When I finished, she was silent. Then she said, 'All right.'

'*All right?*'

'We need to meet,' she said. 'I need to get this on record.'

'There's no time.'

'Come to the department. Higby needs to hear it too.'

'No,' I said.

'For us to do anything – for us to act on it—'

'Dammit.'

'Come in,' she said. 'Do it.'

At ten o'clock that night, Holt, Higby, and I sat down at a conference table in a windowless room at the Sheriff's Office. Years earlier, when I'd told Higby what I saw on the night the Bronson brothers died, we'd started in a room like this. Then Higby had moved us to a formal interview room where a little metal table was bolted to the floor and the walls were thick enough for him to throw me against without rattling them.

Now Holt set a digital recorder on the conference table and hit *Record*.

'It's cold in here,' I said.

'Yeah, we keep it this way,' she said.

'Can you turn it warmer?'

She and Higby settled on to their chairs.

'Tell us everything,' Higby said.

'He has Cynthia,' I said. 'He's planning something.'

Higby rested his thick arms on the table, holding his hands together in a double fist. He looked as unhappy to be sitting with me as I was with him.

I told him what I'd told Holt. 'He has a notebook of drawings,' I said. 'Red *X*-es and crosses like the ones on the foreheads.'

'You sure about that?' Higby said.

'Why would I make it up?'

He bit his bottom lip. If what Holt had said was true, he suspected Harry. But he sure didn't want *me* giving him information that confirmed his thinking.

I said, 'He wrote a couple words in the front. *Deus Vult.*'

Higby glanced at Holt.

'What?' I said.

'You sure?' he said.

'Dammit—'

'All right, all right,' he said. '*God Wills* or *God Wills It*. That's neo-Nazi stuff. The guys who stormed the Capitol used it. And the nuts who rammed a car into a crowd in Charlottesville. It comes from the Crusades. The Catholics yelled it before they slaughtered the Muslims. Tell me more about the other notebook drawings.'

'He only used about fifteen pages,' I said. 'It's like he's just getting started. He filled a page with something that looked like a bike wheel with bent spokes – another with something that looked like a bent-up ceiling fan—'

'Any swastikas?'

'No.'

'Triangles?'

'Some. An upside-down triangle inside a normal one.'

'Yeah, he's putting together a regular alt-right picture book. What about the paintings? You recognized Antonia Soto and Arlenis Canó?'

'And the woman he used to be married to – Karine.'

'How many other people would you say he painted?'

'Maybe eight or ten.'

'No men?'

'No.'

'When we're done talking, I want you to look at a database – see if you recognize anyone.'

I shook my head. 'I need to find Cynthia.'

He glanced at Holt again.

She said, 'How do you plan to do that?'

'I don't know.' I felt the weight of my helplessness. 'I'll figure it out. If I don't, I'll go to the courthouse tomorrow, like he told me to.'

'You need to let us do this,' she said.

'Because that's worked so far?'

She was calm, insistent. 'You need to trust—'

'Uh-uh.' I stood up.

For the first time, Higby raised his voice. 'Sit down.'

I looked away from him.

He said, 'You're going to stay out of the way.'

'Are you going to hold me here?'

'We could do that,' he said.

'No,' Holt said. 'You can go. But Detective Higby is right. You need to keep out of this. If you do what Harry Summers tells you to, you're letting him run the game.'

'You're the second person who has called this a game,' I said. 'The word makes me want to puke.'

'We have resources you don't,' she said. 'We have the means to—'

'Resources and means,' I said, furious. 'He doesn't care about those.'

Higby said, 'And what do *you* have?'

Again, I felt the weight. 'I've got fear,' I said. 'And anger – a lot of anger.'

'Yeah,' Holt said. 'We have those too.'

'Maybe,' I said. 'But I also have a hole in myself big enough to fall through.'

THIRTY-NINE

For a second night, I didn't sleep. I lay in bed, my phone at my side. Then I went downstairs and lay on the couch. Then I went back up and showered, as if water could wash off my dread. Then I lay in bed again.

At four thirty in the morning, I knew where I needed to go. I went down to the kitchen, forced myself to eat a piece of bread, and went out into the dark.

I parked in a guest spot at the Northbank high-rise apartments, waited outside by a row of concrete planters until a gray-haired man in a charcoal suit came out, and slipped into the lobby.

I took an elevator to the thirty-first floor, went to the end of the hall, and tapped on Lehmann's door.

When no one came, I tapped again – lightly, to keep from waking neighbors.

Then I pounded.

A muffled voice spoke from inside. 'What?' Lehmann. He would be looking through the peephole.

'Harry Summers has my girlfriend,' I said.

Several seconds passed. 'Who?'

'Bullshit.'

A security chain rattled and a bolt lock clicked.

Lehmann stood in the open doorway in a pale-yellow bathrobe, his face gray with a night's growth of whiskers. He held a black pistol, which he aimed at my belly.

'I only want to talk,' I said. 'I need to know where—'

He barely shook his head. 'People who only want to talk make appointments at my office.' He held the gun steady. 'Come inside.' He kept his voice down.

I stepped in, and he closed the door, bolted it.

'Harry has Cynthia,' I said.

He put a finger to his lips. 'My son's asleep.' He pointed the pistol toward his sofa. 'Sit down.'

I went to the sofa, stood. A single dim lamp glowed on a table. The two doors from the living room to the interior rooms were closed.

'Harry killed Antonia Soto,' I said. 'He killed Kumar Mehta. He killed Arlenis Canó and Dominick Durant.'

Lehmann eyed me funny. 'I doubt it.'

'Where is he?'

'Your guess is as good as mine.'

'Did *you* tell him about the Valknut group, or did they invite you after he joined because he said he knew you?'

'You must think you're smart, coming here.'

I shook my head. 'You're the only one who it makes sense to talk to.'

'Why don't you take your suspicions to the police?' he said.

I shook my head. 'Where did Harry go? Where does he have Cynthia?'

'You're really in love with that girl, aren't you?'

'*Where?*'

He moved close. 'Men like you are tragic. Infatuation never ends well. It's an open wound. All another man needs to do is reach in and pull out your insides.' He touched the pistol to my belly.

'Tell me how to find Harry, and I'll leave you alone,' I said.

A sound came from behind one of the closed doors.

Lehmann glanced over. I sensed that Harry might come out.

So I grabbed the pistol. Lehmann held on to it. He could've shot me if he'd meant to. He yanked the gun, but I twisted it with both hands. We did a quiet dance. As he stumbled back, I twisted again, and then I had it, and he opened his mouth to protest, but I shoved the barrel against the underside of his chin.

'Where?' I said.

He gasped. 'I don't know.'

'Where do you *think*?'

'I swear, I don't—'

I crammed it into his jawbone.

He said, 'If you're smart, you'll walk out of here. You're—'

I screwed the barrel against his skin, and he tripped backward. I said, 'I'm *what*?' I drove him down to the floor. 'People keep calling this a game.' I pulled the gun away and released the magazine. 'How good are you at playing it?' Then I held the barrel to his forehead. 'Did you chamber a bullet? *Could* the gun still be loaded? People make that mistake all the time. Kids shoot other kids with guns they think are empty. Men shoot themselves in the foot.' I mashed the metal into his head. 'If I pull the trigger, will you die?'

Lehmann's voice broke. 'I don't know.'

I ground the barrel in. 'Think hard.'

'Don't—'

I yelled, 'Then tell me where to find Harry.'

'I don't know,' Lehmann said. 'I swear I don't.'

'I don't care what happens to me,' I said. 'Not the way other people do. *I've* already been punished. Shouldn't I get to hurt someone who deserves it?'

'Not me – I don't—' Lehmann said.

'Yeah,' I said, 'I think you do. Tell me where to find Harry.'

'*I don't know.*'

I pulled the trigger.

The hammer clacked against the empty chamber.

Lehmann screeched.

I slapped the magazine back into the gun and chambered a bullet.

I held the barrel to Lehmann's forehead. 'No more games.'

'Jesus Christ . . .' Lehmann said.

Another sound came from the closed door.

Lehmann shouted, 'Erich!'

I crammed the barrel into his skin. 'Tell me.'

His eyes were pleading. He said, 'For Harry, this is personal. You can't stop someone like that.'

'Yeah, it's personal for me too.'

'If you—'

A door opened. Lehmann's Miniature Pinscher shot out. Lehmann's son followed, swinging a black baseball bat. He charged at me.

I turned and pulled the trigger.

The bullet went wide, hitting a balcony door. Glass exploded.

Erich stopped.

I touched the gun to his dad's head. 'I'll shoot him.'

'No,' Erich said, and dropped the bat on the floor. 'What do you want?'

I talked to Lehmann. 'I don't care how bad Harry got hurt. I

don't care if I hurt you. I'll hurt your son too. Because I don't care.'
His forehead was dotted with welts. Now I held the pistol lightly
against him.

He said, 'If I tell you, you'll leave us alone?'

'I said I would.'

He glanced at his son, then back at me. 'Yellow Water Annex.'

'What?'

'Harry talks about it. His group does drills out there. Simulations.
It's out by the naval air station.'

'What is it?'

'A long time ago, it was a gunnery range. Then the Navy stored
explosives and ammunition there. The big stuff. They abandoned it
twenty-five years ago.'

'Why would he go there now?'

'There are a bunch of old concrete bunkers. It's a good place to
stay out of sight.'

I pulled the gun away. 'What kind of weapons does he have?'

'A revolver. That's all I've seen. He shoots at possums and squir-
rels. But his friends have everything, big and little.'

'OK,' I said.

'That's all I know.'

I said, 'What's going to happen at the immigration rally this
afternoon?'

'I don't know,' he said. 'You've got to believe me.'

'No, I don't,' I said.

'Whatever Harry has done, he hasn't told me.'

'Every time you open your mouth, you lie, don't you?'

'I swear.'

'You lie when you swear too.' But I left him there on the floor
and started toward the door.

'Leave my gun,' he said.

'Hell, no.'

He said, 'What makes you think I won't call Harry and warn
him you're coming?'

I went back. I held the gun to his head, then drew it away.

Shouldn't I get to hurt someone?

I aimed at his right knee. Then I shifted my aim an inch.

I shot a bullet into the floor.

He screeched.

His son grabbed the bat from the floor. I aimed the pistol at him, and he dropped it again.

Lehmann's face twisted. He had tears in his eyes.

I said, 'If I get there and find out he expected me, I'll come back and shoot you and Erich. Maybe I'll die for it too, but I don't care. Either way, you'll be dead.'

FORTY

I charged up a pocked and cracked two-lane strip of concrete toward Yellow Water Annex. The sun was rising, and, in the first light, clumps of grass and weeds growing through the pavement looked like little black animals. The road to the annex had passed through thick woods. As Lehmann said, this was a good place to stay out of sight.

I hit the brakes at a bent-out chain-link gate. Long ago, the Navy had posted signs on either side warning against trespassing on federal land, threatening fines and imprisonment. I steered through.

About sixty bunkers, shaped like low mounds, rose from the sandy soil. At their fronts, double metal doors opened on to concrete aprons. Pavement running the length of the row of buildings had been torn away in spots, exposing dirt and gravel. The trees behind the bunkers were stunted, though, a hundred yards back, cedars and loblolly pines towered over the low growth. A gunman in the dense brush or inside one of the buildings could pick me off. I laid Lehmann's pistol on my lap.

I let the pickup roll forward, watching each bunker for movement and gazing into the shadows where the land dipped toward the woods.

Then I stopped hard and snatched the pistol.

A woman carrying a black object as long and thin as a rifle came from the last bunker, beyond where the pavement ended. She stumbled – hesitated – seemed to straighten – limped out over the uneven ground. She threw the object to the side. She sat down at the edge of the pavement.

I knew then. I flew over the ragged concrete, braking again at the end, tumbling out of the door, running.

Cynthia looked up, her eyes red, as if she'd been staring through smoke.

'Hey,' she said, her voice also as rough as smoke.

Her Bourne-Goff Storage shirt was stained with oil, her jeans torn over one thigh. She was barefoot. A gash angled over the top of her left foot.

'Jesus Christ,' I said. 'Jesus . . .' I sank to the ground beside her.

'I'm all right,' she said.

I was afraid to touch her. 'Did he hurt you?'

She shook her head. 'I'm pissed off. And tired.'

'Where is he?'

'Gone – a couple hours ago.'

Months ago, she'd told me she loved me, and I'd told her I loved her too. Since then, we'd let it rest. *Love* was a heavy word, and we already carried enough between us. As we sat on the dirt at the old explosives and ammunition depot, I said it again. 'I love you.'

She touched her hurt foot and flinched. 'I love you too.' She got up and tested her weight.

'How bad?' I stood beside her.

'I can walk.'

'What happened? How did you—?'

'The bastard was waiting for me in the garage. He had a gun.'

I wanted to cry. 'I'm sorry. So, so—'

'Why? It's not your fault.'

'Yeah,' I said. 'Yeah, it is.'

'No.' Pissed off. '*He* did it. Not you.'

I shook my head. 'I'm sorry.'

She kissed me. Her lips were dry.

She started toward the truck, favoring the injured foot, holding her pain inside. I knew her kind of hardness and knew better than to try to help her. I opened the passenger door, went to the driver's side, and got in.

I started the engine. 'What happened to your foot?'

'He locked me in, and I kicked the door.' She touched the foot again, flinched. 'I think it's broken.'

'I'm sorry . . .'

'Don't say that.'

If she allowed the smallest crack, the shell she protected herself with would disintegrate. I said, 'How did you get out?'

She gestured toward the end of the pavement. A pry bar lay in the grass – the black object she'd thrown. 'I don't think he prepared. I was a last-minute idea. It was dark. I found the bar about twenty minutes ago.'

'He told you who he is?'

'More than I wanted to know,' she said. 'He plans to kill us.'

'I figured.'

I gazed at her – her wide face, her hair ragged after two nights in the bunker – and she stared back, hard.

As we drove to Baptist Hospital, she told me how Harry had stepped from behind a support pillar in the garage and held his revolver against her ribs, how they'd talked through the first night as he hid with her, how a quiet fury had settled over him during the following day.

'He says I remind him of the girl he married in Huahine. He says she was burned too. Not like me, but inside. He was hopping from island to island in the South Pacific, painting the people he saw. Then he met Karine. He says she sometimes was fine, but other times it seemed like her mind turned to ash. Like she was there, but not there. When she got that way, she wandered. That was his word. Wandered. Like she was a stray dog. She went into men's houses. She got in their beds. After she and Harry were together, if she went to other men, Harry beat the men up. Then he beat *her*. He wanted her to himself. He married her. But she kept wandering, and he kept beating her. Then he went too far. He says all he can remember is her eyes and her mouth as he beat her to death.'

'No one arrested him?'

'He dumped her body in the ocean, then took off and came back here. He expected someone to come after him, but no one did.'

'That happened a long time ago,' I said. 'Why is he doing this now?'

'He said a man gets fed up. I asked what he was fed up with. He said I should look around – *Wasn't it obvious?* I told him it wasn't, so he said I was stupid, like Karine. I said I was nothing like her – I would never wander to *his* bed. He said that was all right – he could still beat me. I told him if he touched me, I would tear his balls off. He laughed and said, yeah, I was just like her.'

'Maybe that's why he killed Antonia. She did what she wanted and didn't seem to care what people thought. She was bold.'

'He talked like he and Antonia had a connection – like he meant something to her.'

'Maybe in his own mind,' I said. 'How about Kumar Mehta?'

'Harry called him every jagoff racist name he seemed to be able to come up with. He thinks the man disrespected him.'

'Where did he even meet him?'

'He painted the clubhouse at Mandarin Reach. I guess Kumar Mehta would go by and watch him. He would give him advice like he owned the place – like he was talking to a servant.'

When I first went to Mandarin Reach, worksite tape had been stretched around the clubhouse. Inside, pictures had leaned against newly painted walls. Kumar Mehta's attitude must have been too much for Harry – a little old brown-skinned man telling him what to do.'

'How about Arlenis and Dominick?'

'He said less about them. He seems to feel bad about her . . . but not him. He saw her drawing in a park downtown. He says she also reminded him of Karine. He gave her some hints about art. It sounds like she appreciated them about as much as he appreciated Kumar Mehta's advice. She called him a sleazebag. He called her a whore. Then he stalked her. He says he would've let her go if he hadn't seen her with her pretty, blond boyfriend. He couldn't allow that.'

'Did he tell you where he was going this morning?'

'Nothing that made any sense. He said he needed to *get ready for the show*. I asked what was going on. That was the only time I thought he would actually hit me. I asked if I could go with him. He seemed to think that was funny. He said I would need to stay home from this party. Then he locked me in the building.'

'Demetrius Jones is planning another rally at the courthouse this afternoon. Harry's planning to be there. He said I should go. He talked about making a sacrifice. How many guns does he have?'

'I only saw the one.'

The highway bent toward downtown. We cut toward the hospital.

'The first night, he asked about the burns on my legs,' she said. 'He wanted the details – exactly what happened, exactly how it felt. At first, I thought he felt bad for me. That was better than him killing me, so I told him everything I remembered. Then I realized he was enjoying the story. It fascinated him. When I told him about the nylon in the blanket melting into my skin, he said turpentine and mineral spirits burn like that – they cling. I asked him why he knew this. He said he uses them as paint thinners. Then he went off about how white people burned Black people out of Tulsa with turpentine bombs a hundred years ago, and how old weapons are as much better than new ones as old paintings are better than contemporary art, and that's why he still uses a revolver. He spooked me. I asked him why he was telling me about this. He said I should be a good girl and not ask so many questions. I told him if he talked to me that way, I would tear his balls off.'

We exited on to a street to the hospital. Doctors and nurses in scrubs were walking from their cars, cups of coffee in their hands. Others, coming off the night shift, passed as they walked to the garage. When we pulled to the curb by the emergency room, Cynthia said, 'What will you do?'

I said I would park and meet her in the waiting room.

'No.' She eased from the truck, recoiling when she put weight on her hurt foot. 'Get him.'

'Uh-uh. I need to be with you. I'll call Holt.'

Again, she looked pissed off. 'Get the cocksucker.' She closed the door.

FORTY-ONE

As I drove back to the highway, I called Holt. 'It's Harry Summers,' I said. 'He had Cynthia, but she got away. He told her what he did.'

Holt was silent.

'There's a rally at the courthouse this afternoon at three,' I said. 'He'll hit it – I don't know with what, but he'll hit it hard. He may bring others with him.'

'Slow down,' Holt said. 'How . . .?' She didn't say *how what*. Just *how*.

I said, 'Send someone to talk to Cynthia at the Baptist ER. She'll tell you all you need to know.'

I hung up. The phone rang almost immediately, identifying Holt as the caller. I silenced it, then dialed Demetrius Jones.

He picked up in a loud room, surrounded by other voices.

'Cancel the rally,' I said.

'What?'

'Harry Summers is going to attack it. Call it off.'

'We can't do that.'

'People will get hurt—'

'Do you *know* that?'

'He killed Antonia Soto and the others. Two nights ago, he grabbed my girlfriend. Now he's talking about the rally.'

'The police will be there,' he said.

'How fast can they stop him?'

A woman in the room called Demetrius's name, and he told her to hang on a moment. Then he moved away from the noise. 'Every day is a risk for these families. Every day, ICE might come through the door and rip their lives apart. Every day, some asshole might victimize them. Nothing about today is different, except there will be news cameras. I hope to God you're wrong and we can get our message across, then sneak away without getting detained, but if Harry Summers comes and exposes his hatred, people will see what these families are up against.'

'He won't *expose his hatred*. He'll have a gun, and he might bring friends. Cancel the rally.'

'No,' he said. 'You should come.'

'You're going to get someone killed.'

'Yeah, I sure hope not.'

I drove out of downtown toward Safe Haven, Lehmann's pistol tucked under the driver's seat. I needed more than the one gun if Holt failed to stop Harry before the rally.

A half hour later, I turned into the entrance. For the first time since I'd interviewed there, a chain was locked across the gravel road. I accelerated and hit it.

The chain snapped.

When I pulled up in front of Judy's house, Zemira was steering a wheelbarrow toward the lynx enclosure.

She watched as I went up on the porch and pounded on the door.
'They aren't here,' she said.
'Where are they?'
'Why?'
'*Where are they?*'
'They went into the city for a doctor's appointment. Diane's having a hard time swallowing.'
'Huh?'
'The world keeps turning—'
'I need Judy's help.'
'You lost any chance of that a while ago.'
'Does she have a gun?'
'What?'
'A gun.' I tried the door handle. It was unlocked. I went in.

Zemira came up the steps and followed me into the house. 'What the hell, Franky? Why do you think—?'
'She must have something. In case the cats . . .'
She moved in front of me, to stop me from going farther into the house.

So I told her about the four people Harry had killed – and about Cynthia – and about the immigrant families rally.

She looked more confused than convinced, but she let me step around her and into Judy and Diane's bedroom. They had a four-poster bed, a dark-wood dresser, an armchair, and a glass-fronted cabinet of porcelain bowls. I looked under the bed, then went to the closet. A gun rack with four rifles and a shotgun was fixed to a wall. On a shelf above the rack were a boxed nine-millimeter Luger and cartons of ammunition.

'You can't do this,' Zemira said.
'I need your help,' I said.
'Are you crazy?'
'I'm doing the right thing.'
She shook her head. 'You're doing a seriously fucked-up thing.'
'Help me,' I said. 'If he brings others, I need others too.'
'No way.'

I took the cartons of ammunition from the shelf and laid them on the bed. I removed the rifles and shotgun from the rack and put them by the ammunition. 'Grab the Luger,' I said.

She shoved me away from the bed. 'Leave – *now.*'

I balled a fist.

She stepped toward me, offering her face. 'Is this really who you are?' she said.

I could hit her. I could carry the guns to the truck. In seconds, I could be speeding out over the gravel road.

She yelled, 'Is it?'

I yelled back, 'I don't know.' But I lowered my fist.

She stood between me and the bed. She breathed hard. 'Go. Just go.'

I could brush her aside.

'Go,' she said again, quietly.

I left.

I eased out over the gravel road. Driving into Safe Haven, I'd felt like I was sticking my arm into one of the cat enclosures at feeding time. Driving out, I felt like I hung together by sinews.

I touched the gas, cutting from the road toward downtown, and the engine stuttered and died. The truck rolled to a stop. On the third try, the engine turned over, and I eased forward, accelerated, and accelerated more. Five minutes later, I merged on to the Interstate and stayed in the right lane until the Philips Highway exit.

El Jimador served breakfast from six until ten a.m. and then closed until eleven thirty, when it reopened for lunch. At nine thirty, two men in work boots and dirty work clothes sat in a booth across from an older man in cowboy boots and a plaid button-up shirt, their plates greasy with the remains of fried eggs. The sequined sombrero Carlos Medina had worn in celebratory photos was nowhere in sight.

The wide-eyed woman I'd talked to the last time I'd come gave me a sour look when I asked to talk to one of the co-owners. She went through the swinging door into the kitchen.

The heavyset owner came out and gestured at the table where we'd talked before. He went to a drink machine, filled a cup with Sprite, and made a show of peeling the paper from a straw.

When he sat down, I explained what I wanted.

He listened, blank-faced. Then he scratched his ear. He said, 'You're a real asshole for asking that. A real goddamned *hijo de puta.*'

'I'm trying to stop people from getting killed,' I said.

'And you think me and my friends standing out there is the way to do it? Do you know what they call a Mexican who picks fights? Target practice. Do you know what they call a man with a green card who even talks about this kind of thing? A deportee.'

'I thought you would want to help,' I said.

'How do you think this would make things better?'

'It's hard to imagine it would make them worse.'

'Then you don't understand anything.' He stood up from the table. 'You need to leave my restaurant.' He walked toward the kitchen. 'Don't come back.'

I went out to the truck. Above me, the North Florida sky was solid blue.

As I climbed in, the man with the cowboy boots came from the restaurant. He was short and sturdy. He'd oiled his black hair and combed it back.

'Hey, amigo,' he said.

I stared at him.

'I will join you.' He gestured back inside. 'One of my men will come.' If the others were construction workers or laborers of some kind, he must be their boss.

'Why would you want to do that?'

'I watch the news. I listen to my wife and friends. It's not what I want,' he said. 'But I don't see a choice.'

'You don't know me. I don't know you.'

'I don't like to fight,' he said. 'I have three kids. I have a business. But what good is any of it if someone like this man can take it away because he thinks I should have nothing?' His teeth were little and bright white.

I shook my head.

'There's a saying,' he said. *'En tiempos de guerra todo agujero hace trinchera.* "In times of war, every hole is a trench." Do you have anyone better than me?'

I drove back to my apartment.

I couldn't ask the Mehtas to help. Aadhya had enough anger to take a stand at the rally, even if her husband didn't, but Pratul was in juvenile detention, and if something happened to her, who could he cling to?

The Durants? Money was power, but their kind of power seemed useless against a man like Harry. If anything, it would strengthen him, showing him that, in spite of what we told ourselves, people weren't born equal – some had an advantage over others from the moment they took their first breath, *before* that first breath – and so why shouldn't Harry resent those he believed were breathing *his* air?

I called Jerry Dickerson. He answered with the same calm, pleasant voice he always seemed to have at the beginning of a conversation. 'Franky?'

'Putting Harry Summers' paintings on the news shook things up,' I said.

'Quite nicely,' he said.

'Not so nicely.' I gave him a quick version of what had happened since he released the pictures.

'Then the police have their man,' he said.

'Not yet.' I gave him about a minute more on what I thought was about to happen.

'As a lawyer, I advise you to do as Detective Holt has told you,' he said. 'Stay away. Keep your hands clean. I also advise you that as a friend.'

'Since when have you been my friend?' I asked.

'You can't control what happens to others now, but you can control what happens to you.'

'After the rally, I might need you,' I said.

'I advise against doing anything that would make my services necessary.'

'Yeah,' I said, 'I hear you.

I steered into the Riverview parking lot and pulled into a spot outside my apartment. The rally would start in less than five hours. I was exhausted. I'd barely eaten in two days. I needed to force food down my throat, and after that I would shower and lie down.

I stuck Lehmann's pistol under the seat and went inside. Cynthia had called our apartment *home*. I tried to believe it. Maybe when she came from the hospital – in a cast or splint, her wounded foot stitched together. Maybe after the rally.

I went to the stairway. As I stepped on the bottom stair, I noticed that the sliding back door had been knocked off its tracks. At the same moment, I sensed the weight of someone approaching from behind me, saw a trick of a shadow. I started to turn, but a hand reached around me and held a razor blade to my neck.

Harry.

'You goddamned fool,' he said.

The blade sliced my neck. The metal felt like ice. Then I was falling.

FORTY-TWO

I lay on the floor.

Harry hovered over me, holding a box cutter.

The pain came – ice burning.

'Get up,' Harry said.

'I'm bleeding,' I said.

'*Up*,' he said.

I lay still.

'It's a scratch,' he said. 'If I wanted you dead, I'd've cut deeper. If I wanted you paralyzed, I'd've gone in from behind. There's a time to rend—'

'Fuck you.'

'And there's a time to sew. Did you know that Botticelli sewed two pieces of canvas together for "The Birth of Venus"? Tintoretto did the same thing for "The Dreams of Men." You can do beautiful work that way.'

'Who's Botticelli? Who's Tintoretto?'

'It's just that kind of comment that makes me want to go ahead and kill you now. But' – he cocked his head as if considering the best angle to paint me from – 'for everything a season. Don't worry, killing time is coming, for you . . . and your girlfriend.'

'Uh-uh,' I said. 'Not her. She got out. She's safe.'

'Nice try.'

'She pried the door open at the annex. She walked out.'

He jerked. 'Well, I'll be damned. The two of you have a way of infuriating me.' He eyed me from another angle. 'Get up.'

'No.'

With his startling speed, he flung himself on top of me and held the tip of the blade against my forehead.

My arms felt heavy, laden. I swung one up and smashed a fist into his chin.

He yelled, 'Ha' – as if shocked and pleased at once. He stared down at me. 'That's the spirit.' He stood again. 'Now, get up.'

I sat. Blood ran from my neck into my collar. 'What do you want?'

'I told you. I'm getting everything ready. I need to know what I'm working with. Stand up.'

'Why?'

'Because I told you to.'

He was a little man, but he loomed over me. I touched my fingers to my neck. They came away slick. 'I know nothing,' I said.

'If I believed that, you would be dead. Whenever I paint a house, I look at every board before I write the contract. If there's dry rot, I need to know. If there's sandblasting, I need to know. Tell me what I need to know.'

'You like to hear yourself talk, don't you?' I wiped my hand on the floor. 'I know what you told Cynthia. I know what you told *me*. I know I'm going to stop you.'

He seemed to get a kick out of that.

I said, 'Who's doing this with you? Lehmann?'

'Who have you talked to? Who have you told?'

I pushed myself to my feet. He stepped back, holding the box cutter toward me.

'I talked to the police,' I said. 'I talked to the rally organizers. I talked to people who can help stop you.'

He narrowed his eyes. 'No, you didn't.'

Blood was soaking my shirt, spreading its warmth across my chest. My neck throbbed. 'Don't ask if you won't believe me. Let me ask *you* a question. *Why?*'

'Why what?'

'Why all of this? All the hurt. The killing. I know about Karine. Your sister told me—'

'She shouldn't have.'

'Cynthia told me more. I worked out a little from your paintings. But what Karine did – it had nothing to do with the others you've killed. Karine hurt you. No one else did. They were just people doing the things people do. They didn't care about you.'

'I cared about them.'

'So you killed them.'

'You won't understand – you and a lot of other brainwashed people, following the wrong shepherd.'

'Tell me about Lehmann.'

'What about him?'

'Did you ask him to talk to your Valknut group?'

He smiled out of one side of his mouth. 'You know about that too, do you? It was the other way around. He took me along. We've been friends a long time. Since we were kids.'

'Before he moved downtown,' I said.

'That's right,' he said. 'And after. I spent a lot of happy days on Sugar Hill. Way up high.'

'There was no hill.'

'That's a matter of perspective. Right at the top, there was a park – Wilder Park. Twenty-five, thirty acres. Lawns and fields and a pond, a little library. Lower down, there were the houses and businesses. It was a little village inside the city.'

'Sounds wonderful.'

'It was heaven . . . or could've been.' He jabbed his blade at me. 'Mostly Black by then, though you had some Chinese girls and old Greeks too. They caused the problems.'

'Yeah? What kind of problems?'

'The place was too sweet for those people. They thought they could live on all that sweetness. The city wouldn't have that, so they razed the buildings, leveled Sugar Hill – laid the interstate through the middle. Those people wanted too much. They sucked the sugar-tit dry. They denied me.'

'*Those people?*'

'Sure.'

I fingered my neck. 'What happened to you there?'

'It happened to all of us.' He gazed at me. 'Once you demolish it, you can't rebuild it. You break it, it's yours – forever.'

'What is?'

'Anything. Everything. Sugar Hill.' He smiled his one-sided smile. 'I busted my balls there for the first time with a girl named Charlise. We were twelve. All the kids fought – fists, rocks, knives. I slept in the sun in Wilder Park. I stole cigarettes from Daylight Groceries. I did everything for the first time there. I became a man. It was the purest place I've ever been.'

I rushed him. Slick with blood, I tore across the room. He thrust the box cutter at my face, and I launched into his chest, all my weight, all my muscle, driving him back and down.

He fell.

The box cutter clattered across the floor. I let go of him and crawled after it, got it – spun toward him. He sprang to his feet between me and the front door, stood as if I'd never knocked him down.

He grinned at me. 'There's a time, there's a time,' he said. 'Until then . . .' He turned and went out the door with that strange speed.

I went after him.

As I stepped outside, he was crossing the parking lot to a rusty red Silverado pickup. I sprinted over the pavement. He got in and started the engine.

The truck shot toward me. I dodged, and it skidded across the loose gravel. It headed to the exit and, without slowing, rounded on to the street.

I ran to the Sierra Grand and grabbed Lehmann's pistol. I went out to the exit. Harry was gone.

I went inside and locked the front door. My bloody shirt clung to my chest and belly. I set the sliding back door on its tracks and latched it. I climbed the stairs, peeled off my clothes, and stepped into the shower.

The spray scorched my neck. Blood sheared from my chest, pooling at my feet. After a while, the cut numbed. The water on the shower floor streaked and cleared.

When I stepped out, the wound bled freely again. I bathed it with sink water until it was pink and raw. Then I wrapped gauze around my throat – and around and around again – as if I meant to hang myself.

I went downstairs to the couch.

I was sitting there an hour later when Cynthia called. She'd broken her second metatarsal. The doctor had given her twelve stitches and a tetanus shot, codeine for the pain. She had come down from the boost of adrenaline that got her out of the bunker. She asked how I was doing.

If I spoke of what had happened, what would she do? Rush to me? What would *I* do if she came? Curl into myself, crippled, all but dead?

'Everything's OK.'

'You sound funny,' she said.

'No.'

She said, 'I'll call an Uber and get a ride home.'

'Stay there,' I said. Harry might come back. Even if he stayed away, she would be returning to a bloody floor, a bloody bathroom sink, the wreck Harry had made of me. Whatever we'd been making of the apartment would be ruined. Razed. 'I'll pick you up,' I said.

But when we hung up, I stayed on the couch.

Another hour passed. My neck throbbed. When Cynthia called again, I let her go through to voicemail.

At one o'clock, two hours before the rally, I checked Lehmann's pistol. The magazine held six rounds, the chamber another.

I went outside, gazed across the parking lot, and got in the pickup. The engine turned over on the first try.

I pulled out to the street and headed toward Philips Highway. When I'd moved from the Cardinal Motel, my neighbor Jimmy, palming a joint into my hand, had said, *Remember where you came from.* In my imagination, the place would remain even if the city crumbled around it. *Remember where.* Then Jimmy had said, *If you ever need a pair of fists, you know where I am.*

I drove to the motel.

FORTY-THREE

At a quarter to three, with Jimmy beside me in the pickup, I parked at a meter across from the courthouse. A couple dozen uniformed cops stood in the crowd on the plaza. About ten immigrant families – maybe fifty men, women, and kids in all – stood inside a cordon at the base of the courthouse steps. Demetrius Jones chatted with a woman with gray dreadlocks.

The afternoon had warmed, and the sky was a blue that seemed to have no depth or end. The courthouse was brilliant in the sun.

At the top of the steps, four decorative pillars might have symbolized something, but they seemed to bear no weight. A row of palm trees grew on each side of the broad walkway leading to the steps.

Jimmy stared through the windshield at the crowd. He had the musky, smoky smell of a man who rarely bathed but kept a job and a girlfriend anyway.

'I underestimated you, Franky,' he said, glancing at the passersby on the sidewalk. 'All those months living next door, I figured you for a frightened little bitch.' He half shouted, 'Life's a rodeo.'

'Calm,' I said.

He grinned at me. 'You've got bloody bandages on your neck like Dracula butt-fucked you, and you're telling me to be calm? You pick me up, looking for a brawl, and you want me to talk civilized?'

'Yeah,' I said.

'All right, man, but you're giving me mixed messages.'

Five minutes later, a black Ford Expedition rolled up alongside us with three men inside – the boss in the cowboy boots from El Jimador, one of the workers who'd sat in the booth with him, and, in the back seat, a stringy-haired man in a windbreaker. The man in cowboy boots nodded and angled into a spot in front of me.

When they came over, he introduced the stringy-haired man as his worker's cousin. 'He's dependable,' he said. He looked at my neck. 'What happened to you?'

'Don't worry about it.' I left Lehmann's pistol on the floor in front of the seat for easy access. Standing by the pickup, I described Harry to the others. I said we needed to watch for anyone else who might attack the crowd. 'If we see somebody with weapons, the pickup will be unlocked,' I said. The pistol was loaded and ready for anyone who needed it.

At five to three, the immigrant families assembled on the courthouse steps. Demetrius tested a wireless mic, his voice cracking, echoing. The crews from three TV stations checked their equipment and lined up shots. The cops looked bored.

'All right,' I said, and we started across the street.

Then a dusty VW pulled past, Zemira at the wheel. She touched her horn and parked at the end of the block. As we crossed the plaza, she fell in beside me.

'Why are you here?' I asked.

'You would lose your head without me,' she said, and glanced at the others. 'I didn't know you had friends.'

'Who's to say how much good they are. Who's to say how much good you are either.'

'Yeah, that's questionable. What happened to your neck?'

Before I could answer, Demetrius spoke into the mic, thanking the crowd for coming and asking the news reporters to avoid identifying any of the families by name. Along with the TV crews, a hundred people or so listened, with more arriving from cars and others pausing as they came out of the courthouse.

Demetrius said, first in English and then in Spanish, 'Justice for one means justice for all.' He added, only in English, 'We are a big enough people – a good enough people, a *just* enough people – to open our doors when others need shelter.'

A few in the crowd waved signs – *We Have a Dream! ¡Legalización Para Todos! Immigrant Rights Are Human Rights!* Everyone clapped, except, on one side, a group of eight white men and women dressed in matching American flag shirts, and, on the other side, a man with a ponytail.

I stood at the back, watching, waiting.

Demetrius told the stories of three of the families beside him – one from Guadalajara, one from Mogadishu, one from San Salvador. As he spoke of the danger the fifteen-year-old son in the San Salvadoran family had escaped by fleeing from the Mara Salvatrucha gang, he crossed the steps and put an arm around the boy's shoulders. Then he repeated what he'd said before. 'We are a big enough people.'

I walked behind the crowd and circled toward the man with the ponytail, then worked to the front and went along the cordon by the bottom step. Off to the side, a *Fox News* reporter spoke to a camera. CBS and WJAX reporters stood farther back as camera operators zoomed in on the faces of the immigrant families.

Deborah Holt – in blue jeans and a short blue jacket, her pistol on her belt – stood by the CBS crew. Bill Higby – in jeans and a windbreaker – stood next to her. When he noticed me looking, he stepped toward me, then seemed to reconsider. He glanced up at the sky.

On the steps, a baby in the arms of an ebony-skinned woman shrieked and then was quiet. Demetrius paused, and laughter spread through the crowd.

'Many a day I feel that way,' Demetrius said. 'Many a day.'

He called on a long-haired woman from Vanguard Reform to join him, saying she'd done the outreach that made the rally possible.

A cool breeze blew across the plaza, and the mother of the shrieking baby held her child close.

I walked along the side of the crowd, past the group in the flag T-shirts, to the back.

A Nissan hatchback with tinted windows pulled to the curb across the street from where I'd parked. Three men in business suits climbed out, and the driver, still at the wheel, popped the hatch. Each man removed a box that weighed enough to require both hands. When the last of them set his on the street and closed the door, the hatchback sped away.

I caught Zemira's eye. We cut across the plaza toward the men.

They stood together and talked, glancing at the rally. Then, as we approached, they carried their boxes to the side, toward a set of doors at the far end of the courthouse.

'Hmm,' Zemira said. We watched until they disappeared inside.

With new arrivals, the crowd doubled in size. The uniformed cops stood at the edges or wandered through the middle. Higby walked along the back. He turned and went up along the side again.

I walked into the crowd.

As Demetrius spoke of the contributions immigrant families made to the economy, the group in flag shirts started chanting, 'De-port,' elongating the first syllable, and then, 'America for Americans.'

As if signaled by the interruption, a pack of skinny men ran from the end of the courthouse. They were pale and wore a mix of black golf shirts and black leather jackets. They came toward the crowd, yelling a confused mix of slogans – *Unite the Right! Immigrant pedophiles! Eradicate! White and proud! Fucking foreigners!*

Holt floated toward them, her hand by her hip holster. I pushed through the crowd, following her.

Five uniformed cops moved out in front of us. They lined up side by side, facing the pack, forming a barrier.

Across the plaza, the construction boss, his worker, and the worker's cousin sprinted toward my pickup.

I looked for Harry – in the crowd, out by the street, at the end of the courthouse building.

One of the skinny men yelled, 'Halt' – barking the word like an army command.

The others stopped, yards from the cops.

The one who seemed to be the leader yelled, 'Stand by.'

For a moment, the plaza was silent.

Then Demetrius coughed into his microphone. He tried a laugh. 'Well, it takes all kinds,' he said.

One of the men in flag T-shirts yelled, 'Not *your* kind.'

Demetrius asked a Mexican family to come to the microphone. A man in an oversized belt, his wife in a blue sleeveless dress, and two boys who weren't quite ten shuffled past the others on the steps.

As the man spoke in halting English about their life in Durango before they crossed the border, I moved back through the crowd.

The man said he and his wife came when they were eighteen years old. They went first to Chicago, where they worked in restaurants. Then they lived in Milwaukee for a year. Their boys, one born in each city, were citizens, but he and his wife had no documents. They left Milwaukee and came south. This was their home now, he said, but their home didn't accept them. 'We know this place, but the place does not know us. We are illegal. That is a terrible word, but it is true. Illegal.' He took a deep breath. 'But we are not immoral, and we are not wrong. All we need is a chance.' He smiled at his sons and said, 'We want due process. Freedom from detention. Fair treatment. Easy to understand.'

Standing at the base of the steps, in front of the families, Higby eyed me.

Then he shoved a large man out of the way and charged toward me. He pushed through the crowd, shouldering past women, parting groups with his big hands, knocking them aside. The look on his face – I'd seen it before. Nine years earlier, he'd slammed me against a wall in an interview room at the Sheriff's Office and roared what his eyes already said – *You did it, goddammit, you did it*. He'd smashed his accusation into me until I bent and broke and said I did what I hadn't done. The certainty of his rage had terrified me – it terrified me still – the conviction in his words, which became my words, as though a boy could be guilty of being weak.

A woman with a *No One Is Illegal* sign yelled at him as he pushed by. Her companion – a man half Higby's size – stood as if to block him. Higby thrust him aside.

I turned to run.

That's when I saw Harry coming across the open plaza from the street.

He was alone. He wore black pants and a white button-up dress shirt, as if he was going to church. Over his chest, he had, in reverse, a little gray backpack.

He drew a jar from the pack, a Bic lighter from his pocket. He stopped, lit a rag, which was screwed into the lid, and lobbed the jar toward me. It smashed on the pavement. A puddle of fire bloomed.

He drew out a second jar, lit it, and threw it.

It hit a man in the back and fell to the ground without breaking.

Two women near the man crouched as if to save themselves from the sudden assault. Dozens ran, pushing past others who were unaware of what was happening.

Behind me, Higby shouted – his voice rising through Demetrius's speech.

Harry ran into the gap left by the fleeing spectators. He pulled out a third jar and lit it. He heaved it toward the immigrant families.

It hit the bottom step and exploded. A curtain of flames rose between him and the people he meant to kill.

He dropped the backpack.

He drew his revolver from his belt.

He aimed it at me – hesitated – then stepped past me.

He shot through the curtain of flames.

Once.

Twice.

A third time.

A thick-bellied woman in a purple dress fell, hit in the chest. A boy, sixteen or seventeen, struck in the knee, staggered down two steps before his leg buckled.

Higby shoved through. He shouted again and then fired his own gun – six times fast.

Harry stiffened. Three pocks of blood stained his dress shirt. He held his revolver steady, aiming at the families. Then he pitched straight back and cracked against the pavement.

A bent smile exposed his front teeth. His mouth contorted like the mouths of the women in his paintings, his eyes as fiery as theirs. He made a sound, a wet belch, a ridiculous, pathetic noise.

Thirty seconds after he burst on to the plaza, he was dead.

FORTY-FOUR

That night, I sat in the cubicle Holt shared with Higby. The area housing the homicide unit echoed with loud talk, angry outbursts, and, now and then, a nervous laugh. Off-duty detectives had interrupted their dinners and family time to come in. Some of them gathered in a conference room across from the cubicle. A muffled megaphone spoke outside an exterior wall, talking to reporters who'd gathered out front on Bay Street.

After Harry fell dead, cops had run through the plaza, guns drawn, screaming at everyone to lie flat on the pavement, checking garbage cans for hidden explosives, then widening a circle to the streets around the courthouse. They found the pistol in my pickup. Officers surrounded the truck, then backed away as if there might be an unseen danger. I told one of them the truck was mine, and he took me to the woman who was in charge. I tried to explain.

They arrested me. I rode to the Sheriff's Office in a police cruiser with my hands cuffed behind my back.

As they marched me into the station, Holt climbed from her Grand Marquis.

She made the cops take off the cuffs.

'Lucky for you,' she said, as she walked me to her cubicle. She went to find Higby, and they disappeared into the conference room together, shutting the door behind them.

For more than an hour, I waited and listened. The police had also arrested the group in flag T-shirts – then quickly let them go. They were interviewing the black-shirted and -jacketed men who'd charged toward the rally from the side of the courthouse. The woman in the purple dress and the teenager shot in the knee were in surgery.

I stood up. If no one stopped me, I would leave. But as I walked toward the exit, a detective in a sweat-stained yellow button-up came out of a room where he'd been talking to the man who'd told his friends to *halt*. 'Bunch of knuckleheads,' he said, then gave me a second look. 'Where are *you* going?'

I went back to the cubicle and sat.

Forty minutes later, Holt came from the conference room. She pulled her chair from her desk and sat across from me.

'This shouldn't have happened. We should have had our eyes on him a long time ago.'

'I told you he—'

'And you shouldn't have been at the rally. For God's sake, what were you thinking?'

'I—'

'I'm not asking for an answer,' she said. 'You know Higby saved your life, don't you?'

'No, he didn't.'

'He saw Summers coming for you.'

'Harry didn't want to kill me.'

'From what I saw, he did.'

'He had the chance if he wanted it,' I said.

'He wanted to kill the immigrant families more than you, that's all. When he saw Higby, he made a choice.'

I shook my head. 'No.'

'I saw every bit of it – as helpless as you.'

'I wasn't helpless.'

'Except for Higby, Harry Summers would've shot you and a lot of others.'

I said, 'You know Harry couldn't have done this alone, don't you?'

'We're talking to the group who showed up after the rally started. So far, we see no connection. Every indication is Summers was solo.'

'How about Lehmann?'

'We'll talk to everyone. This will take time. There's a process.'

'Right. Can I go?'

She pressed her lips. 'Not just yet.'

'I need to get my neck looked at. It hurts like hell. I'm still bleeding.'

'You look like you're doing OK.'

'Are you charging me with something?'

'We're sorting it out.'

A man in thick-framed glasses stuck his head out of the conference room door. 'Holt?'

She glanced at him. 'Just a sec.' She turned back to me. 'I've got something for you to do while you wait.' She left the cubicle and went down past the room where the detective in the yellow button-up had stopped me. A minute later, she returned with a blue binder.

The homicide unit had put together a book of unsolved murders from the past fifteen years, each victim marked with a colored tab. 'Take a look,' she said.

'For what?'

'Anything that rings a bell. Summers killed four people in the last two months, a fifth decades ago if what he told you about this girl Karine is true. What about the years between?' She set the binder on the desk.

'I don't know anyone he dealt with outside of Chartein Farm.'

'Just do me a favor and look,' she said.

Then she went to the conference room.

For another hour, I gazed at photos, skimming descriptions of the victims. They were mostly men, young and ragged, their bodies found in drug houses, alongside railroad tracks, in highway-side ditches.

When Holt came out of the room, I pushed the binder away. 'No,' I said.

She sighed. 'There's almost always a history. Something will come out.' She sighed. 'We're going to cut you loose for the night.'

'It's about time.'

'Do you want to say anything to Higby first?'

'No.'

She smiled, sadly. 'I'll tell him you said thanks.'

I walked away in a daze.

How close had I come to getting killed by Harry? He'd arrived at the plaza and one long moment later lay on his back, dead. He barely had time to suck in a breath and exhale. *I* barely had time.

Because of Higby.

Had this man who'd tried to take my life away nine years earlier saved me? Had he killed a man to save a man he wanted to kill?

What did Holt want me to say to him? *Thanks for shooting Harry instead of me?*

The world was a chaos of contradictions. Would it make sense after Holt and Higby wrote their reports, sorting the facts, adjusting chronologies, drawing maps and diagrams?

This will take time. There's a process.

Eight years in prison, three of them on death row. Time and process. A year of freedom that was hardly freedom. More time, more process. My history of suffering.

There's almost always a history.

Something will come out.

I stopped.

Always a history.

When and where.

I busted my balls for the first time.

I became a man.

I did everything for the first time.

Everything.

I turned around and went back to the cubicle.

Holt was at her desk, staring into space.

'Hey,' I said. 'Do you have older books of killings? From about fifty years ago?'

'Why?'

'Do me a favor,' I said.

'Why?'

'Please.'

She curled her lips, got up, and walked out past the conference room. When she came back, she handed me a black binder, the cover peeling with age. It was a cold-case book covering a period of seven years, long ago. Inside were eleven full-page photos of murder victims – eight men of various ages, three teenage girls – followed by sheets of general information and reference codes.

I studied the photos of the girls. 'Her,' I said about the first one. 'Her,' I said about the third.

'Really?' Holt said.

'Harry painted them. The pictures are on his walls.'

Holt looked at the photos. 'This was . . . Are you sure?'

'He would've been about their age,' I said.

She rubbed her face with her hand. Then she went back into the conference room. She returned with Higby.

She said, 'Let's go see what you think you see.'

FORTY-FIVE

We rode out through the dark to Chartein Farm. Higby cracked open his window, and the odor of his sweat eddied in the car. I'd first smelled it nine years earlier. I knew his stink as intimately as I knew my own. On any other night, it would have sickened me with fear.

I rolled down my window.

A mile before the poultry farm, the scent of wood smoke blew in. Then a glow appeared over the dark woods.

'A fire?' Holt said.

We turned in at the sign Harry had painted of two chickens. Deep in the property, flames licked at the air.

We rolled past Everett Peters's dark trailer and up the drive toward the chicken houses. We cut on to the dirt road leading to the Charteins' house and the row of cottages behind it. The flames rose fifteen or twenty feet into the night from one of the back buildings.

We sped toward the house and around it.

A group of sixteen or seventeen men and women – Mr and Mrs Chartein, Peters, others who worked on the farm – stood in the dark in front of Harry's cottage, watching it burn.

Holt, Higby, and I got out and joined them. The old wood building crackled and hissed. When the fire touched an unburned spot, it flared.

Holt asked Mrs Chartein, 'Why?'

'What good would it do?' she said.

'We could have found answers,' Holt said. There was no anger in her voice, only sadness. 'For the families. For everyone.'

The heat was immense. No one backed away.

'It's better to be done with it,' Mrs Chartein said.

'Better for who?' Holt asked.

'It's done,' Mrs Chartein said.

Then a tall man, who'd been standing at the side, walked over. A woman followed.

Carlos Medina and Clara Soto.

They came and faced Holt and Higby.

'Huh,' Holt said.

'I'm not going anywhere,' Carlos said. 'I'm not running away.'

Mrs Chartein said, 'Carlos has been here since he got out of jail. If anyone is to be held responsible, blame my husband and me. We gave him a place to stay – a place to be safe.'

Clara said, 'I talked them into it. They didn't want him here.'

Just before Jerry Dickerson had sprung Carlos from jail, Clara had argued with the Charteins by one of the chicken houses in the darkness before dawn. Afterward, the Charteins had claimed she'd wanted them to pay for the high-priced lawyer. But that was a lie. The co-owner of El Jimador had already put up the money. Had Clara and the Charteins really been arguing over where to hide Carlos once he was out?

Now Mrs Chartein and Clara almost begged Holt and Higby to arrest them for helping a man escape taking responsibility for killings he hadn't committed.

'It's done,' Mrs Chartein said again.

FORTY-SIX

When I returned the pickup truck to Safe Haven two days after Harry's attack, Judy came down from her front porch to take the keys.

'You've got guts, I'll say that much.' She looked at my eyes as if she was trying to see inside. 'It takes courage to do what needs to be done.'

Cynthia had followed me in her car, her broken foot braced in an orthopedic boot. She waited with the windows up.

I turned to go.

Judy said, 'Did you like your job here?'

'I don't know.'

'That's what I thought.' Across the property, one of the lions made a grunting roar. 'You have anything better going on right now?'

'No.'

'I figured.'

'I need to go,' I said.

'Where?' Judy said. 'Where will you go?'

'I'll find something.'

'Unless something finds you first?'

'Right.' I started toward Cynthia's car.

Judy walked with me. 'I admire nerve – and commitment.'

'I guess they've gotten you this place,' I said.

'Maybe this place isn't your cause,' she said. 'But in the meantime, we need someone.'

I stopped. 'To shovel the shit?'

She smiled. 'Shit needs to be shoveled.'

'I'll take my shovel somewhere else.'

'It's not all shit,' she said. 'Zemira's in the refrigerator shed, sorting a load from Jenquist. She could use a hand. Ollie gave us a cow.'

I looked at her.

She said, 'You can always quit if it doesn't work out.'

'Or you can fire me again.'

'It's a possibility.'

'You know I'll screw up again.'

'Yeah, I figure.'

I talked to Dr Patel about Harry. 'Maybe the Valknut group gave him a focus for his pain over Karine,' he said. 'A way to rationalize what he'd done to her. And once he rationalized it, he needed to kill the others – to show himself he was right.'

'No,' I said. 'He also killed girls before he met Karine.'

'I don't know,' he said. 'Sometimes I wish I understood exactly what goes on in the head of a man like him. Most of the time, I'm glad I don't.'

Lehmann denied any connection to Harry – publicly in a press conference and, from what Deborah Holt told me when we met, privately with a lawyer beside him.

'Unless you catch a man like him with his finger on the trigger,' Holt said, 'he'll cover himself with so much political smoke and constitutional doubletalk you can barely see him.'

'I can see him.'

'Stay away from him,' she said. 'For your own good. For *every-one's* good.'

That weekend, Cynthia and I drove out to Yellow Water Annex.

We walked from bunker to bunker. We stared into the dark interiors, which seemed to recede like holes into the earth. Behind the buildings, the woods were quiet. High in the sky, a jet drew a contrail. We stood in the heavy silence.

What would a man like Lehmann do if pulled from his high-rise and held in a place like this?

If push came to shove.

Cynthia and I picked the third bunker from the end, two down from the one where Harry had held her. The doors were solid, the walls thick. We cleared the inside of trash and metal scraps, anything a captive might use as a weapon or tool. We swept the place clean.